P9-APN-011

Philip Roth

Fawcett Crest Books
by Philip Roth:

THE GHOST WRITER
ZUCKERMAN UNBOUND

Other Books
by Philip Roth

Goodbye, Columbus
Letting Go
When She Was Good
Portnoy's Complaint
Our Gang
The Breast
The Great American Novel
My Life as a Man
Reading Myself and Others
The Professor of Desire
A Philip Roth Reader

Philip Roth

"Is one of those rare authors who honors the language and brings honor to it while remaining accessible.... Roth's metier is angst... his particular gift humor, not merely funny but trenchant, biting, illuminating."

Cosmopolitan

The Anatomy Lesson

"Funny, masterly... Nathan Zuckerman... exists as an assemblage of subtle, comic and often moving words.... In a year and a half of pain Zuckerman finds ample time to review his life and especially his other body, the corpus of his works. The rich complexity of that review, its dark comedy, demonstrates better than any argument what mature command of prose fiction Philip Roth has achieved across 25 years of honest work. ... Roth's novels, this one particularly, are full of well-realized characters, of depth and insight and reverberation, of sympathy for the human race and passion for its spirit.... in comedy Roth arrives at a deep structure fully as powerful and fully as realized as Kafka's cockroach or Melville's whale. That he should also entertain with satire and caricature and the best invective anyone has written in many a year only adds robust variation to the great pleasure of his work."

Chicago Sun-Times

(Please turn the page for more ciritcal acclaim of *The Anatomy Lesson*.)

The Anatomy Lesson

The Anatomy Lesson

Philip Roth

FAWCETT CREST • NEW YORK

For Richard Stern

The chief obstacle to correct diagnosis in painful conditions is the fact that the symptom is often felt at a distance from its source.

—*Textbook of Orthopaedic Medicine*
JAMES CYRIAX, M.D.

The Collar

When he is sick, every man wants his mother; if she's not around, other women must do. Zuckerman was making do with four other women. He'd never had so many women at one time, or so many doctors, or drunk so much vodka, or done so little work, or known despair of such wild proportions. Yet he didn't seem to have a disease that anybody could take seriously. Only the pain— in his neck, arms, and shoulders, pain that made it difficult to walk for more than a few city blocks or even to stand very long in one place. Just having a neck, arms, and shoulders was like carrying another person around. Ten minutes out getting the groceries and he had to hurry home and lie down. Nor could he bring back more than one light bagful per trip, and even then he had to hold it cradled up against his chest like somebody eighty years old. Holding the bag down at his side only worsened the pain. It was painful to bend over and make his bed. To stand at the stove was painful, holding nothing heavier than a spatula and waiting for an egg to fry. He couldn't throw open a window, not one that required any strength. Consequently, it was the women who opened the windows for him: opened his windows, fried his egg, made his bed, shopped for his food, and effortlessly, manfully, toted home his bundles. One woman on her own could have done what was needed in an hour or two a day, but Zuckerman didn't have one woman any longer. That was how he came to have four.

To sit up in a chair and read he wore an orthopedic collar, a spongy lozenge in a white ribbed sleeve that he fastened around his neck to keep the cervical vertebrae aligned and to prevent him from turning his head unsupported. The support and the restriction of movement were supposed to diminish the hot line of pain that ran from behind his right ear into his neck, then branched downward beneath the scapula like a menorah held bottom side up. Sometimes the collar helped, sometimes not, but just wearing it was as maddening as the pain itself. He couldn't concentrate on anything other than himself in his collar.

The text in hand was from his college days, *The Oxford Book of Seventeenth Century Verse*. Inside the front cover, above his name and the date inscribed in blue ink, was a single penciled notation in his 1949 script, a freshman aperçu that read, "Metaphysical poets pass easily from trivial to sublime." For the first time in twenty-four years he turned to the poems of George Herbert. He'd got the book down to read "The Collar," hoping to find something there to help him wear his own. That was commonly believed to be a function of great literature: antidote to suffering through depiction of our common fate. As Zuckerman was learning, pain could make you awfully primitive if not counteracted by steady, regular doses of philosophical thinking. Maybe he could pick up some hints from Herbert.

> . . . Shall I be still in suit?
> Have I no harvest but a thorn
> To let me blood, and not restore
> What I have lost with cordiall fruit?
> Sure there was wine
> Before my sighs did drie it: there was corn

> Before my tears did drown it.
> Is the yeare only lost to me?
> Have I no bayes to crown it?
> No flowers, no garlands gay? all blasted?
> All wasted?
> ...But as I rav'd and grew more fierce and wilde
> At every word
> Me thought I heard one calling, *Childe*:
> And I reply'd, *My Lord*.

As best he could with his aching arm, he threw the volume across the room. Absolutely not! He refused to make of his collar, or of the affliction it was designed to assuage, a metaphor for anything grandiose. Metaphysical poets may pass easily from trivial to sublime, but on the strength of the experience of the past eighteen months, Zuckerman's impression was of proceeding, if at all, in the opposite direction.

Writing the last page of a book was as close as he'd ever come to sublimity, and that hadn't happened in four years. He couldn't remember when he'd written a *readable* page. Even while he was wearing the collar, the spasm in the upper trapezius and the aching soreness to either side of the dorsal spine made it difficult to type just the address on an envelope. When a Mount Sinai orthopedist had ascribed his troubles to twenty years of hammering away at a manual portable, he at once went off to buy an IBM Selectric II; however, when he tried at home to get to work, he found that he ached as much over the new, unfamiliar IBM keyboard as he had over the last of his little Olivettis. Just a glimpse of the Olivetti stowed away in its battered traveling case at the back of his bedroom closet and the depression came rolling in— the way Bojangles Robinson must have felt looking at his old dancing shoes. How simple, back when he was still healthy, to give it a shove and make room on his desk for his lunch or his notes or his reading or his mail.

How he'd loved to push them around, those silent un-complaining sparring partners—the pounding he'd been giving them since he was twenty! There when he paid his alimony and answered his fans, there to lay his head beside when overcome by the beauty or ugliness of what he'd just composed, there for every page of every draft of the four published novels, of the three buried alive— if Olivettis could talk, you'd get the novelist naked. While from the IBM prescribed by the first orthopedist, you'd get nothing—only the smug, puritanical, work-manlike hum telling of itself and all its virtues: I am a Correcting Selectric II. I never do anything wrong. Who this man is I have no idea. And from the look of things neither does he.

Writing manually was no better. Even in the good old days, pushing his left hand across the paper, he looked like some brave determined soul learning to use an ar-tificial limb. Nor were the results that easy to decipher. Writing by hand was the clumsiest thing he did. He danced the rumba better than he wrote by hand. He held the pen too tight. He clenched his teeth and made ag-onized faces. He stuck his elbow out from his side as though beginning the breast stroke, then hooked his hand down and around from his forearm so as to form the letters from above rather than below—the contor-tionist technique by which many a left-handed child had taught himself how not to smear his words as he pro-ceeded across the page from left to right back in the era of the inkwell. A highly recommended osteopath had even concluded that the cause of Zuckerman's problems was just this: the earnest left-handed schoolboy, straining to overcome the impediment of wet ink, who had begun microscopically to twist the writer's spine off the vertical axis and screw it down cockeyed into his sacrum. His rib cage was askew. His clavicle was crooked. His left scapula winged out at its lower angle like a chicken's.

Even his humerus was too tightly packed into the shoulder capsule and inserted in the joint on the bias. Though to the untrained eye he might appear more or less symmetrical and decently proportioned, within he was as misshapen as Richard III. According to the osteopath, he'd been warping at a steady rate since he was seven. Began with his homework. Began with the first of his reports on life in New Jersey. "In 1666 Governor Carteret provided an interpreter for Robert Treat and also a guide up the Hackensack River to meet with a representative of Oraton, the aged chief of the Hackensacks. Robert Treat wanted Oraton to know that the white settlers wished only peace." Began at ten with Newark's Robert Treat and the euphonious elegance of *interpreter* and *representative*, ended with Newark's Gilbert Carnovsky and the blunt monosyllables *cock* and *cunt*. Such was the Hackensack up which the writer had paddled, only to dock at the port of pain.

When sitting upright at the typewriter became too painful, he tried leaning back in an easy chair and doing the best he could with his imperfect longhand. He had the collar to brace his neck, the firm, uncushioned, back of the upholstered chair to support his spine, and a piece of beaverboard, cut to his specifications, laid across the arms of the chair to serve as a portable desk for his composition books. His place was certainly quiet enough for total concentration. He'd had his big study windows double-glazed so that nobody's television or phonograph would blare through from the building backing onto his brownstone apartment, and the ceiling had been soundproofed so he wouldn't be disturbed by the scratching of his upstairs neighbor's two Pekinese. The study was carpeted, a deep copper-brown wool, and the windows were hung to the floor with creamy velvet curtains. It was a cozy, quiet, book-lined room. He'd spent half his life sealed off in rooms just like it. Atop the small cabinet

where he kept his vodka bottle and his glass were favorite
old photographs in Plexiglas frames: his dead parents as
newlyweds in his grandparents' backyard; ex-wives
blooming with health on Nantucket; his estranged brother
leaving Cornell in 1957, a magna cum laude (and a tabula
rasa) in a cap and gown. If during the day he spoke at
all, it was only small talk to those pictures; otherwise,
enough silence even to satisfy Proust. He had silence,
comfort, time, money, but composing in longhand set
off a throbbing pain in his upper arm that in no time at
all made him sick to his stomach. He kneaded the muscle
with his right hand while he continued to write with
the left. He tried not thinking about it. He pretended
that it wasn't *his* upper arm hurting but somebody else's.
He tried to outwit it by stopping and starting. Stopping
long enough helped the pain but hurt the writing; by
the tenth time he'd stopped he had nothing left to write,
and with nothing to write, no reason to be. When he
tore off the neck collar and threw himself to the floor,
the ripping sound of the Velcro fastener coming undone
could have been emitted by his guts. Every thought and
feeling, ensnared by the selfness of pain.

In a children's furniture store on Fifty-seventh Street
he had bought a soft red plastic-covered playmat that
was permanently laid out in his study now, between his
desk and his easy chair. When he could no longer bear
sitting up, he stretched supine upon the playmat, his
head supported by *Roget's Thesaurus*. He'd come to con-
duct most of the business of his waking life on the playmat. From there, no longer laden with an upper torso
or saddled with fifteen pounds of head, he made phone
calls, received visitors, and followed Watergate on TV.
Instead of his own spectacles, he wore a pair of prism
glasses that enabled him to see at right angles. They
were designed for the bedridden by a downtown optical
firm to which he'd been referred by his physiotherapist.

Through his prism glasses he followed our President's chicanery—the dummy gestures, the satanic sweating, the screwy dazzling lies. He almost felt for him, the only other American he saw daily who seemed to be in as much trouble as he was. Flat out on the floor, Zuckerman could also see whichever of his women was seated upright on the sofa. What the woman in attendance saw were the rectangular opaque undersides of the protruding glasses and Zuckerman explaining Nixon to the ceiling.

He tried from the playmat to dictate fiction to a secretary, but he hadn't the fluency for it and sometimes went as long as an hour without a word to say. He couldn't write without seeing the writing; though he could picture what the sentences pictured, he couldn't picture the sentences unless he saw them unfold and fasten one to the other. The secretary was only twenty and, during the first few weeks particularly, got too easily caught up in his anguish. The sessions were torture for both of them, and generally ended with the secretary down on the playmat. Intercourse, fellatio, and cunnilingus Zuckerman could endure more or less without pain, provided he was supine and kept the thesaurus beneath his head for support. The thesaurus was just the right thickness to prevent the back of his skull falling below the line of his shoulders and setting off the pain in his neck. Its inside cover was inscribed "From Dad— You have my every confidence," and dated "June 24, 1946." A book to enrich his vocabulary upon graduation from grade school.

To lie with him on the playmat came the four women. They were all the vibrant life he had: secretary-confidante-cook-housekeeper-companion—aside from the doses of Nixon's suffering, they were the entertainment. On his back he felt like their whore, paying in sex for someone to bring him the milk and the paper. They told him their troubles and took off their clothes and lowered the orifices for Zuckerman to fill. Without a taxing vocation or a hopeful prognosis, he was theirs to do with as they wished; the more conspicuous his helplessness, the more forthright their desire. Then they ran. Washed up, downed a coffee, kneeled to kiss him goodbye, and ran off to disappear in real lives. Leaving Zuckerman on his back for whoever rang the bell next.

Well and working, he'd never had time for liaisons like these, not even when he'd been tempted. Too many wives in too few years to allow for a consortium of mistresses. Marriage had been his bulwark against the tremendous distraction of women. He'd married for the order, the intimacy, the dependable comradery, for the routine and regularity of monogamous living; he'd married so as never to waste himself on another affair, or go crazy with boredom at another party, or wind up alone in the living room at night after a day alone in his study. To sit alone each night doing the reading that he required to concentrate himself for the next day's solitary writing was too much even for Zuckerman's single-mindedness, and so into the voluptuous austerity he had enticed a woman, one woman at a time, a quiet, thoughtful, serious, literate, self-sufficient woman who didn't require to be taken places, who was content instead to sit after dinner and read in silence across from him and his book.

Following each divorce, he discovered anew that unmarried a man had to take women places: out to restaurants, for walks in the park, to museums and the opera and the movies—not only had to go to the movies but afterwards had to discuss them. If they became lovers, there was the problem of getting away in the morning while his mind was still fresh for his work. Some women expected him to eat breakfast with them, even to talk to them over breakfast like other human beings. Sometimes they wanted to go back to bed. *He* wanted to go back to bed. It was certainly going to be more eventful in bed than back at the typewriter with the book. Much less frustrating too. You actually could complete what you set out to accomplish without ten false starts and sixteen drafts and all that pacing around the room. So he dropped his guard—and the morning was shot.

No such temptations with the wives, not as time went by.

But pain had changed it all. Whoever spent the night was not only invited to breakfast but asked to stay on for lunch if she had the time (and if no one else was to turn up till dinner). He'd slip a wet washcloth and a bulging ice pack under his terry-cloth robe, and while the ice anesthetized his upper trapezius (and the orthopedic collar supported his neck), he'd lean back and listen in his red velvet chair. He'd had a fatal weakness for high-minded mates back when all he ever thought about was toiling away; excellent opportunity, immobilization, to sound out less predictably upright women than his three ex-wives. Maybe he'd learn something and maybe he wouldn't, but at least they would help to distract him, and according to the rheumatologist at NYU, distraction, pursued by the patient with real persistence, could reduce even the worst pain to tolerable levels.

The psychoanalyst whom he consulted took a contrary position: he wondered aloud if Zuckerman hadn't given up fighting the illness to *retain* (with a fairly untroubled conscience) his "harem of Florence Nightingales." Zuckerman so resented the crack he nearly walked out. Given up? What could he do that he hadn't—what was left that he was unwilling to try? Since the pains had begun in earnest eighteen months before, he'd waited his turn in the offices of three orthopedists, two neurologists, a physiotherapist, a rheumatologist, a radiologist, an osteopath, a vitamin doctor, an acupuncturist, and now the analyst. The acupuncturist had stuck twelve needles into him on fifteen different occasions, a hundred and eighty needles in all, not one of which had done a thing. Zuckerman sat shirtless in one of the acupuncturist's eight treatment cubicles, the needles hanging from him, and reading *The New York Times*—sat obediently for fifteen minutes, then paid his twenty-five dollars and rode back uptown, jangling with pain each time the cab took a pothole. The vitamin doctor gave him a series of five vitamin B-12 shots. The osteopath yanked his rib cage upward, pulled his arms outward, and cracked his neck sharply to either side. The physiotherapist gave him hot packs, ultrasound, and massage. One orthopedist gave him "trigger-point" injections and told him to throw out the Olivetti and buy the IBM; the next, having informed Zuckerman that he was an author too, though not of "best-sellers," examined him lying down and standing up and bending over, and, after Zuckerman had dressed, ushered him out of his office, announcing to his receptionist that he had no more time that week to waste on hypochondriacs. The third orthopedist prescribed a hot bath for twenty minutes every morning, after which Zuckerman was to perform a series of stretching exercises. The baths were pleasant enough—Zuckerman listened to Mahler through the open doorway—but the exercises, simple as they were, so exacerbated all his pains that within the week he rushed back to the first orthopedist, who gave him a second series of trigger-point injections that did no good. The radiologist X-rayed his chest, back, neck, cranium, shoulders, and arms. The first neurologist who saw the X-rays said he wished his own spine was in such good shape; the second prescribed hospitalization, two weeks of neck traction to alleviate pressure on a cervical disc—if not the worst experience of Zuckerman's life, easily the most humbling. He didn't even want to think about it, and generally there was nothing that happened to him, no matter how bad, that he didn't

want to think about. But he was stunned by his cowardice. Even the sedation, far from helping, made the
powerlessness that much more frightening and oppres-
sive. He knew he would go berserk from the moment
they fastened the weights to the harness holding his head.
On the eighth morning, though there was no one in the
room to hear him, he began to shout from where he was
pinned to the bed, "Let me up! Let me go!" and within
fifteen minutes was back in his clothes and down at the
cashier's cage settling his bill. Only when he was safely
out onto the street, hailing a cab, did he think, "And
what if something really terrible were happening to you?
What then?"

Jenny had come down from the country to help him
through what was to have been the two weeks of traction.
She made the round of the galleries and museums in the
morning, then after lunch came to the hospital and read
to him for two hours from *The Magic Mountain*. It had
seemed the appropriate great tome for the occasion, but
strapped inert upon his narrow bed, Zuckerman grew
increasingly irritated by Hans Castorp and the dynamic
opportunities for growth provided him by TB. Nor could
life in New York Hospital's room 611 be said to measure
up to the deluxe splendors of a Swiss sanatorium before
the First World War, not even at $1,500 a week. "Sounds
to me," he told Jenny, "like a cross between the Salzburg
Seminars and the stately old *Queen Mary*. Five great meals
a day and then tedious lectures by European intellectuals,
complete with erudite jests. All that philosophy. All
that snow. Reminds me of the University of Chicago."

He'd first met Jenny while visiting the retreat of some
friends on a wooded mountainside in a village up the
Hudson called Bearsville. The daughter of a local school-
teacher, she'd been down to art school at Cooper Union
and then three years on her own with a knapsack in
Europe, and now, back where she'd begun, was living

alone in a wood shack with a cat and her paints and a Franklin stove. She was twenty-eight, robust, lonely, blunt, pink-complexioned, with a healthy set of largish white teeth, baby-fine carrot-colored hair, and impressive muscles in her arms. No long temptress fingers like his secretary Diana—she had *hands*. "Someday, if you like," she said to Zuckerman, "I'll tell you stories about my jobs—'My Biceps and How I Got Them.'" Before leaving for Manhattan, he'd stopped off at her cabin unannounced, ostensibly to look at her landscapes. Skies, trees, hills, and roads just as blunt as she was. Van Gogh without the vibrating sun. Quotations from Van Gogh's letters to his brother were tacked up beside the easel, and a scarred copy of the French edition of the letters, the one she'd lugged around Europe in her knapsack, lay in the pile of art books by the daybed. On the fiberboard walls were pencil drawings: cows, horses, pigs, nests, flowers, vegetables—all announcing with the same forthright charm, "Here I am and I am real."

They strolled through a ravaged orchard out behind the cabin, sampling the crop of gnarled fruit. Jenny asked him, "Why does your hand keep stealing up to your shoulder?" Zuckerman hadn't even realized what he was doing; the pain, at this point, had only cornered about a quarter of his existence, and he still thought of it as something like a spot on his coat that had only to be brushed away. Yet no matter how hard he brushed, nothing happened. "Some sort of strain," he replied. "From stiff-arming the critics?" she asked. "More likely stiff-arming myself. What's it like alone up here?" "A lot of painting, a lot of gardening, a lot of masturbating. It must be nice to have money and buy things. What's the most extravagant thing you've ever done?" The most extravagant, the most foolish, the most vile, the most thrilling—he told her, then she told him. Hours of questions and answers, but for a while no further than that. "Our great sexless rapport," she called it, when they spoke for long stretches on the phone at night. "Tough luck for me, maybe, but I don't want to be one of your girls. I'm better off with my hammer, building a new floor." "How'd you learn to build a floor?" "It's easy."

One midnight she'd called to say she'd been out in the garden bringing in the vegetables by moonlight. "The natives up here tell me it's going to freeze in a few hours. I'm coming down to Lemnos to watch you lick your wounds." "Lemnos? I don't remember Lemnos." "Where the Greeks put Philoctetes and his foot."

She'd stayed for three days on Lemnos. She squirted the base of his neck with anesthetizing ethyl chloride; she sat unclothed astride his knotted back and massaged between his shoulder blades; she cooked them dinner, coq au vin and cassoulet—dishes tasting strongly of bacon—and the vegetables she'd harvested before the frost; she told him about France and her adventures there with men and women. Coming from the bathroom at bedtime, he caught her by the desk looking into his datebook. "Oddly furtive," he said, "for someone so open." She merely laughed and said, "You couldn't write if you didn't do worse. Who's 'D'? Who's 'G'? How many do we come to all together?" "Why? Like to meet some of the others?" "No thanks. I don't think I want to get into that. That's what I thought I was phasing myself out of up on my mountaintop." On the last morning of that first visit he wanted to give her something—something other than a book. He'd been giving women books (and the lectures that went with them) all his life. He gave Jenny ten $100 bills. "What's this for," she said. "You just told me that you couldn't stand coming down here looking like a yokel. Then there's the curiosity about extravagance. Van Gogh had his brother, you have me. Take it." She returned three hours later with a scarlet cashmere cloak, burgundy boots, and a big bottle of Bal à Versailles. "I went to Bergdorf's," she said rather shyly, but proudly—"here's your change," and handed him two quarters, a dime, and three pennies. She took off all her yokel clothes and put on just the cloak and the boots. "Know what?" she said, looking in the mirror. "I feel like I'm pretty." "You *are* pretty." She opened the bottle and dabbed at herself with the stopper; she perfumed the tip of her tongue. Then again to the mirror. A long look. "I feel tall." That she wasn't and wouldn't be. She phoned from the country that evening to tell him about her mother's reaction when she stopped by the house, wearing the cloak and smelling of Bal à Versailles, and explained it was a gift from a man. "She said, 'I wonder what your grandmother will say about that coat.'" Well, a harem's a harem, Zuckerman thought. "Ask your grandmother's size and I'll get her one too."

The two weeks of hospital traction began with Jenny reading to him in the afternoons from *The Magic Mountain*, then back at his apartment at night drawing pictures in her sketchbook of his desk, his chair, his bookshelves, and his clothes, pictures that she taped to the wall of his room the next time she came to visit. Each day she made a drawing of an old American sampler with an uplifting adage stitched in the center, and this too she taped to the wall he could see. "To deepen your outlook," she told him.

The only antidote to mental suffering is physical pain.

KARL MARX

One does not love a place the less for having suffered in it.

JANE AUSTEN

If one is strong enough to resist certain shocks, to
solve more or less complicated physical difficulties,
then from forty to fifty-one is again in a new relatively normal tideway.

V. VAN GOGH

She devised a chart to trace the progress of the treatment on his outlook. At the end of seven days it looked
like this:

DAY	Elan	Humor	Sanity	Appetite	Congeniality	Stoicism	Libido	Pettiness (lack of)	Pissing and Moaning	Courtesy to Jenny
1	A	A	A	A	A	A	F	A	A	A
2	B	A	B	A	A	A	F	C	C	A
3	A	A	A	A	A	A	F	B	B	A
4	C	B	C	A	C	B	A	C	C	A
5	C	B	A	C	B	A	F	B	B	B
6	C	C	C	C	C	C	C	C	B	A
7	F	D	F	F	C	D	F	D	B	F
8										
9										
10										
11										
12										
13										
14										

On the eighth afternoon, when she arrived with her drawing pad at room 611, Zuckerman was gone; she found him at home, on the playmat, half drunk. "Too much inlook for the outlook," he told her. "Too all-encompassing. Too isolating. Broke down."

"Oh," she said lightly, "I don't think this constitutes much of a breakdown. I couldn't have lasted an hour."

"Life smaller and smaller and smaller. Wake up thinking about my neck. Go to sleep thinking about my neck. Only thought, which doctor to turn to when this doesn't help the neck. There to get well and knew I was getting worse. Hans Castorp better at all this than I am, Jennifer. Nothing in that bed but me. Nothing but a neck thinking neck-thoughts. No Settembrini, no Naphta, no snow. No glamorous intellectual voyage. Trying to find my way out and I only work my way further in. Defeated. Ashamed." He was also angry enough to scream.

"No, the problem was me." She poured him another drink. "I wish I were more of an entertainer. I only wish I weren't this tough lump. Well, forget it. We tried—it didn't work."

He sat at the kitchen table rubbing his neck and finishing the vodka while she made her bacony lamb stew. He didn't want her out of his sight. Levelheaded Jenny, let's make the underside of domesticity the whole thing—live with me and be my sweet tough lump. He was about ready to ask her to move in. "I said to myself in bed, 'Come what may, when I get out of here I throw myself back into work. If it hurts it hurts and the hell with it. Muster all your understanding and just overcome it.'"

"And?"

"Too elementary for understanding. Understanding doesn't touch it. Worrying about it, wondering about it, fighting it, treating it, trying to ignore it, trying to figure out what it is—it makes my ordinary inwardness look like New Year's Eve in Times Square. When you're in pain all you think about is not being in pain. Back and back and back to the one obsession. I should never have asked you to come down. I should have done it alone. But even this way I was too weak. You, a witness to this."

"Witness to what? Come on, for *my* outlook it was just fine. You don't know how I've loved running around here wearing a skirt. I've been taking care of myself a long time now in my earnest, blustery way. Well, for you I can be softer, gentler, calmer—you've provided a chance for me to provide in a womanly way. No need for anybody to feel bad about that. It's guilt-free time, Nathan, for both of us. I'll be of use to you, you be of use to me, and let's neither of us worry about the consequences. Let my grandmother do that."

Choose Jenny? Tempting if she'd have it. Her spunk, her health, her independence, the Van Gogh quotations, the unwavering will—how all that quieted the invalid frenzy. But what would happen when he was well? Choose Jenny because of the ways in which she approximates Mrs. Zuckermans I, II, and III? The best reason not to choose her. Choose like a patient in need of a nurse? A wife as a Band-Aid? In a fix like this, the only choice is not to choose. Wait it out, as is.

It was the severe depression brought on by the eight days imprisoned in traction—and by the thought of waiting it out as is—that sent him running to the psychoanalyst. But they didn't get on at all. He spoke of the appeal of illness, the returns on sickness, he told Zuckerman about the psychic payoff for the patient. Zuckerman allowed that there might well be profits to be reckoned in similarly enigmatic cases, but as for himself, he hated being sick: there was no payoff that could possibly compensate for his disabling physical pain. The "secondary gains" the analyst identified couldn't begin to make up for the primary loss. But perhaps, the analyst suggested, the Zuckerman who was getting paid off wasn't the self he perceived as himself but the ineradicable infant, the atoning penitent, the guilty pariah—perhaps it was the remorseful son of the dead parents, the author of *Carnovsky*.

It had taken three weeks for the doctor to say this out loud. It might be months before he broke the news of the hysterical conversion symptom.

"Expiation through suffering?" Zuckerman said. "The pain being my judgment on myself and that book?"

"Is it?" the analyst asked.

"No," Zuckerman replied, and three weeks after it had begun, he terminated the therapy by walking out.

One doctor prescribed a regimen of twelve aspirin per day, another prescribed Butazolidin, another Robaxin, another Percodan, another Valium, another Prednisone; another told him to throw all the pills down the toilet, the poisonous Prednisone first, and "learn to live with it." Untreatable pain of unknown origins is one of the vicissitudes of life—however much it impaired physical movement, it was still wholly compatible with a perfect state of health. Zuckerman was simply a well man who suffered pain. "And I make it a habit," continued the no-nonsense doctor, "never to treat anybody who isn't ill. Furthermore," he advised, "after you leave here, steer clear of the psychosomologists. You don't need any more of that." "What's a psychosomologist?" "A baffled little physician. The Freudian personalization of every ache and pain is the crudest weapon to have been bequeathed to these guys since the leech pot. If pain were only the expression of something else, it would all be hunky-dory. But unhappily life isn't organized as logically as that.

Pain is in addition to everything else. There are hysterics, of course, who can mime any disease, but they constitute a far more exotic species of chameleon than the psychosomologists lead all you gullible sufferers to believe. You are no such reptile. Case dismissed."

It was only days after the psychoanalyst had accused him, for the first time, of giving up the fight that Diana, his part-time secretary, took Zuckerman—who was able still to drive in forward gear but could no longer turn his head to back up—took him out in a rent-a-car to the Long Island laboratory where an electronic pain suppressor had just been invented. He'd read an item in the business section of the Sunday *Times* announcing the laboratory's acquisition of a patent on the device, and the next morning at nine phoned to arrange an appointment. The director and the chief engineer were in the parking lot to welcome him when he and Diana arrived; they were thrilled that Nathan Zuckerman should be their first "pain patient" and snapped a Polaroid picture of him at the front entrance. The chief engineer explained that he had developed the idea to relieve the director's wife of sinus headaches. They were very much in the experimental stages, still discovering refinements of technique by which to alleviate the most recalcitrant forms of chronic pain. He got Zuckerman out of his shirt and showed him how to use the machine. After the demonstration session, Zuckerman felt neither better nor worse, but the director assured him that his wife was a new woman and insisted that Zuckerman take a pain suppressor home on approval and keep it for as long as he liked.

Isherwood is a camera with his shutter open, I am the experiment in chronic pain.

The machine was about the size of an alarm clock. He set the timer, put two moistened electrode pads above and below the site of the pain, and six times a day gave himself a low-voltage shock for five minutes. And six times a day he waited for the pain to go away—actually he waited for it to go away a hundred times a day. Having waited long enough, he then took Valium or aspirin or Butazolidin or Percodan or Robaxin; at five in the evening he said the hell with it and began taking the vodka. And as tens of millions of Russians have known for hundreds of years, that is the best pain suppressor of all.

By December 1973, he'd run out of hope of finding a treatment, drug, doctor, or cure—certainly of finding an honest disease. He was living with it, but not because he'd learned to. What he'd learned was that something decisive had happened to him, and whatever the unfathomable reason, he and his existence weren't remotely what they'd been between 1933 and 1971. He knew about solitary confinement from writing alone in a room virtually every day since his early twenties; he'd served nearly twenty years of that sentence, obediently and on his best behavior. But this was confinement without the writing and he was taking it only a little better than the eight days harnessed to room 611. Indeed, he had never left off upbraiding himself with the question that had followed him from the hospital after his escape: What if what was happening to you were really terrible?

Yet, even if this didn't register terrible on the scale of global misery, it felt terrible to him. He felt pointless, worthless, meaningless, stunned that it should *seem* so terrible and undo him so completely, bewildered by defeat on a front where he hadn't even known himself to be at war. He had shaken free at an early age from the sentimental claims of a conventional, protective, worshipful family, he had surmounted a great university's beguiling purity, he had torn loose from the puzzle of passionless marriages to three exemplary women and from the moral propriety of his own early books; he had worked hard for his place as a writer—eager for recognition in his striving twenties, desperate for serenity in his celebrated thirties—only at forty to be vanquished by a causeless, nameless, untreatable phantom disease. It wasn't leukemia or lupus or diabetes, it wasn't multiple sclerosis or muscular dystrophy or even rheumatoid arthritis—it was nothing. Yet to nothing he was losing his confidence, his sanity, and his self-respect.

He was also losing his hair. Either from all the worrying or all the drugs. He saw hair on the thesaurus when he rose from a session on the playmat. Hair came away by the combful as he prepared himself at the bathroom mirror for his next empty day. Shampooing in the shower, he found the strands of hair looped in the palms of his hands doubling and tripling with every rinse—he expected to see things getting better and with each successive rinsing they got worse.

In the Yellow Pages he found "Anton Associates Trichological Clinic"—the least outlandish ad under "Scalp Care"—and went off to the basement of the Commodore Hotel to see if they could make good on their modest promise to "control all controllable hair problems." He had the time, he had the hair problem, and it would be something like an adventure voyaging from the playmat to midtown one afternoon a week. The treatments couldn't be less effective than what he'd been getting at Manhattan's finest medical facilities for his neck, arms, and shoulders. In happier times he might have resigned himself with little more than a pang to the dismaying change in his appearance, but with so much else giving way in life, he decided "No, no further": vocationally obstructed, physically disabled, sexually mindless, intellectually inert, spiritually depressed—but not bald overnight, not that too.

The initial consultation took place in a sanitary white office with diplomas on the wall. The sight of Anton, a vegetarian and a yoga practitioner as well as a scalp specialist, made Zuckerman feel a hundred and lucky even to have retained his teeth. Anton was a small and vibrant man in his sixties who looked to be still in his forties; his own hair, gleaming like a black polished helmet, stopped just short of cheekbone and brow. As a boy in Budapest, he told Zuckerman, he had been a champion gymnast and ever since had devoted himself to the preservation of physical well-being through exercise, diet, and ethical living. He was particularly chagrined, while taking Zuckerman's history, to learn of the heavy drinking. He asked if Zuckerman was under any undue pressure: pressure was a leading cause of premature hair loss. "I'm under pressure," Zuckerman replied, "from prematurely losing hair." He wouldn't go into the pain, couldn't narrate that enigma to yet another expert with a wallful of diplomas. He wished, in fact, that he'd stayed at home. His hair at the center of his life! His receding hairline where his fiction used to be! Anton turned a lamp on Zuckerman's scalp and lightly combed the thinning hair from one side to the other. Then he extracted from the teeth of the comb the hairs that had come loose during the examination and piled them carefully onto a tissue for analysis in the lab.

Zuckerman felt no bigger than his topmost bald spot as he was led along a narrow white corridor into the clinic—a dozen curtained cubicles with plumbing, each just large enough to hold a trained trichological technician and a man losing his hair. Zuckerman was introduced to a small, delicate young woman in a white unbelted smock reaching to below her knees and a white bandanna that gave her the look of a stern and dedicated nun, a novice in a nursing order. Jaga was from Poland;

her name, explained Anton, was pronounced with a "Y" but spelled with an initial "J." Mr. Zuckerman, he told Jaga—"the well-known American writer"—was suffering premature hair loss.

Zuckerman sat down before the mirror and contemplated his hair loss, while Anton elaborated on the treatment: white menthol ointment to strengthen the follicles, dark tar ointment to cleanse and disinfect, steamer to stimulate circulation, then fingertip massage, followed by Swedish electric massage and two minutes under the ultraviolet rays. To finish off, No. 7 dressing and fifteen drops of the special hormone solution, five to the hairline at each of the temples, five where it was thinnest at the crown. Zuckerman was to apply the drops himself every morning at home: the drops to promote growth and then, sparingly, the pink dressing to prevent splitting and breaking of the hair ends he had left. Jaga nodded, Anton bounded off to the lab with his pile of specimens, and in the cubicle his treatment began, recalling to Zuckerman a second Mann protagonist with whom he now shared a dubious affinity: Herr von Aschenbach, tinting his locks and rouging his cheeks in a Venetian barbershop.

At the end of the hour session, Anton returned to guide Zuckerman back to the office. Facing each other across Anton's desk, they discussed the laboratory results.

"I have completed the microscopical examination of your hair and scalp scrapings. There is a condition which we call folliculitis simplex, which means there is clogging of the hair follicles. Over a period of time it has led to some loss of hair. Also, by robbing the hair of its natural sebum flow it has created dryness of the hair, with consequent breakage and splitting—which could lead to further loss of hair. I am afraid," said Anton, attempting in no way to soften the blow, "that there are quite a lot of follicles of the scalp which are devoid of hair. I am hoping that with some at least the papilla is only impaired and not destroyed. In this case regrowth can take place to some extent, in those areas. But only time will give us the answer to this. However, apart from the empty follicles, I feel that the prognosis in your case is good and that, with correct regular treatment and your help, your hair and scalp should respond and be restored to a healthy condition. We should be able to stop the clogging, obtain a freer flow of sebum, and restore the elasticity to the hair; then it will grow strong once again, making the overall appearance quite a bit thicker. The most important thing is that the loss of hair must not be allowed to continue."

It was the longest, most serious, most detailed and thoughtful diagnosis that Zuckerman had ever got from anyone for anything he had suffered in his life. Certainly the most optimistic he had heard in the last eighteen months. He couldn't remember ever having had a book reviewer who'd given a novel of his as full, precise, and accurate a reading as Anton had given his scalp. "Thank you, Anton," Zuckerman said.

"But."

"Yes?"

"There is a but," said Anton gravely.

"What is it?"

"What you do at home is just as important as what we do when you attend here for treatment. Number one, you must not drink to excess. You must stop this immediately. Number two, whatever is causing you undue pressure you must come to terms with. That there is undue pressure, I need no microscope to discover; I have only to look at you with my two eyes. Whatever it may be, you must eliminate it from your life. And quickly. Otherwise, Mr. Zuckerman, I must be honest with you: we are fighting a losing battle."

* * *

In the full-length mirror on his bathroom door, he saw at the start of each day a skinny old man holding Nathan's pajamas: denuded scalp, fleshy hips, bony frame, softening belly. Eighteen months without his regular morning exercises and his long afternoon walks and his body had aged twenty years. Awakening as always promptly at eight, he worked now—worked with the same stubborn resolve with which formerly he could mount a morning-long assault on a single recalcitrant page—to fall back to sleep until noon. Steady, dogged, driven Zuckerman, unable ordinarily to go half an hour without reaching for a pad to write on or a book to underline, now with a bed sheet pulled over his head to shorten the time until evening, when he could hit the bottle. Self-regulating Zuckerman emptying another fifth, self-controlled Zuckerman sucking the last of a roach, self-sufficient Zuckerman helplessly clinging to his harem (enlarged to include his trichological technician). Anything to cheer him up or put him out.

His comforters told him it was only tension and he should learn to relax. It was only loneliness and would disappear once he was back reading after dinner across from another worthy wife. They suggested that he was always finding new ways to be unhappy and didn't know how to enjoy himself unless he was suffering. They agreed with the psychoanalyst that the pain was self-inflicted: penance for the popularity of *Carnovsky*, come-uppance for the financial bonanza—the enviable, comfortable American success story wrecked by the wrathful cells. Zuckerman was taking "pain" back to its root in *poena*, the Latin word for punishment: poena for the family portrait the whole country had assumed to be his, for the tastelessness that had affronted millions and the shamelessness that had enraged his tribe. The crippling of his upper torso was, transparently, the punishment called forth by his crime: mutilation as primitive justice. If the writing arm offend thee, cut it off and cast it from thee. Beneath the ironic carapace of a tolerant soul, he was the most unforgiving Yahweh of them all. Who else could have written so blasphemously of Jewish moral suffocation but a self-suffocating Jew like Nathan? Yes, your illness is your necessity—that was the gist of it—and what prevents your recovery is you, you choosing to be incurable, you bullying into submission your own inbuilt will to be well. Unconsciously, Zuckerman was frightened of everything—another assumption generally accepted among his diagnosticians: frightened of success and frightened of failure; frightened of being known and frightened of being forgotten; frightened of being bizarre and frightened of being ordinary; frightened of being admired and frightened of being despised; frightened of being alone and frightened of being among people; frightened, after *Carnovsky*, of himself and his instincts, and frightened of being frightened. Cowardly betrayer of his verbal life—collaborator with the enemies of his filthy mouth. Unconsciously suppressing his talent for fear of what it'd do next.

But Zuckerman wasn't buying it. His unconscious wasn't that unconscious. Wasn't that conventional. His unconscious, living with a published writer since 1953, understood what the job entailed. He had great faith in his unconscious—he could never have come this far without it. If anything, it was tougher and smarter than he was, probably what *protected* him against the envy of rivals, or the contempt of mandarins, or the outrage of Jews, or the charge by his brother Henry that what had shocked their ailing father into his fatal coronary in 1969 was Zuckerman's hate-filled, mocking best-seller. If the Morse code of the psyche was indeed being tapped out along the wires of physical pain, the message had to be more original than "Don't ever write that stuff again."

Of course one could always interpret a difficulty like this as a test of character. But what was twenty years of writing fiction? He didn't need his character tested. He already had enough obstinacy to last a lifetime. Artistic principles? Up to his ears in them. If the idea was to marshal still more grim determination in the face of prolonged literary labors, then his pain was sadly misinformed. He could accomplish that on his own. Doomed to it by the mere passage of time. The resolute patience he already possessed made life more excruciating by the year. Another twenty like the last twenty and there'd be no frustration to challenge him.

No, if the pain intended to accomplish something truly worthwhile, it would not be to strengthen his adamancy but to *undo* the stranglehold. Suppose there was the message flashing forth from a buried Nathan along the fibers of his nerves: Let the others write the books. Leave the fate of literature in their good hands and relinquish life alone in your room. It isn't life and it isn't you. It's ten talons clawing at twenty-six letters. Some animal carrying on in the zoo like that and you'd think it was horrifying. "But surely they could hang a tire for him to swing on—at least bring in a little mate to roll around with him on the floor." If you were to watch some certified madman groaning over a table in his little cell, observe him trying to make something sensible out of qwertyuiop, asdfghjkl, and zxcvbnm, see him engrossed to the exclusion of all else by three such nonsensical words, you'd be appalled, you'd clutch his keeper's arm and ask, "Is there nothing to be done? No antihallucinogen? No surgical procedure?" But before the keeper could even reply, "Nothing—it's hopeless," the lunatic would be up on his feet, out of his mind, and shrieking at you through his bars: "Stop this infernal interference! Stop this shouting in my ears! How do I complete my life's great work with all these gaping visitors and their noise!"

Suppose pain had come, then, not to cut him down to size like Herbert's "Lord," or to teach him civility like Tom Sawyer's Aunt Polly, or to make him into a Jew like Job, but to rescue Zuckerman from the wrong calling. What if pain was offering Zuckerman the best deal he'd ever had, a way out of what he should never have got into? The right to be stupid. The right to be lazy. The right to be no one and nothing. Instead of solitude, company; instead of silence, voices; instead of projects, escapades; instead of twenty, thirty, forty years more of relentless doubt-ridden concentration, a future of diversity, of idleness, of abandon. To leave what is given untransformed. To capitulate to qwertyuiop, asdfghjkl, and zxcvbnm, to let those three words say it all.

Pain to bring Nathan purposeless pleasure. Maybe a good dose of agony is what it took to debauch him. Drink? Dope? The intellectual sin of light amusement, of senselessness self-induced? Well, if he must. And so many women? Women arriving and departing in shifts, one barely more than a child, another the wife of his financial adviser? Usually it's the accountant who cheats the client, not the other way around. But what could he do if pain required it? He himself had been removed from command, released from all scruple by the helpless need. Zuckerman was to shut up and do what he was told—leave off rationing out the hours, stop suppressing urges and super-supervising every affair, and from here on, *drift*, just drift, carried along by whatever gives succor, lying beneath and watching as solace is delivered from above. Surrender to surrender, it's the time.

Yet if that really was the psyche's enjoinder, to what end? To *no* end? To the end of ends? To escape completely the clutches of self-justification? To learn to lead a wholly indefensible, unjustified life—and to learn to like it? If so, thought Zuckerman, if that is the future that my pain has in mind, then this is going to be the character test to top them all.

2

Gone

Zuckerman had lost his subject. His health, his hair, and his subject. Just as well he couldn't find a posture for writing. What he'd made his fiction from was gone— his birthplace the burnt-out landscape of a racial war and the people who'd been giants to him dead. The great Jewish struggle was with the Arab states; here it was over, the Jersey side of the Hudson, his West Bank, occupied now by an alien tribe. No new Newark was going to spring up again for Zuckerman, not like the first one: no fathers like those pioneering Jewish fathers bursting with taboos, no sons like their sons boiling with temptations, no loyalties, no ambitions, no rebellions, no capitulations, no clashes quite so convulsive again. Never again to feel such tender emotion and such a desire to escape. Without a father and a mother and a homeland, he was no longer a novelist. No longer a son, no longer a writer. Everything that galvanized him had been extinguished, leaving nothing unmistakably his and nobody else's to claim, exploit, enlarge, and reconstruct.

These were his distressing thoughts, reclining on the playmat unemployed.

His brother's charge—that *Carnovsky* had precipitated their father's fatal coronary—hadn't been easy to forget. Memories of his father's last years, of the strain between them, the bitterness, the bewildering estrangement, gnawed away at him along with Henry's dubious accusation; so did the curse his father had fastened upon him with his dying breath; so did the idea that he had written what he had, as he had, simply to be odious, that his work embodied little more than stubborn defiance toward a respectable chiropodist. Having completed not a page worth keeping since that deathbed rebuke, he had half begun to believe that if it hadn't been for his father's frazzled nerves and rigid principles and narrow understanding he'd never have been a writer at all. A first-generation American father possessed by the Jewish demons, a second-generation American son possessed by their exorcism: that was his whole story.

Zuckerman's mother, a quiet, simple woman, dutiful and inoffensive though she was, always seemed to him a slightly more carefree and emancipated spirit. Redressing historical grievances, righting intolerable wrongs, changing the tragic course of Jewish history—all this she gladly left for her husband to accomplish during dinner. He made the noise and had the opinions, she contented herself with preparing their meal and feeding the children and enjoying, while it lasted, the harmonious family life. A year after his death she developed a brain tumor. For months she'd been complaining of episodes of dizziness, of headache, of little memory lapses. Her first time in the hospital, the doctors diagnosed a minor stroke, nothing to leave her seriously impaired; four months later, when they admitted her again, she was able to recognize her neurologist when he came by the room, but when he asked if she would write her name for him on a piece of paper, she took the pen from his hand and instead of "Selma" wrote the word "Holocaust," perfectly spelled. This was in Miami Beach in 1970, inscribed by a woman whose writings otherwise consisted of recipes on index cards, several thousand thank-you notes, and a voluminous file of knitting instructions.

Zuckerman was pretty sure that before that morning she'd never even spoken the word aloud. Her responsibility wasn't brooding on horrors but sitting at night getting the knitting done and planning the next day's chores. But she had a tumor in her head the size of a lemon, and it seemed to have forced out everything except the one word. That it couldn't dislodge. It must have been there all the time without their even knowing.

Three years this month. December 21. In 1970 it had been a Monday. The neurologist told him on the phone that the brain tumor could take anywhere from two to four weeks to kill her, but when Zuckerman reached her room from the airport the bed was already empty. His brother, who'd arrived separately by plane an hour before, was in a chair by the window, jaw fixed, face a blank, looking, for all his size and strength, as though he were made of plaster. One good whack and he'd just be pieces on the floor. "Mother's gone," he said.

Of all the words that Zuckerman had read, written, spoken, or heard, there were none he could think of whose rhetorical effectiveness could ever measure up to those two. Not she's going, not she will go, but *she's gone*.

Zuckerman hadn't seen the inside of a synagogue since the early sixties, when he used to ride forth each month to defend *Higher Education* on the temple lecture trail. The nonbeliever wondered nonetheless if his mother oughtn't to be buried in the Orthodox manner—washed with water, wrapped in a shroud, and laid in a plain wood box. Even before she'd begun to be troubled by the first disabling signs of her fatal illness, four years of tending to an invalid husband had already reduced her to a replica of her own late mother in advanced old age, and it was in the hospital morgue, blankly staring at the prominent ancestral nose set in the small, childlike family skull, that curving sickle from which the sloping wedge of the careworn face sharply dropped away, that he thought of an Orthodox burial. But Henry wanted her wearing the soft gray crepe dress she'd looked so pretty in the night he and Carol had taken her over to Lincoln Center to hear Theodore Bikel, and Zuckerman saw no reason to argue. He was trying really to *place* this corpse, to connect what had happened to his mother with what had happened to her mother, whose funeral he'd witnessed as a child. He was trying to figure out where, in life, they were. As for the attire in which she should molder away, let Henry have what he wished. All that mattered was to get this last job done as unbruisingly as possible; then he and Henry needn't agree on anything or speak to each other ever again. Her welfare was all that had kept them in touch anyway; over her empty hospital bed they'd met for the first time since their father's Florida funeral the year before.

Yes, she was all Henry's now. The angry edge to his organizational efficiency made it unmistakable to everyone that inquiries relating to her burial were to be addressed to the younger son. When the rabbi came around to their mother's apartment to plan the chapel service— the same softly bearded young rabbi who'd officiated at their father's graveside—Nathan sat off by himself saying nothing, while Henry, who'd just gotten back from the mortician's, questioned the rabbi about the arrangements. "I thought I'd read a little poetry," the rabbi told him, "something about growing things. I know how she loved her plants." They all looked over at the plants as though they were Mrs. Zuckerman's orphaned babies. It was far too soon to see anything straight—not the plants on the windowsill, or the noodle casserole in the refrigerator, or the dry-cleaning ticket in her purse. "Then I'll read some psalms," the rabbi said. "I'd like to conclude, if you wouldn't mind, with some personal observations of my own. I knew your parents from the Temple. I knew them well. I know how much they enjoyed together as a husband and wife. I know how they loved their family." "Good," said Henry. "And you, Mr. Zuckerman?" the rabbi asked Nathan. "Any memories you'd like to share? I'll be glad to include them in my remarks." He took a pad and pencil from his jacket to note down whatever the writer had to tell him, but Nathan merely shook his head. "The memories," said Zuckerman, "come in their own time." "Rabbi," said Henry, "*I'll* deliver the eulogy." Earlier he'd said that he didn't think he'd have the emotional wherewithal to get through it. "If you could," said the rabbi, "despite your grief, that would be wonderful." "And if I cry," replied Henry, "that won't hurt either. She was the best mother in the world."

So: the historical record was to be set straight at last. Henry would cleanse from the minds of her Florida friends the libelous portrait in *Carnovsky*. Life and art are distinct, thought Zuckerman; what could be clearer? Yet the distinction is wholly elusive. That writing is an act of imagination seems to perplex and infuriate everyone.

Carol arrived on an evening plane with their two oldest kids and Henry put them up with him at a hotel over on Collins Avenue. Zuckerman slept at his mother's alone. He didn't bother making the bed up anew but, between the sheets that had covered her only two nights before, planted his face in her pillow. "Mama, where are you?" He knew where she was, at the mortician's wearing her gray crepe dress; nonetheless, he couldn't stop asking. His little mother, five feet two, had disappeared into the enormity of death. Probably the biggest thing she'd ever entered before was L. Bamberger's department store on Market Street in Newark.

Till that night Zuckerman hadn't known who the dead were or just how far away. She murmured into his dreams, but no matter how hard he strained to hear, he could not understand. An inch separated them, nothing separated them, they were indivisible—yet no message could make it through. He seemed to be dreaming that he was deaf. In the dream he thought, "Not gone; beyond gone," and awoke in the dark, bubbling saliva, her pillow soaked with his spittle. "Poor child," he said, feeling for her as though *she* were the child, his child, as though she'd died at ten instead of sixty-six. He felt a pain in his head the size of a lemon. It was her brain tumor.

Coming out of sleep that morning, struggling to be freed from a final dream of a nearby object at a dreadful distance, he began readying himself to find her beside him. Mustn't be frightened. The last thing she'd ever do would be to come back to frighten Nathan. But when he opened his eyes to the daylight and rolled over on his side there was no dead woman on the other half of the bed. There was no way to see her beside him again.

He got up to brush his teeth, then came back into the bedroom and, still in his pajamas, stepped into the closet among her clothes. He put his hand in the pocket of a poplin raincoat that looked hardly ever to have been worn, and found a freshly opened packet of Kleenex. One of the tissues lay folded in the pocket's seam. He touched it to his nose, but it smelled only of itself.

From a square plastic case down in the pocket he extracted a transparent rain bonnet. It was no bigger than a Band-Aid, folded up to about a quarter-inch thickness, but that it was tucked away so neatly didn't necessarily mean that she had never used it. The case was pale blue, stamped "Compliments of SYLVIA'S, Distinctive Fashions, Boca Raton." The "S" in Sylvia's was entwined in a rose, something she would have appreciated. Little flowers always bordered her thank-you notes. Sometimes his wives had got the flowered thank-you notes for as little as a thoughtful long-distance call.

In her other pocket, something soft and gauzy. Withdrawing the unseen thing gave him a bad moment. It wasn't exactly like his mother to be carrying her underwear in her pocket like a drunk. Had the tumor impaired her thinking in pitiful little ways none of them had even known? But it wasn't a bra or her underpants, only a stocking-colored chiffon hood, something to wear home from the beauty parlor. Newly set hair, hers, or so he was ready to believe, holding the hood up to his nose and searching for some fragrance he remembered. The sharp smells, the decisive noises, the American ideals, the Zionist zeal, the Jewish indignation, all that to a boy was vivid and inspiring, almost superhuman, had belonged to his father; the mother who'd been so enormous to him for the first ten years of his life was as diaphanous in recollection as the chiffon hood. A breast, then a lap, then a fading voice calling after him, "Be careful." Then a long gap when there is nothing of her to remember, just the invisible somebody, anxious to please, reporting to him on the phone the weather in New Jersey. Then the Florida retirement and the blond hair. Neatly dressed for the tropics in pink cotton slacks and a monogrammed white blouse (wearing the pearl pin he'd bought years before in Orly Airport and brought home for her from his first summer in France), a little brown-skinned blond-haired woman waiting down at the end of the corridor when he gets off the elevator with his bag: the unconstrained grin, the encompassing dark eyes, the sad clinging embrace, instantly followed by the gratitude. Such gratitude! It was as though the President of the United States had arrived at the condominium to call upon some lucky citizen whose name and address had been drawn from a hat.

The last thing he found in her pocket was an item scissored out of *The New York Times*. Must have been sent to her by someone back home. She'd slipped it out of the envelope down by the mailbox, then put it into her pocket on the way to the beauty parlor or to Sylvia's in Boca Raton. The headaches and the dizziness still incorrectly diagnosed, she'd driven off with a friend on a rainy afternoon to look at a dress. When it got to be 4 p.m., the two widows would have decided on a restaurant for the early-bird dinner. Looking down the menu, she would have thought: "This is what Victor would order. This is what Nathan would order. This is what Henry would order." Only then would she choose for herself. "My husband," she would tell the waitress, "loved ocean scallops. If they're fresh, and the nice big ones, I'll have the ocean scallops, please."

One short paragraph in the *Times* clipping had been squared off with rough pencil markings. Not by her. Any frame she drew would have been finely made with a freshly sharpened point. The paragraph was from an article in the "New Jersey Section" dated Sunday, December 6, 1970. She died fifteen days later.

Similarly, Newark has produced many famous people, ranging from Nathan Zuckerman, the author, to Jerry Lewis, the comedian. Elizabeth's most famous offspring are military men: General Winfield Scott, a 19th-century Army man, and Adm. William "Bull" Halsey, a World War II hero.

In a kitchen cabinet he found a yellow plastic watering can decorated with white daisies and held it under the tap. He went into the living room to sprinkle her wilting plants. So sick and lost and forgetful that last week, she'd not even tended her garden. Zuckerman turned on the FM station she'd had the dial tuned to and, listening to her favorite music—famous show tunes smothered in strings—proceeded with the watering can along the windowsill. He believed he recognized plants from New Jersey and his high-school days. Could that be? So many years as her companions? He raised the blind. Out past the new condominium that had gone up next door, he saw a wide slice of the bay. So long as her husband was alive, they used to look at the bay ritually from the bedroom balcony every evening after dinner and the TV news. "Oh, Nathan, you should have seen the colors last night at sunset—only you would have the words to describe it." But after Dr. Zuckerman's death, she couldn't face all that ineffable beauty alone and just keep watching television, no matter what was on.

There was no one out sailing yet. It wasn't even seven. But two stories below, in the parking lot between the two buildings, a very old man in bright green slacks and a bright green cap and a canary-yellow sweater was taking his constitutional, walking uncertainly back and forth between rows of shining cars. Stopping to lean on the hood of a new two-toned Cadillac, his own perhaps, he looked up to where Zuckerman was standing in his pajamas at the picture window. He waved, Zuckerman waved back and for some reason showed him the watering can. The man called out but too weakly to be heard above the radio. On her FM station they were playing an uninterrupted medley of the tunes from *Finian's Rainbow*. "How are things in Glocca Morra, this fine day . . . ?" A spasm of emotion went through him: this fine day in Glocca Morra, where was she? Next they'd play "All the Things You Are" and break him down completely. That was the record to which she'd taught him the box step so that he could dance at his bar mitzvah reception. After he'd finished all his homework they would practice on the rugless floor between the dining- and living-room Orientals, while Henry, with an imaginary clarinet between his fingers, pretended to be Artie Shaw. Henry would mouth the words as Helen Forrest sang—anything to get into the act, even half asleep in his pajamas and slippers. At the evening reception, catered in a Bergen Street hall several rungs down from the Schary Manor, everybody in the family applauded (and all his young friends mockingly cheered) as Nathan and Mrs. Zuckerman stepped out under the rainbow lighting and began to fox-trot. When the boy bandleader lowered his sax and started to croon the lyrics—"You are/The promised kiss of springtime"—she looked proudly in the eyes of her thirteen-year-old partner—his hand placed inches away from where he imagined that even inadvertently he might touch the strap of her brassiere—and softly confided in his ear, "You *are*, darling."

The apartment, purchased ten years earlier by his father, had been decorated with the help of daughter-in-law Carol. On the longest wall hung two large reproductions framed in faded wormwood, a white Paris street by Utrillo and the hills of a lilac-colored island by Gauguin. The bright linen chosen by the women for the cushions of the bamboo living-room set showed branches of trees bearing lemons and limes. Tropical Eden, that was the idea, even as the strokes hammered her husband down into his grave. She'd done her best, but the organic opposition did better, and she'd lost.

There was nothing to do for her sadness. If ever there had been, the chance was gone.

While he was still watching the old man down in the parking lot totter from one row of cars back to the other, a key turned in the door. Despite the unequivocal gleam off the bay—that dancing of light in which the living exult, proclaiming, "Sunny existence knows nothing of death!"—the likelihood of her reappearance seemed suddenly as strong as it had while he lay on the bed dazed from the hours of dreaming on her pillow. Maybe he was still dazed up on his feet.

There was nothing to fear from her ghost. She'd return only to get a look at him, to see that he hadn't lost weight in the three months since his last visit, she'd return only to sit with him at the table and listen to him talk. He remembered when he'd first come home from college, the Wednesday evening of his first Thanksgiving vacation—how, with a great unforeseen gush of feeling, he'd told her about the books he was absorbed in at school. This was after they'd cleaned up the dinner dishes; his brother had left even before dessert for the AZA basketball game down at the Y, and his father was back in the office, dealing with the last of the day's paperwork. Zuckerman remembered her apron, her housedress, the dark graying hair, remembered the old Newark sofa recovered—the year he went off to Chicago—in a sober, utilitarian, stain-resistant "Scotch plaid." She was stretched out on the living-room sofa, smiling faintly at all he was explaining to her, and imperceptibly falling asleep. He put her right out discussing Hobbes and the social contract. But how she loved that he knew it all. What a sedative that was, the most powerful she'd ever dared to take until, after her husband's death, they got her on phenobarbital.

All this sentiment. He wondered if it was only to compensate for the damage that he was reputed to have done her with the portrait of the mother in *Carnovsky*, if that was the origin of these tender memories softening him up while he watered her plants. He wondered if watering the plants wasn't itself willed, artificial, a bit of heart-pleasing Broadway business as contrived as his crying over her favorite kitsch show tune. Is this what writing has done? All that self-conscious self-mining— and now I can't even be allowed to take purely the shock of my own mother's death. Not even when I'm in tears am I sure what gives.

He had to smile when he saw who came in: no, it wasn't the specter of his mother returned from the dead with a key to the door so as to hear from him now about Locke and Rousseau but a small, bottom-heavy, earth-bound stranger, the color of bittersweet chocolate. She was dressed in a roomy turquoise slacks suit and wore a wig of shiny black curls. This would be Olivia, the eighty-three-year-old cleaning woman. Who he was, this man in pajamas humming to Mrs. Zuckerman's music and watering her plants with her flowered can, she was not so quick to figure out.

"Who you!" she shouted and, stamping her foot, showed him the way out.

"You're Olivia. Take it easy, Olivia. I'm Mrs. Zuckerman's son. I'm Nathan. From New York. I slept here last night. You can close the door and come in." He extended his hand. "I'm Nathan Zuckerman."

"My God, you like t' scared me to death. My heart just flutterin'. You say you Nathan?"

"Yes."

"What you do for a livin'?"

"I'm the writer."

She walked straight up to shake his hand. "Well, you a good-lookin' man, ain't you?"

"You're a good-looking woman. How do you do?"

"Where's your momma?"

He told her and she dropped backwards onto the sofa. "My Miz Zuckerman? My Miz Zuckerman? My beautiful Miz Zuckerman? That cain't be! I seen her last Thursday. All dressed up—goin' out. Wearin' that white coat with the big collar. I say to her, 'Oh, Miz Zuckerman, how beautiful you looks.' She *cain't* be dead, not my Miz Zuckerman!"

He sat beside her on the sofa, holding and stroking her hand until finally she was able to be consoled.

"You wants me to clean up anyway?" Olivia asked.

"If you feel you can, why not?"

"You wants me to fix you a egg?"

"No, I'm all right, thanks. You always come this early?"

"Most usually I gets here six-thirty sharp. Me and Miz Zuckerman, we likes a early start. Oh, I cain't believe that woman is dead. People always dyin', but you never get used to it. The nicest woman in the world."

"She went quickly, Olivia. Without any pain."

"I say to Miz Zuckerman, 'Miz Zuckerman, your place so clean it hard for me to *make* it clean.'"

"I understand."

"I tells her all the time, 'You wastin' your money on me. Everything so sparklin' here, I just rubs around to make it more sparklin' but I cain't.' I never comes in here we don't hug and kiss soon as we sees each other. That woman she kind to everybody. They comes in here, the other ladies, and she sit in her chair, that one, and they start peskerin' her to give 'em some advice. The widow mens, they's no different. She go downstairs with them and she stand there and she show them how to fold up their laundry out of the dryin' machine. They wants to marry her practically the day your father pass. The man upstairs want to take her on a fancy cruise, and some other ones down in the lobby, they's linin' up like little boys to takes her Sunday afternoon to the movie. But she love your daddy too much for any monkey business. Not her. She don't play that. She always sayin' to me, after Dr. Zuckerman pass, 'I was lucky all my life, Olivia. I had the three best mens in the world.' She tell me all the tales from when you and the dentist was little boys. What you write them books about?"

"Good question," he said.

"Okay, you can go right back to what you was doin'. I gon' get myself along now." And as though she'd just stopped by to chew the fat, she got up and went off to the bathroom with her shopping bag. She came out wearing a red cotton beret and, over her slacks, a long red apron. "Wants me to spray the shoe closet?"

"Whatever you usually do."

"Most usually I sprays. Keep the shoes good."

"Then do it."

* * *

Henry's eulogy lasted nearly an hour. Nathan kept count as Henry slipped each page beneath the last. Seventeen—some five thousand words. It would have taken him a week to write five thousand words, but Henry had done it overnight, and in a hotel suite with three young children and a wife. Zuckerman couldn't write if there was a cat in the room. That was one of the differences between them.

A hundred mourners were gathered in the mortuary chapel, mostly lonely widowed Jewish women in their sixties and seventies who'd been transplanted South after a lifetime in New York and New Jersey. By the time Henry had finished, they all wished they'd had such a son, and not only because of his height, posture, profile, and lucrative practice: it was the depth of the filial devotion. Zuckerman thought, If sons were like that, I'd have had one myself. Not that Henry was out to put something over on them; it was by no means a ludicrously idealized portrait—the virtues were all hers. Yet they were virtues of the kind that make life happy for a little boy. Chekhov, drawing on material resembling Henry's, had written a story one-third that length called "The Darling." However, Chekhov wasn't undoing the damage of *Carnovsky*.

From the cemetery they went back to their cousin Essie's apartment, across the hall from their mother's, to receive and feed the mourners. Some of the women asked Henry if they might have his eulogy. He promised to oblige as soon as he got back to the office, where his receptionist would make photocopies and mail them off. "He's the dentist," Zuckerman overheard one of the widows saying, "and he writes better than the writer." Zuckerman learned from several of her friends how his mother taught the widowers to fold their laundry when they took it out of the dryer. A vigorous-looking man with a white fringe of hair and a tanned face came over to shake his hand. "Maltz is my name—sorry about your mother." "Thank you." "You left New York when?" "Yesterday morning." "How was the weather? Very cold?" "Not too bad." "I should never have come here," Maltz said. "I'll stay till the lease runs out. Two more years. If I live, I'll be eighty-five. Then I go home. I have fourteen grandchildren in north Jersey. Somebody'll take me in." While Mr. Maltz spoke, a woman wearing dark glasses stood to the side and listened. Zuckerman wasn't sure if she could see, though she appeared to be by herself. He said, "I'm Nathan, how do you do?" "Oh, I know who you are. Your mother talked about you all the time." "Did she?" "I told her, 'Next time he comes, Selma, bring him around—I could give him plenty of stories to write.' My brother owns a nursing home in Lakewood, New Jersey, and the things he sees you could make a book out of. If somebody wrote it, it might do the world some good." "What does he see?" Zuckerman asked. "What doesn't he see. An old lady there sits by the door, by the entrance to the home, all day long. When he asks her what she's doing, she says, 'I'm waiting for my son.' Next time the son visits, my brother says to him, 'Your mother sits by the door waiting for you every day. Why don't you come to visit her a little more often?' And you know what he says? I don't even have to tell you what he says. He says, 'Do you know what the traffic is like getting over to Jersey from Brooklyn?'"

They stayed for hours. They talked to him, to Henry, to each other, and though nobody asked for a drink, they ate up most of the food, and Zuckerman thought, No, it can't be easy on these people down here when somebody in the building dies—everybody wonders if he's going to be next. And somebody is.

Henry flew back with the children to New Jersey and his patients, leaving Carol behind with Nathan to go through the apartment and decide what to give away to the Jewish charities—Carol, so that there'd be no fights. She never fought with anyone—"the sweetest disposition in the world," by the in-laws' reports. She was a peppy, youthful thirty-four, a girlishly pretty woman who cut her hair short and fancied woolen knee socks and about whom Zuckerman could say very little more, though she'd been his brother's wife for almost fifteen years. She always pretended when he was around to know nothing, to have read nothing, to have no thoughts on any subject; if he was in the same room, she wouldn't even dare to recount an anecdote, though Zuckerman often heard from his mother how "thoroughly delightful" she could be when she and Henry entertained the family. But Carol herself, in order to reveal nothing he could criticize or ridicule, revealed to him nothing at all. All he knew for sure about Carol was that she didn't want to wind up in a book.

They emptied the two shallow drawers at the top of his mother's dresser and spread her little boxes between them on the dining table. They opened them one at a time. Carol offered Nathan a ring bearing a tag that read "Grandma Shechner's wedding band." He remembered from childhood how it had astounded him to hear of her taking it from her mother's finger moments after she had died: his mother had touched a corpse and then come home and made their dinner. "You keep it," said Nathan—"the jewelry should go to the girls someday. Or to Leslie's wife." Carol smiled—Leslie, her son, was ten. "But you must have something of hers," she pleaded. "It isn't right, our taking it all." She didn't know what he had already—the white piece of paper with the word "Holocaust" on it. "I didn't want to throw it away," the neurologist had said to him; "not until you'd seen it." Nathan had thanked him and put it in his wallet; now *he* couldn't throw it away.

In one of the boxes Carol came upon the round gold
pin his mother had received for being president of the
PTA back when he and Henry were in grade school: on
the face, the name of their school engraved above a flow-
ering tree; on the reverse side, the inscription "Selma
Zuckerman, 1944–45." I'd be better off, he thought,
carrying that around in my wallet. He told Carol to take
it for Henry, however. In his eulogy, Henry had gone
on for nearly a page about her PTA presidency and what
a proud child that had made him.

Opening a tortoiseshell box Zuckerman found a stack
of knitting instructions. The handwriting was hers, so
were the precision and the practical thinking. "1 row sc
all around, held in to keep flat . . . front same as back
up to armhole . . . sleeve 46 sts K 2 P 2 for 2½/add 1 st
each end every 5 rows . . ." Each sheet of instructions was
folded in half and bore on the outside the name of the
grandchild, the niece, the nephew, the daughter-in-law
for whom she was preparing her gift. He read the names
of each of his wives in his mother's writing. "Vest for
Betsy." "Raglan cardigan—Virginia." "Laura's navy
sweater." "Suppose I take this," Zuckerman said. He tied
the bundle with a five-inch snippet of pinkish-white yarn
that he found at the bottom of the tortoiseshell box—a
sample, he thought, to be matched up at the yarn shop
for some project being planned only the day before yesterday. There was a snapshot at the bottom of the box,
a picture of himself. Severe unsmiling face, dark low
hairline, clean polo shirt, khaki Bermudas, white sweat
socks, suitably dirtied white tennis sneakers, and clutched
in his hand, a Modern Library Giant. His tall skinny
frame looked to him tense with impatience for the whole
enormously unknown future. On the back of the snapshot
his mother had written, "N., Labor Day 1949. On his
way to college." It had been taken on the rear lawn of
the Newark house by his father. He remembered the

brand-new Brownie box camera and how his father was absolutely certain that the sun was supposed to shine into the camera. He remembered the Modern Library Giant: *Das Kapital*.

He waited for Carol to say it: "And this is the woman the world will remember as Mrs. Carnovsky, this woman who adored you." But having seen how his mother had identified the picture, she made no accusations. All she did was put one hand over her eyes as though the radiance off the bay was momentarily too much. She'd been up all night too, Nathan realized, helping Henry compose his seventeen pages. Perhaps she'd written them. She was supposed to have written wonderfully exhaustive letters to her in-laws, itemizing all she and Henry had seen and eaten when they were off on their vacation trips. She read prodigiously too, and not the books he might have imagined from the mask of innocuous niceness that she invariably showed him. Once, while using the upstairs phone in South Orange, Zuckerman had gone through the pile of books on the table at her side of the bed: a note-covered pad thrust into the second volume of a history of the Crusades, a heavily underlined paperback copy of Huizinga on the Middle Ages, and at least six books on Charlemagne borrowed from the Seton Hall University library, historical works written in French. Back in 1964, when Henry drove to Manhattan and stayed up all night in Nathan's apartment trying to decide whether he had the right to leave Carol and the children for the patient with whom he was then having an affair, he had positively rhapsodized over her "brilliance," calling her, in an exceptional outburst of lyricism, "my brain, my eyes, my understanding." When they were traveling abroad on Henry's vacation, her fluent French enabled them to see everything, go everywhere, to have a really wonderful time; when he'd made his first small investments, Carol had read up on stocks and bonds and given him more good practical advice than the guy at Merrill Lynch; her backyard full of flowers, a spectacular success written up and photographed for the local weekly, had been planted only after a winter of patient planning on graph paper and studying landscape gardening books. Henry spoke movingly of the strength she'd given her parents when her twin brother died of meningitis in his second year of law school. "If only she'd gone on for her Ph.D." He said this mournfully a dozen times. "She was *made* for a Ph.D."—as though, had the wife as well as her husband (had the wife *instead* of the husband) proceeded after their early student marriage to do three years of postgraduate work, Henry would somehow be free to disregard the claims of loyalty, habit, duty, and conscience—and his forebodings of social censure and eternal doom—and run away with the mistress whose brilliance seemed to reside largely in her sexual allure.

Zuckerman waited for Carol to look up at him and say, "This woman, this touching, harmless woman who saved this picture in this box, who wrote 'N. on his way to college,' that was her reward." But Carol, who after all these years had still not spoken with Nathan, in English or French, about her brother's tragic death, or the waning of the Middle Ages, or stocks, or bonds, or landscape gardening, was not about to open her heart about his shortcomings as a son, not to a trigger-happy novelist like him. But then Carol, as everyone knew, wouldn't fight with anyone, which was why Henry had left her behind to settle the touchy business of who should take home what from their mother's dresser. Perhaps Henry had also left her behind because of the touchier business of the mistress—either another mistress, or maybe still the same one—whom he could more readily arrange to see with a wife away in Florida a few more days. It had been an exemplary eulogy, deserving of all the praise it received—nor did Zuckerman mean to cast doubt upon the sincerity of his brother's grief; still, Henry was only human, however heroically he tried not to show it. Indeed, a son of Henry's filial devotion might even find in the hollow aftermath of such a sudden loss the need for dizzying, obliterating raptures categorically beyond the means of any wife, with or without a Ph.D.

Two hours later Zuckerman was out the door with his overnight bag and his knitting instructions. In his free hand he carried a cardboard-covered book about the size of the school composition books he used for taking notes. Carol had found it at the bottom of the lingerie drawer under some boxes of winter gloves still in their original store wrappings. Reproduced on the cover was a pinkish pastel drawing of a sleeping infant, angelically blond and endowed with regulation ringlets, lashes, and globular cheeks; an empty bottle lay to the side of the billowing coverlet, and one of the infant's little fists rested half open beside its cherry-red tiny bow lips. The book was called *Your Baby's Care*. Printed near the bottom of the cover was the name of the hospital where he'd been born. *Your Baby's Care* must have been presented to her in her room shortly after his delivery. Use had weakened the binding and she had fastened the covers back together with transparent tape—two old strips of tape that had gone brownish-yellow over the decades and that cracked at the spine when Zuckerman opened the book and saw on the reverse of the cover the footprint he'd left there in the first week of life. On the first page, in her symmetrical handwriting, his mother had recorded the details of his birth—day, hour, name of parents and attending physician; on the next page, beneath the title "Notes on Development of the Baby," was recorded his weekly weight throughout his first year, then the day he held up his head, the day he sat up, crept, stood alone, spoke his first word, walked, and cut his first and second teeth. Then the contents—a hundred pages of "rules" for raising and training a newborn child. "Baby care is a great art," the new mother was told; ". . . these rules have resulted from the experience of physicians over many years." Zuckerman put his suitcase on the floor of the elevator and began to turn the pages. "Let the baby sleep in the sun all morning . . . To weigh the baby, undress him completely . . . After the bath, dry him gently with soft, warm towels, patting the skin gently . . . The best stockings for a baby are cotton . . . There are two kinds of croup . . . The morning is the best time for play . . ."

The elevator stopped, the door opened, but Zuckerman's attention was fixed on a small colorless blot halfway down the page headed "Feeding." "It is important that each breast be emptied completely every 24 hours in order to keep up the supply of milk. To empty the breast by hand . . ."

His mother's milk had stained the page. He had no hard evidence to prove it, but then he was not an archaeologist presenting a paper: he was the son who had learned to live on her body, and that body was now in a box underground, and he didn't need hard evidence. If he who had spoken his first word in her presence on March 3, 1934—and his last word on the phone to her the previous Sunday—if he should choose to believe that a drop of her milk had fallen just there while she followed the paragraph instructing a young mother in how to empty her breasts, what was to stop him? Closing his eyes, he put his tongue to the page, and when he opened them again saw that he was being watched through the elevator door by an emaciated old woman across the lobby, leaning in exhaustion on her aluminum walker. Well, if she knew what she'd just seen she could now tell everyone in the building that she'd seen everything.

In the lobby there was a sign up for an Israel Bond Rally at a Bal Harbour Hotel, and hanging beside it a crayoned notice, now out of date, for a Hanukkah festival party in the condominium lobby sponsored by the building's Social Committee. He passed the bank of mailboxes and then came back and looked for hers. "Zuckerman S./414." He set down his suitcase, placed the baby book beside it, and touched the raised letters of the nameplate with his fingers. When World War I began, she was ten. When it ended, she was fourteen. When the stock market crashed, she was twenty-five. She was twenty-nine when I was born and thirty-seven on December 7, 1941. When Eisenhower invaded Europe, she was just my age . . . But none of this answered the cradle-question of where Mama had gone.

The day before, Henry had left instructions for the post office to forward her mail to South Orange. There was a plain white envelope, however, down in the box, probably a condolence note dropped through the slot by a neighbor that morning. In his jacket pocket Nathan had her extra set of house keys; one of her little tags was still attached, labeling them "Extra set of house keys." With the tiniest of the keys he opened the box. The envelope was not addressed. Inside was a pale green index card on which someone who preferred remaining anonymous had printed with a fountain pen

> MAY YOUR MOTHER SUCK
> COCKS IN HELL—
> AND YOU SOON
> JOIN HER!
> YOU DESERVE IT.
>   ONE OF YOUR
>   MANY FOES

In hell no less. An act she never even committed on earth, you stupid son of a bitch. Who'd written him this? The fastest way to find out was to go back upstairs and ask Esther. She knew everybody's business. She also had no aversion to reprisals; her success in life was founded on them. They'd check together through the building directory until Essie had figured out who it was, who living in which apartment, then he'd walk over to Meyer Lansky's hotel to find out from the bell captain who could be hired to do a little job. Why not that for a change, instead of flying back to New York to file the green index card under "Mother's Death"? You could not be a nothing writer fellow forever, doing nothing with the strongest feelings but turning them over to characters to deal with in books. It'd be worth a couple thousand to have the ten fingers that wrote those twenty words smashed beneath some moron's boot. You could probably do it down here on your Diners Club card.

Only whose maimed fingers would they turn out to be? What would the comedy come up with this time— one of the widowers she'd taught how to fold laundry, or the old guy tottering around the parking lot who'd waved to Zuckerman up by the window while he was watering her plants?

A nothing fellow, he flew home to his files. A nasty, nothing fellow, surreptitiously vindictive, covertly malicious, who behind the mask of fiction had punished his adoring mother for no reason. True or false? In a school debate, he could have argued persuasively for either proposition.

Gone. Mother, father, brother, birthplace, subject, health, hair—according to the critic Milton Appel, his talent too. According to Appel, there hadn't been much talent to lose. In *Inquiry*, the Jewish cultural monthly that fifteen years earlier had published Zuckerman's first stories, Milton Appel had unleashed an attack upon Zuckerman's career that made Macduff's assault upon Macbeth look almost lackadaisical. Zuckerman should have been so lucky as to come away with decapitation. A head wasn't enough for Appel; he tore you limb from limb.

Zuckerman didn't know Appel. They'd met only twice—one August out in the Springs on Long Island, strolling by each other at the Barnes Hole beach, then briefly at a big college arts festival where each was sitting on a different panel. These meetings came some years after Appel's review of Zuckerman's first book had appeared in the Sunday *Times*. That review had thrilled him. In the *Times* in 1959, the twenty-six-year-old author had looked to Appel like a wunderkind, the stories in *Higher Education* "fresh, authoritative, exact"—for Appel, almost too pointed in their portraiture of American Jews clamoring to enter Pig Heaven: because the world Zuckerman knew still remained insufficiently transformed by the young writer's imagination, the book, for all its freshness, seemed to Appel more like social documentation, finally, than a work of art.

Fourteen years on, following the success of *Carnovsky*, Appel reconsidered what he called Zuckerman's "case": now the Jews represented in *Higher Education* had been twisted out of human recognition by a willful vulgar imagination largely indifferent to social accuracy and the tenets of realistic fiction. Except for a single readable story, that first collection was tendentious junk, the by-product of a pervasive and unfocused hostility. The three books that followed had nothing to redeem them at all— mean, joyless, patronizing little novels, contemptuously dismissive of the complex depths. No Jews like Zuckerman's had ever existed other than as caricature; as literature that could interest grown people, none of the books could be said to exist at all, but were contrived as a species of sub-literature for the newly "liberated" middle class, for an "audience," as distinguished from serious readers. Though probably himself not an outright anti-Semite, Zuckerman was certainly no friend of the Jews: *Carnovsky*'s ugly animus proved that.

Since Zuckerman had heard most of this before—and usually in *Inquiry*, whose editorial admiration he'd lost long ago—he tried being reasonable for fifteen minutes. *He doesn't find me funny. Well, no sense writing to tell him to laugh. He thinks I depict Jewish lives for the sake of belittling them. He thinks I lower the tone to please the crowd. To him it's vulgar desecration. Horseplay as heresy. He thinks I'm "superior" and "nasty" and no more. Well, he's under no obligation to think otherwise. I never set myself up as Elie Wiesel.*

But long after the reasonable quarter hour had passed, he remained shocked and outraged and hurt, not so much by Appel's reconsidered judgment as by the polemical overkill, the exhaustive reprimand that just asked for a fight. This set Zuckerman's teeth on edge. It couldn't miss. What hurt most was that Milton Appel had been a leading wunderkind of the Jewish generation preceding his own, a contributing editor to Rahv's *Partisan Review*, a fellow at Ransom's Indiana School of Letters, already publishing essays on European modernism and analyses of the exploding American mass culture while Zuckerman was still in high school taking insurgency training from Philip Wylie and his Finnley Wren. In the early fifties, during a two-year stint at Fort Dix, Zuckerman composed a fifteen-page "Letter from the Army," describing the bristling class resentment between black cadre just back from Korea, white commanding officers recalled to active duty, and the young college-educated draftees like himself. Though rejected by *Partisan*, the manuscript was returned with a note which, when he read it, excited him nearly as much as if it had been a letter of acceptance: "Study more Orwell and try us again. M.A."

One of Appel's own early *Partisan* essays, written when

he was just back from World War II, had been cherished reading among Zuckerman's friends at the University of Chicago circa 1950. No one, as far as they knew, had ever written so unapologetically about the gulf between the coarse-grained Jewish fathers whose values had developed in an embattled American immigrant milieu and their bookish, nervous American sons. Appel pushed his subject beyond moralizing into deterministic drama. It could not be otherwise on either side—a conflict of integrities. Each time Zuckerman returned to school from a bruising vacation in New Jersey, he took his copy of the essay out of its file folder ("Appel, Milton, 1918- ") and, to regain some perspective on his falling out with his family, read it through again. He wasn't alone... He was a social type... His fight with his father was a tragic necessity...

In truth, the type of intellectual Jewish boy whom Appel had portrayed, and whose struggles he illustrated with painful incidents from his own early life, had sounded to Zuckerman far worse off than himself. Maybe because these were boys more deeply and exclusively intellectual, maybe because their fathers were more benighted. Either way, Appel didn't minimize the suffering. *Alienated, rootless, anguished, bewildered, brooding, tortured, powerless*— he could have been describing the inner life of a convict on a Mississippi chain gang instead of the predicament of a son who worshipped books that his underschooled father was too ignorant to care about or understand. Certainly Zuckerman at twenty didn't feel tortured *plus* powerless *plus* anguished—he really just wanted his father to lay off. Despite all the solace that essay had given him, Zuckerman wondered if there might not be more comedy in the conflict than Appel was willing to grant.

Then again, Appel's might well have been a more dispiriting upbringing than his own, and the young Appel what he himself would have labeled a "case." According to Appel, it was a source of the deepest shame to him during his adolescence that his father, whose livelihood was earned from the seat of a horse-drawn wagon, could speak to him easily only in Yiddish. When, in his twenties, the time came for the son to break away from the impoverished immigrant household and take a room of his own for himself and his books, the father couldn't begin to understand where he was going or why. They shouted, they screamed, they wept, the table was struck, the door was slammed, and only then did young Milton leave home. Zuckerman, on the other hand, had a father who spoke in English and practiced chiropody in a downtown Newark office building that overlooked the plane trees in Washington Park; a father who'd read William Shirer's *Berlin Diary* and Wendell Wilkie's *One World* and took pride in keeping up; civic-minded, well-informed, a member admittedly of one of the lesser medical orders, but a professional, and in that family the first. Four older brothers were shopkeepers and salesmen; Dr. Zuckerman was the first of the line even to have gone beyond an American grade school. Zuckerman's problem was that his father *half* understood. They shouted and screamed, but in addition they sat down to reason together, and to that there is no end. Talk about torture. For the son to butcher the father with a carving knife, then step across his guts and out the door, may be a more merciful solution all around than to sit down religiously to reason together when there is nothing to reason about.

Appel's anthology of Yiddish fiction, in his own translations, appeared when Zuckerman was at Fort Dix. It was the last thing Zuckerman expected after the pained, dramatic diction of that essay proclaiming the depths of alienation from a Jewish past. There were also the critical essays that had, since then, made Appel's reputation in the quarterlies and earned him, without benefit of an advanced degree, first a lectureship at the New School and then a teaching job up the Hudson at Bard. He wrote about Camus and Koestler and Verga and Gorky, about Melville and Whitman and Dreiser, about the soul revealed in the Eisenhower press conference and the mind of Alger Hiss—about practically everything except the language in which his father had hollered for old junk from his wagon. But this was hardly because the Jew was in hiding. The disputatious stance, the aggressively marginal sensibility, the disavowal of community ties, the taste for scrutinizing a social event as though it were a dream or a work of art—to Zuckerman this was the very mark of the intellectual Jews in their thirties and forties on whom he was modeling his own style of thought. Reading the quarterlies for the essays and fiction of Appel and his generation—Jewish sons born into immigrant families a decade or more after his own father—only corroborated what he'd first sensed as a teenage undergraduate at Chicago: to be raised as a post-immigrant Jew in America was to be given a ticket out of the ghetto into a wholly unconstrained world of thought. Without an Old Country link and a strangling church like the Italians, or the Irish, or the Poles, without generations òf American forebears to bind you to American life, or blind you by your loyalty to its deformities, you could read whatever you wanted and write however and whatever you pleased. Alienated? Just another way to say "Set free!" A Jew set free even from Jews—yet only by steadily maintaining self-consciousness as a Jew. That was the thrillingly paradoxical kicker.

Though Appel's initial motive for compiling his Yiddish anthology was, more than likely, the sheer excitement of discovering a language whose range he could never have guessed from the coarseness of his father's speech, there seemed a deliberately provocative intention too. Far from signaling anything so comforting and inauthentic as a prodigal son's return to the fold, it seemed, in fact, a stand *against*: to Zuckerman, if to no one else, a stand against the secret shame of the assimilationists, against the distortions of the Jewish nostalgists, against the boring, bloodless faith of the prospering new suburbs—best of all, an exhilarating stand against the snobbish condescension of those famous departments of English literature from whose impeccable Christian ranks the literary Jew, with his mongrelized speech and caterwauling inflections, had until yesterday been pointedly excluded. To Appel's restless, half-formed young admirer, there was the dynamic feel of a rebellious act in the resurrection of those Yiddish writers, a rebellion all the more savory for undercutting the anthologist's own early rebellion. The Jew set free, an animal so ravished and agitated by his inexhaustible new hunger that he rears up suddenly and bites his tail, relishing the intriguing taste of himself even while screaming anguished sentences about the agonies inflicted by his teeth.

After reading Appel's Yiddish anthology, Zuckerman went up to New York on his next overnight pass, and on lower Fourth Avenue, on booksellers' row, where he normally loaded up with used Modern Library books for a quarter apiece, searched the stores until he found secondhand copies of a Yiddish grammar and an English–Yiddish dictionary. He bought them, took them back to Fort Dix, and after supper in the mess hall, returned to the quiet empty office where during the day he wrote press releases for the Public Information Officer. There at his desk he sat studying Yiddish. Just one lesson each night and by the time he was discharged he would be reading his literary forefathers in their original tongue. He managed to stick with it for six weeks.

Zuckerman had retained only a very dim sense of Appel's appearance from the mid-sixties. Round-faced, bespectacled, tallish, balding—that's all he came up with. Maybe the looks weren't as memorable as the opinions. A more vivid recollection was of a striking wife. Was he still married to the pretty, delicate, dark woman who'd been walking hand in hand with him along the Barnes Hole beach? Zuckerman recalled rumors of an adulterous passion. Which had she been, the discard or the prize? According to *Inquiry*'s biographical note, Milton Appel was at Harvard for the year, on leave from his Distinguished Professorship at NYU. When literary Manhattan spoke of Appel, it seemed to Zuckerman that the name Milton was intoned with unusual warmth and respect. He couldn't turn up anyone who had it in for the bastard. He fished and found nothing. In Manhattan. Incredible. There *was* talk of a counterculture daughter, a dropout from Swarthmore who took drugs. Good. That might eat his guts out. Then word went around that Milton was in a Boston hospital with kidney stones. Zuckerman would have liked to witness their passing. Someone said that a friend had seen him walking in Cambridge with a cane. From kidney stones? Hooray. That satisfied the ill will a little. Ill will? He was furious, especially when he learned that before publishing "The Case of Nathan Zuckerman" Appel had tried it out on the road, traveled the college lecture circuit telling students and their professors just how awful a writer he was. Then Zuckerman heard that over at *Inquiry* they had received a single letter in his defense. The letter, which Appel had dismissed in a one-line rebuttal, turned out to have been written by a young woman Zuckerman had slept with during a summer on the Bread Loaf staff. Well, he'd had a good time too, but where were the rest of his supporters, all the influential allies? Writers shouldn't—and not only do they tell themselves they shouldn't, but everybody who is not a writer reminds them time and again—writers of course shouldn't, but still they do sometimes take these things to heart. Appel's attack—no, Appel in and of himself, the infuriating fact of his corporeal existence—was all he could think about (except for his pain and his harem).

The comfort that idiot had given the fatheads! Those xenophobes, those sentimental, chauvinist, philistine Jews, vindicated in their judgment of Zuckerman by the cultivated verdict of unassailable Appel, Jews whose political discussions and cultural pleasures and social arrangements, whose simple dinner conversation, the Distinguished Professor couldn't have borne for ten seconds. Their kitsch alone made Appel's gorge rise; their taste in Jewish entertainment was the subject of short scalding pieces he still dutifully published in the back pages of the intellectual journals. Nor could they have borne Appel for long either. His stern moral dissection of their leisure pursuits—had the remarks been delivered around the card table at the Y, instead of in magazines they'd never heard of—would have struck them as cracked. His condemnation of their favorite hit shows would have seemed to them nothing less than anti-Semitic. Oh, he was tough on all those successful Jews for liking that cheap middlebrow crap. Beside Milton Appel, Zuckerman would have begun to look good to these people. That was the real joke. Zuckerman had been raised in the class that *loved* that crap, had known them all his life as family and family friends, visited with them, eaten with them, joked with them, had listened for hours to their opinions even while Appel was arguing in his editorial office with Philip Rahv and acting the gent to John Crowe Ransom. Zuckerman knew them still. He also knew that nowhere, not even in the most satiric of his juvenilia, was there anything to match Appel's disgust at contemplating this audience authenticating their "Jewishness" on Broadway. How did Zuckerman know? Ah, this is what you know about someone you have to hate: he charges you with his crime and castigates himself in you. Appel's disgust for the happy millions who worship at the shrine of the delicatessen and cherish *Fiddler on the Roof* was far beyond anything in Zuckerman's nastiest pages. How could Zuckerman be sure? He hated Appel, that's how. He hated Appel and would never forgive or forget that attack.

Sooner or later there comes to every writer the two-thousand-, three-thousand-, five-thousand-word lashing that doesn't just sting for the regulation seventy-two hours but rankles all his life. Zuckerman now had his: to treasure in his quotable storehouse till he died, the unkindest review of all, embedded as indelibly (and just about as useful) as "Abou Ben Adhem" and "Annabel Lee," the first two poems he'd had to memorize for a high-school English class.

Inquiry's publication of Appel's essay—and the outbreak of Zuckerman's hatred—took place in May 1973. In October, five thousand Egyptian and Syrian tanks attacked Israel on Yom Kippur afternoon. Caught off guard, the Israelis took three weeks this time to destroy the Arab armies and approach the suburbs of Damascus and Cairo. But after the rallying to victory, the Israeli defeat: in the Security Council, the European press, even in the U.S. Congress, condemnation of Jewish aggression. Of all things, in the desperate search for allies, Milton Appel turned to the worst of Jewish writers for an article in support of the Jewish state.

The appeal wasn't put directly, but through their mutual acquaintance Ivan Felt, who had once been Appel's graduate assistant at NYU. Zuckerman, who knew Felt from the artist's colony at Quahsay, had introduced him to his own publisher the year before, and Felt's first novel, soon to be published, would carry a paragraph of appreciation by Zuckerman on the jacket. The contemptuous destructive rage of the sixties was Felt's subject, the insolent anarchy and gleeful debauchery that

had overturned even the most unlikely American lives
while Johnson was devastating Vietnam for the networks.
The book was as raw as Felt but, alas, only half as
overbearing; Zuckerman's guess was that if he could get
all that overbearing nature coursing through the prose,
abandon his halfhearted objectivity and strange lingering
respect for the great moral theme, Ivan Felt might yet
become a real artist in the demonic, spiteful Céline line.
Surely his letters, Zuckerman wrote to Felt, if not his
fiction, would live forever in the annals of paranoia. As
for the brash, presumptuous overconfidence and osten-
tatious egoism, it remained to be seen how much protection they would offer for the long-drawn-out brawl:
Felt was twenty-seven and the literary career yet to begin.

Syracuse— 12/1/73

Nathan—

Xerox paragraph (enclosed) from correspondence
between M. Appel and myself concerning NZ. (Rest
about B.U. vacancy I asked him, and now you, to
support me for.) I stopped at his Harvard pulpit
when in Boston ten days back. Hadn't heard any
echo since galleys went off to him weeks ago. Told
me he'd read a chapter but wasn't "responsive" to
"what that sort of humor represents." Only trying
to strip everything I fear of its "prestige." I said
what's wrong with that, but he wasn't interested,
said he didn't have strong impressions any longer
of my book, his mind far away from fiction. On
Israel's enemies. "They'd kill us all gladly," he told
me. I told him that's how I saw *everything*. When
later I said of Israel, "Who isn't worried?" he thought
I was assuming a profitable role—took it for play-
acting. So out I lashed at the tirade on you. He
said I should have written the magazine if I wanted
to debate. He didn't have the energy or inclination

now—"Other things on my mind." On leaving I
added that one Jew worried about Israel was you.
His paragraph follow-up to that parting shot. Civilized world knows how celebrated paranoid would
rush to respond. Wait to learn what invitation to
clear your conscience whips up in loving soul like
you.

Your public toilet,
I.F.

"Buried anger, troves of it"; this was young Dr. Felt
on the origins of Zuckerman's affliction. When news had
reached him the year before that Zuckerman was hos-
pitalized for a week, he phoned from Syracuse to find
out what was wrong, and stopped by when he was next
in New York. Out in the hallway, in his hooded high-
school windbreaker, he'd taken his comrade by the arms—
arms whose strength was ebbing by the day—and, only
half mockingly, pronounced judgment.

Felt was constructed like a dockworker, strutted about
like a circus strong man, piled layers of clothes on like
a peasant, and had the plain ungraspable face of a successful felon. Compact neck, thick back, shock-absorbent
legs—roll him up and you could shoot him from a
cannon. There were those in the Syracuse English Department waiting in line with matches and powder. Not
that Ivan cared. He'd already ascertained the proper relationship of Ivan Felt to his fellow man. So had Zuckerman, at twenty-seven: Stand alone. Like Swift and
Dostoevsky and Joyce and Flaubert. Obstinate independence. Unshakable defiance. Perilous freedom. No,
in thunder.

It was the first time they'd met on Eighty-first Street.
No sooner had Felt entered the living room and begun
pulling off his jacket, his cap, and the assortment of old
sweaters that he was wearing under the windbreaker and

over the T-shirt, than he was appraising aloud all he saw: "Velvet curtains. Persian carpet. Period mantelpiece. Overhead the ornamented plaster, below the gleaming parquet floor. Ah, but properly ascetic all the same. Not a hint of hedonism yet somehow—*cushy*. Very elegantly underfurnished, Nathan. The pad of a well-heeled monk."

But how Felt sardonically sized up the decor interested Zuckerman less than the new diagnosis. They just kept coming, these diagnoses. Everybody had a slant. The illness with a thousand meanings. They read the pain as his fifth book.

"Buried anger?" Zuckerman asked him. "Where'd you get that idea?"

"*Carnovsky*. Incomparable vehicle for the expression of your inadmissible loathings. Your hatred flows at flood level—so much hatred the heap of flesh can't contain it. Yet, outside the books, you act like you ain't even here. Moderation itself. Altogether, your books give off a greater sense of reality than you do. The first time I saw you, the night you came down into the dining room at Quahsay, the Glittering Guest of the Month, I said to little Gina, the lesbian poet, 'I'll bet that fellow never gets mad outside of those best-sellers.' Do you? Do you know how to?"

"You're tougher than I am, Ivan."

"That's a flattering way of saying I'm nastier than you are."

"When do *you* get angry outside of the writing?"

"I get angry when I want to get rid of somebody. They're in my way. Anger is a gun. I point it and I fire, and I keep firing till they disappear. I'm like you are in the writing outside the writing *and* in the writing. You button your lip. I'll say anything."

By now, with all Felt's layers of clothes unpeeled and

strewn across the floor, the pad of the well-heeled monk looked as if it had just been sacked.

"And," Zuckerman asked, "you believe what you're saying when you say anything?"

Felt looked over at him from the sofa as though Zuckerman were demented. "It doesn't matter whether *I* believe it. You're such a good soldier you don't even understand. The thing is to make *them* believe it. You are a good soldier. You seriously entertain the opposition point of view. You do all that *the right way*. You have to. You're always astonished how you provoke people by pouring out the secrets of your disgraceful inner life. You get stunned. You get *sad*. It's a wonder to you that you're such a scandal. The wonder to me is that you can possibly care. You, down with a case of the Bad-Taste Blues! To require the respect of men and women's tender caresses. Poppa's approval and Momma's love. Nathan Zuckerman! Who'd believe it?"

"And you require nothing? You believe *that*?"

"I sure don't let guilt enter everything, not the way you good soldiers do. It's nothing, guilt—it's self-indulgence. They despise me? They call me names? They don't approve? All the better. A girl tried to commit suicide at my place last week. Dropped by with her pills for a glass of my water. Swallowed them while I was off teaching my afternoon dopes. I was furious when I found her. I phoned for an ambulance, but I'd be damned if I'd go with her. If she had died? Fine with me. Let her die if that's what she wants. I don't stand in their way and nobody stands in mine. I say, 'No, I don't want any more of this—it's not for me.' And I start firing until it's gone. All you need from them is money—the rest you take care of yourself."

"Thanks for the lesson."

"Don't thank me," said Felt. "I learned it in high

school, reading you. Anger. Point it and fire it and just keep firing until they disappear. You'll be a healthy novelist in no time."

Appel's paragraph xeroxed by Felt and sent on to Zuckerman in New York:

Truth to tell, I don't know that there's much we can do—first the Jews were destroyed by gas, and now it may be in oil. Too many around New York are shameful on this matter: it's as if their circumcisions were acquired for other reasons. The people who raised hell about Vietnam are not saying much on Israel (but for a few souls). However, insofar as public opinion matters, or the tiny fraction of it we can reach, let me offer a suggestion that may irritate you, but which I'll make nonetheless. Why don't you ask your friend Nate Zuckerman to write something in behalf of Israel for the Times Op Ed page? He could surely get in there. If I come out in support of Israel there, that's not exactly news; it's expected. But if Zuckerman came out with a forthright statement, that would be news of a kind, since he has prestige with segments of the public that don't care for the rest of us. Maybe he has spoken up on this, but if so I haven't seen it. Or does he still feel that, as his Carnovsky says, the Jews can stick their historical suffering up their ass? (And yes, I know that there's a difference between characters and authors; but I also know that grown-ups should not pretend that it's quite the difference they tell their students it is.) Anyway, brushing aside my evident hostility to his view on these matters, which is neither here nor there, I honestly believe that if he were to come out publicly, it would be of some interest. I think we're

at the point where the whole world is getting ready
to screw the Jews. At such points even the most
independent of souls might find it worth saying a
word.

Well, now he was angry outside of the books. Moderation? Never heard of it. He got down a copy of *Carnovsky*. Had it really been proposed in these pages that
Jews can stick their suffering quote unquote? A sentiment
so scathing just dropped like a shoe? He looked in his
book for the source of Appel's repugnance and found it
a third of the way through: penultimate line of two
thousand words of semi-hysterical protest against a family's obsession with their minority plight—declaration
of independence delivered by Carnovsky to his older sister
from the sanctuary of his bedroom at the age of fourteen.

So: undeluded by what grown-ups were pretending to
their students, Appel had attributed to the author the
rebellious outcry of a claustrophobic fourteen-year-old
boy. This was a licensed literary critic? No, no—an over-
wrought polemicist for endangered Jewry. The letter
could have come from the father in *Carnovsky*. It could
have come from his own real father. Written in Yiddish,
it could have come from Appel's, from that ignorant
immigrant junkman who, if he hadn't driven young Milton even crazier than Carnovsky, had clearly broken his
heart.

He pored over the paragraph like a professional litigant,
drawn back in fury to what galled him most. Then he called
Diana at school. Needed her to type. Had to see her right
away. Anger was a gun and he was opening fire.

Diana Rutherford was a student at Finch, the rich girls'
college around the corner where the Nixons had sent
Tricia. Zuckerman was out mailing a letter the first time
they met. She wore the standard cowpoke denims, jeans

and jacket beaten senseless on the sun-bleached stones of the Rio Grande, then shipped north to Bonwit's. "Mr. Zuckerman," she'd said, tapping him on his shoulder as he dropped the envelope in the box, "can I interview you for the school paper?" Only yards away, two roommates were in stitches over her brashness. This was obviously the college character. "Do you write for the school paper?" he asked her. "No." Confessed with a large guileless smile. Guileless, really? Twenty is the age of guile. "Walk me home," he said; "we'll talk about it." "Great," the character replied. "What's a smart girl like you doing at a place like Finch?" "My family thought I ought to learn how to cross my legs in a skirt." But when they got to his door fifty feet down the block, and he asked if she'd like to come up, the brashness gave out and she sashayed back to her friends.

The next afternoon, when the buzzer rang, he asked who it was through the intercom. "The girl who's not on the school paper." Her hands were trembling when he let her in. She lit a cigarette, then removed her coat, and without waiting to be invited, set about examining the books and the pictures. She took everything in room by room. Zuckerman followed.

In the study she asked, "Don't you have anything out of place here?"

"Only you."

"Look, it'll be no contest if you start off hypersardonic." Her voice quivering, she still spoke her mind. "Nobody like you should have to be afraid of anybody like me."

In the living room again, he took her coat from the sofa and, before hanging it in the closet, looked at the label. Bought in Milano. Setting somebody back many many hundreds of thousands of lire.

"You always this reckless?" he asked.

"I'm writing a paper on you." From the edge of the

sofa she lit the next cigarette. "That's a lie. That's not true."

"You're here on a dare."

"I thought you were somebody I could talk to."

"About what?"

"Men. I can't take much more of them."

He made them coffee and she began with her boyfriend, a law student. He neglected her and she didn't understand why. He phoned in tears in the middle of the night to say that he didn't want to see her but he didn't want to lose her either. Finally she'd written a letter asking him what was going on. "I'm young," she told Zuckerman, "and I want to fuck. It makes me feel ugly when he won't do it."

Diana was a long, narrow girl with a minute behind, small conical breasts, and boyishly clipped dark curls. Her chin was round like a child's, and so were her dark Red Indian eyes. She was straight and circular, soft and angular, and certainly wasn't ugly, except for the pout, the Dead End Kid look around the mouth whenever she began to complain. Her clothes were a child's: tiny suede skirt over a black leotard and, pinched from Momma's closet to amaze the other girls, high-heeled black shoes with open toes and a sequined strap. The face was really a baby's too, until she smiled—that was big and captivating. Laughing she looked like someone who'd seen it all and emerged unscathed, a woman of fifty who'd been lucky.

What she'd seen and survived were the men. They'd been in pursuit since she was ten.

"Half your life," he said. "What have you learned?"

"Everything. They want to come in your hair, they want to beat your ass, they want to call you on the phone from work and get you to finger yourself while you're doing your homework. I'm without illusions, Mr. Zuckerman. Ever since I was in seventh grade a friend of my father's has been calling every month. He couldn't be sweeter to his wife and his kids, but me he's been calling since I'm twelve. He disguises his voice and every time it's the same damn thing: 'How would you like to straddle my cock?'"

"What do you do about it?"

"I didn't know what to do in the beginning except listen. I got frightened. I bought a whistle. To blow into the mouthpiece. To burst his eardrum. But when I blew it finally, he just laughed. It turned him on *more*. This is eight years now. He calls me at school once a month. 'How would you like to straddle my cock?' I say to him, 'Is that it? Is that the whole thing?' He doesn't answer. He doesn't have to. Because it is. Not even to do it. Just to say it. To me."

"Every month, for eight years, and you've done nothing about it except buy a whistle?"

"What am I supposed to do, call the cops?"

"What happened when you were ten?"

"The chauffeur used to play with me when he drove me to school."

"Is that true?"

"The author of *Carnovsky* asks me if that's true?"

"Well, you might be making yourself interesting by making it up. People do that."

"I assure you, it's writers who have to make things up, not girls."

After an hour he felt as if Temple Drake had hitched up from Memphis to talk about Popeye with Nathaniel Hawthorne. He was stunned. It was a little hard to believe in all she said she'd seen—in all she seemed to be saying she was. "And your parents?" he asked her. "What do they say to these chilling adventures with all the terrible men?"

"Parents?" She came catapulting up onto her feet, sprung by that one word alone from the cushioned nest she'd dug down in the sofa pillows. The length of the leotarded legs, the speed and aggression of the delicate fingers, that mocking, cocky beat she took before driving in her point—a budding female matador, Zuckerman decided. She'd certainly look great in the gear. Might be frightened out of her wits to begin with, but he could also see her going in there and doing it. *Come and get me.* She's breaking free and being brave—or trying hard, by tempting fate, to learn. Sure there's a side of her that wants and invites this erotic attention—along with the side that gets angry and confused; but all in all there is something more intriguing here than mere teenage chance-taking. There's a kind of perverse autonomy covering up a very interesting, highly strung girl (and woman, and child, and kid). He could remember what it was like saying, "Come and get me." That of course was before they'd got him. It got him. Whatever you wanted to call it, something had got him.

"Where have *you* been?" she asked. "There *are* no more parents. Parents are over. Look, I've tried to make a go of it with the law student. I thought he'd help me concentrate on this silly school. He studies, he jogs, he doesn't do too much dope, and he's only twenty-three— and for me that's young. I've worked hard on him, damn it, him *and* his hang-ups, and now, now he doesn't want to do it at all. I don't know what the matter is with that boy. I look at him cockeyed and he turns into a baby. Fear, I guess. The sane ones bore you practically to death, and the ones who fascinate you turn out to be nuts. Know what I've been pushed to? What I'm just about ready for? To be married. To be married and to get knocked up, and to say to the contractor, 'Put the pool in over there.'"

Twenty minutes after receiving Zuckerman's call, Diana was sitting in the study with the pages to be typed and

mailed to Appel. He'd filled four long yellow pages
before sliding from his chair to the playmat. Back on his
back he tried to get the throbbing to subside in his upper
arm by kneading the muscle with his fingers. The base
of his neck was on fire too, the toll for the longest
sustained piece of prose he'd composed sitting upright
in over a year. And there were more bullets left in the
chamber. Suppose through careful analysis of those early
essays I demonstrate how Appel harshly denounces Zuckerman because of a distressing conflict with Poppa insufficiently settled in himself—show that it's not only
the menace of Islam that's provoked this reappraisal of
my "case" but Ocean Hill–Brownsville and black anti-
Semitism, the condemnation of Israel in the Security
Council, even the New York teachers' strike; that it's
the media dada of loud Jewish Yippies whose playpen
goals he ludicrously associates with me. Now for *my*
reappraisal of him. It isn't that Appel thinks he was
wrong about Zuckerman in 1959. Or wrong about his
own rootlessness in 1946. Right then, and now that he's
changed his mind, right again. The "mind" may change,
or appear to, but never the inquisitor's passion for punishing verdicts. Behind the admirable flexibility of judicious reappraisal the theoretical substructure is still
blast-proof concrete: none of us as *seriozny* as Appel. "The
Irrefutable Rethinkings of Milton Appel." "Right and
Rigid in Every Decade: The Polemical Spasms of a Hanging Judge." He came up with titles by the dozen.

"I've never heard anybody like you on the phone,"
Diana said. She sat submerged in her secretarial cam-
ouflage: shapeless overalls and a bulky sweater intended
originally to help him dictate his fiction. When she
showed up in the child's skirt, little dictation was ever
taken. The skirt was another reason to give up. "You
should see yourself," she said. "Those prism glasses, that
contorted face. You should see what you look like. You

let something like this get inside you and it builds and builds until your head comes off. And with your hair in it. That's exactly why you're losing your hair. It's why you have all this pain. *Look* at you. Have you looked in a mirror?"

"Don't you get angry about things? I'm angry."

"Yes, sure, of course I do. There's always somebody in the background of anybody's life driving you mad and giving you cystitis. But I *think* about them. I do my yoga. I run around the block and I play tennis and I try to get rid of it. I can't live like that. I'd have an upset stomach for the rest of my life."

"You don't understand."

"Well, I think I do. You have it at school."

"You can't equate this with school."

"Well, you can. You get the same kind of knocks at college. And they're damn hard to get over. Especially when they seem to you totally unjust."

"Type the letter."

"I'd better read it first."

"Not necessary."

Through the prism glasses he impatiently watched her reading it, meanwhile kneading away at his upper arm to try to subdue the pain. What helped sometimes with the deltoid muscle was the electronic pain suppressor. But would the neurons even register that low-voltage shock, what with this supercharge of indignation lighting up his brain?

"I'm not typing this letter. Not if this is what it says."

"What the hell business is it of yours what it says?"

"I refuse to type this letter, Nathan. You're a crazy man when you start on these things, and this letter is crazy. 'If the Arabs were undone tomorrow by a plague of cheap solar power, you wouldn't give my books a second thought.' You're off your head. That makes no sense. He wrote what he wrote about your books because that is what he thinks. Period. Why even *care* what these people think, when you are you and they are nobody? *Look* at you. What a vulnerable, resentful mouth! Your hair is actually standing on end. Who is this little squirt anyway? Who is Milton Appel? I never read any books by him. They don't teach him at school. I can't fathom this in a man like you. You're an extremely sophisticated, civilized man—how can you be caught in a trap by these people and let them upset you to such a degree?"

"You're a twenty-year-old girl from an ultraprivileged Christian-Connecticut background, and I accept that you have no idea what this is all about."

"Well, a lot of people who aren't twenty and don't have ultraprivileged Christian-Connecticut backgrounds wouldn't understand either, not if they saw you looking like this. 'Why those Jews in *Higher Education*, all too authentic to you in 1959, are suddenly the excreta of a vulgar imagination is because the sole Jewish aggression sanctioned in 1973 is against Egypt, Syria, and the PLO.' Nathan, you can't believe the PLO is why he wrote that piece."

"But it *is*. If it wasn't for Yasir Arafat he'd never be on my ass. You don't know what frazzled Jewish nerves are like."

"I'm learning. Please, take a Percodan. Smoke some pot. Have a vodka. But *calm down*."

"You get over to that desk and type. I pay you to type for me."

"Well, not that much. Not enough for this." Again she read aloud from his letter. "'In your view, it really isn't deranged Islam or debilitated Christianity that's going to deal us the death blow anyway, but Jewish shits who write books like mine, carrying the hereditary curse of self-hate. And all to make a dollar. Six million dead— six million sold. Isn't that the way you really see it?' Nathan, this is all ludicrous and overstated. You're a man of forty and you're flailing out like a schoolboy who's been made to stand in the corner."

"Go home. I greatly admire your self-possession in telling me off like this, but I want you to go away."

"I'll stay till you calm down."

"I'm not calming down. I've been calm long enough. Go."

"Do you really think it's intelligent to be so unforgiving about this great wrong that's been committed against you? This enormous wrong?"

"Oh, should I forgive him?"

"Yes. You see, I *am* a Christian. I do believe in Christ. And in people like Gandhi. And *you're* going back to that dreadful dreadful Old Testament. That stonelike book. Eye for eye and teeth for teeth and never forgive anybody. Yes, I'm saying that I believe in forgiving my enemies. I can't believe in the end that it isn't healthier for everybody."

"Please don't prescribe peace and love. Don't make me a member of your generation."

"Gandhi wasn't a member of my generation. Jesus isn't a member of my generation. St. Francis of Assisi wasn't a member of my generation. As you God damn well know, *I'm* not even a member of my generation."

"But I'm not Jesus, Gandhi, St. Francis, or you. I'm a petty, raging, vengeful, unforgiving Jew, and I have been insulted one time too many by another petty, raging, vengeful, unforgiving Jew, and if you intend to stay, then type what I've written, because it cost me bloody hell in my aching joints to write it."

"Okay. If you're such a Jew, and these Jews are all so central to your thinking—and that they have this hold *is* unfathomable to me, really—but if you really are stuck on Jews like this, and if Israel does mean something to you, then sure I'll type—but only if you dictate an essay about Israel for *The New York Times*."

"You don't understand. That request from him, after what he's published in *Inquiry*, is the final insult. In *Inquiry*, run by the kind of people he used to attack before he began attacking people like me!"

"Only it is not an insult. He's asked you what he's asked because people know who you are, because you can be so easily *identified* with American Jews. What I can't understand is what you're in such a state about. Either do it or don't do it, but don't take it as an insult when it wasn't meant as one."

"What *was* it meant as? He wants me to write an article that says I'm not an anti-Semite anymore and that I love Israel with all my heart—and that he *can* stick up his ass."

"I can't believe that's what he wants you to write."

"Diana, when somebody who has said about me and my work and the Jews what this guy has, then turns around and says why don't you write something nice about us for a change—well, how can you fail to understand that this is particularly *galling* to me? 'Write something in behalf of Israel.' But what about the hostility to Jews that's at the heart of every word I publish? To propagate that caricature in *Inquiry*, publicly to damn *me* as the caricaturist, and then in private to suggest this piece—and with some expectation at least of the crypto anti-Semite's acquiescence! 'He has prestige with segments of the public that don't care for the rest of us.' Right—the scum, the scum whom his novels are fashioned to please. If Zuckerman, a Jew adored by the scum for finding Jews no less embarrassing and distasteful than they do, were to make the argument *for* the Jews *to* the scum, 'it would be of some interest.' You bet! Like a case of schizophrenia is of interest! On the other hand, when Appel speaks up in a Jewish crisis, 'it's expected.' Sign of deep human engagement and predictably superior compassion. Sign of nothing less than the good, the best, the most responsible Jewish son of them all. These Jews, these Jews and their responsible sons! First he says I vilify Jews under the guise of fiction, now he wants me to lobby for them in *The New York Times*! The comedy is that the real visceral haters of the bourgeois Jews, with the *real* contempt for their everyday lives, are these complex intellectual giants. They *loathe* them, and don't particularly care for the smell of the Jewish proletariat either. All of them full of sympathy suddenly for the ghetto world of their traditional fathers now that the traditional fathers are filed for safekeeping in Beth Moses Memorial Park. When they were alive they wanted to strangle the immigrant bastards to death because they dared to think they could actually be of consequence without ever having read Proust past *Swann's Way*. And the ghetto—what the ghetto saw of these guys was their heels: out, out, screaming for air, to write about great Jews like Ralph Waldo Emerson and William Dean Howells. But now that the Weathermen are around, and me and my friends Jerry Rubin and Herbert Marcuse and H. Rap Brown, it's where oh where's the inspired orderliness of those good old Hebrew school days? Where's the linoleum? Where's Aunt Rose? Where is all the wonderful inflexible patriarchal authority into which they wanted to stick a knife? Look, I obviously don't want to see Jews destroyed. That wouldn't make too much sense. But I am not an authority on Israel. I'm an authority on Newark. Not even on Newark. On the Weequahic section of Newark. If the truth be known, not even on the whole of the Weequahic section. I don't even go below Bergen Street."

"But it's not a matter of whether you're an authority. It's a matter of people reading what you say because at the moment you're very famous."

"So is Sammy Davis. So is Elizabeth Taylor. They're even more famous. And they're real Jews who haven't ruined their credentials writing vulgar books. They haven't set loose the illicit forces that are now corrupting the culture. Why doesn't he ask them, if he wants somebody famous? They'd jump at the chance. Besides, that I'm famous for what I'm famous for is precisely what makes me reprehensible to Appel. *That's* what he's scolding me about. He actually seems to have read that book as a manifesto for the instinctual life. As if he'd never heard of obsession. Or repression. Or repressed obsessive Jews. As if he isn't one himself, the fucking regressive nut! Diana, I have nothing to say, at Appel's request, about Israel. I can write an essay about a novelist, and even that takes six months, but I can't write an essay about international politics, not for anyone. I don't do it, I never have. I am not Joan Baez. I am not a great thinker like Leonard Bernstein. I am not a political figure—he flatters me to suggest that I am."

"But you're a Jewish figure. Whether you want to be or not. And as you seem to want to be, you might as well do it. Why are you making it so difficult? Just state your opinion. It's as simple as that. Where you stand."

"I will not make atonement on the Op Ed page for the books he's accused me of writing! I cracked a few jokes about playing stinky-pinky in Newark and you'd think I'd blown up the Knesset. Don't start confusing me with your Wasp clarity—'there is no problem.' There is! This is not my maiden appearance in the pages of *Foreskin* as their Self-Hating Jew of the Month."

"But that is a petty little ghetto quarrel of no interest to *anyone*. How many Jews can dance on the head of a pin? *No one cares.* You can't really remember what some silly magazine has said about you—your mind would just be muck. If the magazine is as awful as you say, why should you even bother to worry? Besides, the one subject is so big and the other is so tiny, and the two have come together for you in a very strange way that I *cannot* understand, no matter how many ways you explain it. To me it seems like you're balancing a very large mountain against a very tiny molehill, and, truthfully, if anybody had told me you were like this before I met you... or that Jews were like this. I just thought they were immigrants—period. No, I *don't* understand. Maybe I'm only twenty, but you're forty years old. Is this really what happens when people hit forty?"

"You bet. They've had it up to fucking here. This is *exactly* what happens. Twenty years into your livelihood, and whether you know how to do it, whether you should be doing it at all, still a matter of public debate! And still in doubt yourself. How do I even know that Appel isn't right? What if my writing's as bad as he says? I hate his guts, and obviously the sixties have driven him batty, but that doesn't make him a fool, you know. He's one of the few of them around who make any sense at all. Let's face it, even the worst criticism contains some truth. They always see something you're trying to hide."

"But he *exaggerates* it. It's all out of proportion. He doesn't see the good things. He won't even acknowledge that you're funny. That's ridiculous. He only sees crudely what you fail at. Well, everybody has failings."

"But suppose he's right. Suppose nobody needs my books. Suppose I don't even need them. Am I funny? And if I am, so what? So are the Ritz Brothers. Probably funnier. Suppose what he implies is true and I've poisoned their sense of the Jewish reality with my vulgar imagination. Suppose it's even half true. What if twenty years of writing has just been so much helplessness before a compulsion—submission to a lowly, inconsequential compulsion that I've dignified with all my principles, a compulsion probably not all that different from what made my mother clean the house for five hours every day. Where am I then? Look, I'm going to medical school."

"Pardon?"

"Medical school. I'm pretty sure I've got the grades. I want to be a doctor. I'm going back to the University of Chicago."

"Oh, shut up. So far, this conversation has just been depressing. Now it's idiotic."

"No, I've been thinking about this for a long time. I want to be an obstetrician."

"At your age? Really? In ten years you'll be fifty. Pardon me, but that's an old man."

"And in sixty years I'll be a hundred. But I'll worry about that then. Why don't you come with me? You can transfer your credits from Finch. We'll do our homework together."

"Do you want to write the piece about Israel or not?"

"No. I want to forget Israel. I want to forget Jews. I should have the day I left home. Take your penis out in public and of course the squad car comes around—but, really, this has gone on now a little too long. The way I found to spring myself from everything that held me captive as a boy, and it's simply extended the imprisonment to my fortieth year. Enough of my writing, enough of their scolding. Rebellion, obedience—discipline, explosion—injunction, resistance—accusation, denial—defiance, shame—no, the whole God damn thing has been a colossal mistake. This is not the position in life that I had hoped to fill. I want to be an obstetrician. Who quarrels with an obstetrician? Even the obstetrician who delivered Bugsy Siegel goes to bed at night with a clear conscience. He catches what comes out and everybody loves him. When the baby appears they don't start shouting, 'You call that a baby? That's not a baby!' No, whatever he hands them, they take it home. They're grateful for his just having been there. Imagine those butter-covered babies, Diana, with their

little Chinese eyes, imagine what seeing that does to the
spirit, *that* every morning, as opposed to grinding out
another two dubious pages. Conception? Gestation?
Gruesome laborious labor? The mother's business. You
just wash your hands and hold out the net. Twenty years
up here in the literary spheres is enough—now for the
fun of the flowing gutter. The bilge, the ooze, the gooey
drip. The stuff. No words, just stuff. Everything the
word's in place of. The lowest of genres—life itself.
Damn right I'll be fifty next time I look. No more words!
On to the delivery room before it's too late. Headlong
into the Cloaca Maxima and all the effusions thereof.
Leave Finch and fly out to Chicago with me. You can
go to school at my alma mater."

"Leave Finch and I lose my trust fund. You don't want
me anyway. You want a nursemaid. You want a gov-
erness."

"Would it make any difference if I said I'd marry
you?"

"Don't fuck with me."

"But would it?"

"Yes, it would, of course it would. Do it. Do it now.
Let's get married tonight. Then we'll run away from your
life and you'll become a doctor and I'll become a doctor's
wife. I'll take the phone calls. I'll make the appoint-
ments. I'll boil your instruments. The hell with my trust
fund. Let's do it now. Let's go out tonight and get the
license and the blood tests."

"My neck hurts too much tonight."

"That's what I figured. You're full of shit, Nathan.
There's only one thing for you to do and that's *to get on
with it*. WRITE ANOTHER BOOK. *Carnovsky* is not
the end of the world. You cannot make yourself a life of
misery out of a book that just happened to have been a
roaring success. It cannot stop you in your tracks like

this. Get up off the floor, get your hair back, straighten out your neck, and write a book that isn't *about* these Jews. *And then the Jews won't bug you.* Oh, what a pity you can't shake free. That you should still be aroused and hurt by this! Are you *always* fighting your father? I know it may sound like a cliché, probably it would be with somebody else, but in your case I happen to think that it's true. I look through these books on your shelves, your Freud, your Erikson, your Bettelheim, your Reich, and every single line about a father is underlined. Yet when you describe your father to me, he doesn't sound like a creature of any stature at all. He may have been Newark's greatest chiropodist, but he sure doesn't sound like much of a challenge otherwise. That a man of your breadth of intelligence and your total freedom in the world . . . that *this* should beat you down. That you should be so broken down from these *Jews.* You hate this critic Appel? You don't ever want to stop hating him? He's done you such a grievous injury? Okay, the hell with this crazy little four-page letter—go bonk him on the nose. Are Jews scared of physical confrontations? My father would go and punch him in the nose if he thought he'd been insulted the way you do. But you aren't man enough to do that, and you aren't man enough just to forget it—you aren't even man enough to write for the Op Ed page of *The New York Times*. Instead you lie there in your prism glasses and make up fairy tales about medical school, and having a doctor's office with a picture on the desk of a doctor's wife, and coming home FROM work and going out TO RELAX, and when someone on a plane faints and a stewardess asks if anybody here is a doctor, you can stand up and say I am."

"Why the hell not? They never come around when someone faints and ask if anybody here is a writer."

"More of your black-and-blue humor. Go back to school

again, to study, to be the professor's pet and make the Dean's List and get an ID card for the library and all the student activities. At forty. You know why I wouldn't marry you? I would say no anyway because I couldn't marry anybody so weak."

3

The Ward

One morning only a few days later, one very depressing morning in December 1973, after he'd been up much of the night vainly trying to compose into his tape recorder a more reasonable reply to Milton Appel, Zuckerman came down to the mailbox in his orthopedic collar to see why the postman had rung. He wished he'd brought a coat along: he was thinking of continuing out into the cold and on to the corner to jump from the roof of the Stanhope Hotel. He no longer seemed worth preserving. From 1 to 4 a.m., with the noose of a narrow electric heating pad encircling his cervical spine, he'd gone another fifteen rounds with Appel. And now the new day: what equally useful function could he perform through the interminable hours awake? Cunnilingus was about it. Step right up, sit right down. It was all he was good for. Blotted out everything else. That and hating Appel. Smothered with mothers and shouting at Jews. Yes, illness had done it: Zuckerman had become Carnovsky. The journalists had known it all along.

The problem with jumping is smashing your skull. That can't be pleasant. And if he wound up merely severing his spinal cord on the hotel canopy—well, he'd be bedridden for life, a fate hundreds of thousands of times worse than what already was making him miserable. On the other hand, a failed suicide that didn't completely cripple him might provide a new subject— more than could be said so far for success. But what if the pain vanished halfway down, went the way it came, leaped from his body as he sailed from the roof—what then? What if he saw in every salient detail a next book, a new start? Halfway down is probably just where that happens. Suppose he walked to the Stanhope simply as an experiment. Either the pain disappears before I reach the corner or I enter the hotel and wait for the elevator. Either it disappears before I get into the elevator or I go up to the top floor and out through the fire exit onto the roof. I walk straight to the parapet and look sixteen floors down to the traffic, and this pain comes to realize that I'm not kidding, that sixteen floors is a very respectable distance, that after a year and a half *it is time to leave me alone.* I lean out toward the street and I say to the pain—and I mean what I say—"One minute more and I *jump!*" I'll *scare* it out of me.

But all he scared with such thoughts was himself.

Two manila envelopes in the mailbox, so tightly wedged together that he skinned his knuckles in the excitement of prying them out. The medical-school catalogue, his application forms! What he hadn't dared to tell Diana was that already, weeks before, he'd sent off this inquiry to the University of Chicago. From his seat in the doctors' waiting rooms, watching the patients come and go, he'd begun to think: Why not? Four decades, four novels, two dead parents, and a brother I'll never speak to again—looks from the evidence like my exorcism's done. Why *not* this as a second life? They talk in earnest to fifty needy people every day. From morning to night, bombarded by stories, and none of their own devising. Stories intending to lead to a definite, useful, authoritative conclusion. Stories with a clear and practical purpose: *Cure me.* They follow carefully all the details, then they go to work. And either the job is doable or undoable, while mine is both at best and mostly not.

Tearing open the bigger of the two envelopes—well, he hadn't known a thrill quite like it since the fall of 1948, when the first of the college mail began to arrive. Each day he raced home after his last class and, over his quart of milk, madly read about the life to come; not even the delivery of the first bound edition of his first published book had promised such complete emancipation as those college catalogues. On the cover of the catalogue now in his hand, a light-and-shadow study of a university tower, stark, soaring, academic Gibraltar, the very symbol of the unassailable solidity of a medical vocation. Inside the front cover, the university calendar. *Jan. 4–5: Registration for Winter quarter . . . Jan. 4: Classes meet . . .* He quickly turned to find "Requirements for Admission" and read until he reached "Selection Policy" and the words that would change everything.

> The Committee on Admissions strives to make its decision on the basis of the ability, achievement, personality, character, and motivation of the candidates. Questions of race, color, religion, sex, marital status, age, national or ethnic origin, or geographic location have no bearing in the consideration of any application for the Pritzker School of Medicine.

They didn't care that he was forty. He was in.

But one page back, bad news. Sixteen hours of chemistry, twelve of biology, eight of physics—merely to qualify, twice as much coursework as he'd been expecting. In science. Well, the sooner the better. When classes meet on January 4, I'll be there to ignite my Bunsen burner. I'll pack a bag and fly out to Chicago—over my microscope in a month! Lots of women his age were doing it—what was to stop him? A year's grind as an undergraduate, four of medical studies, three of residency, and at forty-eight he'd be ready to open an office. That would give him twenty-five years in practice—if he could depend on his health. It was the change of professions that would *restore* his health. The pain would just dwindle away; if not, he'd cure himself: it would be within his power. But never again to give himself over to doctors who weren't interested enough or patient enough or simply curious enough to see a puzzle like his through to the end.

That's where the writing years would be of use. A doctor thinks, "Everybody ends badly, nothing I can do. He's just dying and I can't cure life." But a good writer can't abandon his character's suffering, not to narcotics or to death. Nor can he just leave a character to his fate by insinuating that his pain is somehow deserved for being self-induced. A writer learns to stay around, has to, in order to make sense of incurable life, in order to chart the turnings of the punishing unknown even where there's no sense to be made. His experience with all the doctors who had misdiagnosed the early stages of his mother's tumor and then failed him had convinced Zuckerman that, even if he was washed up as a writer, he couldn't do their job any worse than they did.

He was still in the hallway removing sheaves of application blanks from the university envelope when a UPS deliveryman opened the street door and announced a package for him. Yes, it appeared to be happening: once the worst is over, even the parcels are yours. Everything is yours. The suicide threat had forced fate's hand—an essentially unintelligent idea that he found himself believing.

The box contained a rectangular urethane pillow about a foot and a half long and a foot wide. Promised to him a week before and forgotten by him since. Everything was forgotten in the workless monotony of his empty five hundred days. The evening's marijuana didn't help either. His mental activity had come to focus on managing his pain and managing his women: either he was figuring out what pills to take or scheduling arrivals and departures to minimize the likelihood of collision.

He'd been put on to the pillow at his bank. Waiting in line to cash a check—cash for Diana's connection—trying to be patient despite the burning sensation running along the rim of his winged left scapula, he'd been tapped lightly from behind by a pint-sized white-haired gentleman with an evenly tanned sympathetic face. He wore a smart double-breasted dove-gray coat. A dove-gray hat was in the gloved hand at his side. Gloves of dove-gray suede. "I know how you can get rid of that thing," he told Zuckerman, pointing to his orthopedic collar. The mildest Old Country accent. A helpful smile.

"How?"

"Dr. Kotler's pillow. Eliminates chronic pain acquired during sleep. Based on research done by Dr. Kotler. A scientifically designed pillow made expressly for sufferers like yourself. With your wide shoulders and long neck, what you're doing on an ordinary pillow is pinching nerves and causing pain. Shoulders too?" he asked. "Extend into the arms?"

Zuckerman nodded. Pain everywhere.

"And X-rays show nothing? No history of whiplash, no accident, no fall? Just on you like that, unexplained?"

"Exactly."

"All acquired during sleep. That's what Dr. Kotler discovered and how he came up with his pillow. His pillow will restore you to a pain-free life. Twenty dollars plus postage. Comes with a satin pillowcase. In blue only."

"You don't happen to be Dr. Kotler's father?"

"Never married. Whose father I am, we'll never know."

He handed Zuckerman a blank envelope out of his pocket. "Write on this: name, along with mailing address. I'll see they send one tomorrow, C.O.D."

Well, he'd tried everything else, and this playful old character clearly meant no harm. With his white wavy hair and nut-colored face, in his woolens and skins of soft dove-gray, he seemed to Zuckerman like somebody out of a children's tale, one of those elfin elderly Jews, with large heart-shaped ears and dangling Buddha lobes, and dark earholes that looked as though they'd been dug to a burrow by a mouse; a nose of impressive length for a man barely reaching Zuckerman's chest, a nose that broadened as it descended, so that the nostrils, each a sizable crescent, were just about hidden by the wide, weighted tip; and eyes that were ageless, polished brown protruding eyes such as you see in photographs taken of prodigious little fiddlers at the age of three.

Watching Zuckerman write his name, the old man asked, "N. as in Nathan?"

"No," replied Zuckerman. "As in Neck."

"Of course. You are the young fellow who has handed me those laughs. I thought I recognized you but I wasn't sure—you've lost quite a number of hairs since I saw your last photo." He removed one glove and extended his hand. "I am Dr. Kotler. I don't make a production out of it with strangers. But you are no stranger, N. Zuckerman. I practiced in Newark for many, many years, began there long before you were born. Had my office in the Hotel Riviera down on Clinton and High before it was purchased by Father Divine."

"The Riviera?" Zuckerman laughed and forgot for the moment about his scapula. N. as in Nostalgia. This *was* a character out of a child's tale: his own. "The Riviera is where my parents spent their honeymoon weekend."

"Lucky people. It was a grand hotel in those days. My first office was on Academy Street near the *Newark Ledger*.

I started with the lumbago of the boys from the paper and an examining table I bought secondhand. The fire commissioner's girl friend had a lingerie shop just down the street. Mike Shumlin, brother of theatrical producer Herman, owned the Japtex shops. So you're our writer. I was expecting from the way you hit and run you'd be a little bantamweight like me. I read that book. Frankly the penis I had almost enough of by the five hundredth time, but what a floodgate of memories you opened up to those early, youthful days. A kick for me on every page. You mention Laurel Garden on Springfield Avenue. I attended Max Schmeling's third fight in the U.S., staged by Nick Kline at Laurel Garden. January 1929. His opponent, an Italian, Corri, was KO'd in one and a half minutes of the first round. Every German in Newark was there—you should have heard them. Saw Willie La Morte beat Corporal Izzie Schwartz that summer—flyweight championship, fifteen rounds. You mention the Empire Burlesque on Washington, near Market. I knew the old guy who managed it, grizzled old guy named Sutherland. Hinda Wassau, the blond Polish striptease queen—knew her personally. One of my patients. Knew producer Rube Bernstein, who Hinda married. You mention the old Newark Bears. I treated young Charlie Keller for his knee. Manager George Selkirk, one of my dearest friends. You mention the Newark Airport. When it opened up, Jerome Congleton was mayor. I attended the dedication. One hangar in those days. There the morning they cut the ribbon on the Pulaski Skyway. What a sight—a viaduct from ancient Rome rising out of the Jersey marshes. You mention the Branford Theater. Favorite place of mine. Saw the first stage shows, featuring Charley Melson and his band. Joe Penner and his 'Wanna Buy a Duck' routine. Oh, Newark was my turf then. Roast beef at Murray's. Lobsters at Dietsch's. The tube station, gateway to New York. The locust trees along the street with their skinny twisted pods. WJZ with Vincent Lopez. WOR with John B. Gambling. Jascha Heifetz at the Mosque. The B. F. Keith theater—the old Proctor's—featuring acts direct from the Palace on Broadway. Kitty Doner, with her sister Rose and her brother Ted. Ted sang, Rose danced. Mae Murray making a grand personal appearance. Alexander Moissi, the great Austrian actor, at the Shubert on Broad Street. George Arliss. Leslie Howard. Ethel Barrymore. A great place in those days, our dear Newark. Large enough to be big-time, small enough to walk down the street and greet people you knew. Vanished now. Everything that mattered to me down the twentieth-century drain. My birthplace, Vilna, decimated by Hitler, then stolen by Stalin. Newark, my America, abandoned by the whites and destroyed by the colored. That's what I thought the night they set the fires in 1968. First the Second World War, then the Iron Curtain, now the Newark Fire. I cried when that riot broke out. My beautiful Newark. I loved that city."

"So did we all, Dr. Kotler. What are you doing in New York?"

"Good practical question. Living. Eight years now. Man in exile. Child of the times. I gave up my wonderful practice, my cherished friends, took my books and my mementos, packed the last of my pillows, and established myself here at the age of seventy. Life anew in my eighth decade on earth. Now on my way to the Metropolitan Museum. I go for the great Rembrandt. I'm studying his masterpieces a foot at a time. Quite a discipline. Very rewarding. The man was a magician. Also studying Holy Scriptures. Delving into all the translations. Amazing what's in there. Yet the writing I don't like. The Jews in the Bible were always involved in highly dramatic moments, but they never learned to write good drama. Not like the Greeks, in my estimation. The Greeks heard a sneeze and they took off. The sneezer becomes the hero, the one who reported the sneeze becomes the messenger, the ones who overheard the sneeze, they became the chorus. Lots of pity, lots of terror, lots of cliff-hanging and suspense. You don't get that with the Jews in the Bible. There it's all round-the-clock negotiation with God."

"You sound like you know how to keep going."

Wish I could say the same for myself; I wish, he thought childishly, you could teach me.

"Do as I like, Nathan. Always have. Never denied myself what counted. And I believe I know what counted. I've been some use to others too. Kept a balance, you might say. I want to send you a pillow. Free of charge. For the wonderful memories you brought back to life. No reason for you to be in this pain. You don't sleep on your stomach, I trust."

"On my side and on my back, as far as I know."

"Heard this story a thousand times. I'm sending a pillow and a case."

And here they were. Also, tucked in the box, a type-written note on the doctor's stationery: "Remember, don't place Dr. Kotler's Pillow on top of an ordinary pillow. It does the job by itself. If there is no significant improvement in two weeks, phone me at RE 4–4482. With long-standing problems, manipulation could be required at the outset. For recalcitrant cases there are hypnotic techniques." The letter was signed "Dr. Charles L. Kotler, Dolorologist."

And if, by itself, the pillow worked and the pain completely vanished? He couldn't wait for night to fall so he could take it to sleep. He couldn't wait for it to be January 4 and the first day of class. He couldn't wait for 1981—that was when he'd be opening his office. 1982 at the latest. He'd pack the dolorologist's pillow for Chicago—and he'd leave the harem behind. With Gloria Galanter he'd gone too far, even for a man as disabled as himself. With *Roget's Thesaurus* under his head and Gloria sitting on his face, Zuckerman understood just how little one can depend upon human suffering to produce ennobling effects. She was the wife, the coddled and irreplaceable wife, of the genial wizard who'd weaned Zuckerman reluctantly away from his triple-A bonds and nearly doubled his capital in three years. Marvin Galanter was such a fan of *Carnovsky* that in the beginning he'd refused even to bill Zuckerman for his services; at their first meeting the accountant told Nathan that he would pay any penalties out of his own pocket, should the IRS challenge the shelters. *Carnovsky*, Marvin claimed, was his own life story; for the author of that book, there was nothing whatsoever that he wouldn't do.

Yes, he must divest himself at least of Gloria—only he couldn't resist her breasts. Alone on the playmat, following the rheumatologist's suggestion to try to find some means to distract himself from his pain, he sometimes thought of nothing but her breasts. Of the four women in the harem, it was with Gloria that his helplessness hit bottom—while Gloria herself seemed the happiest, in a strange and delightful way seemed the most playfully independent, tethered though she was to his wretched needs. She distracted him with her breasts and delivered his food: Greenberg's chocolate cakes, Mrs. Herbst's strudel, Zabar's pumpernickel, beluga in pots from the Caviarteria, the lemon chicken from Pearl's Chinese Restaurant, hot lasagna from "21." She sent the chauffeur all the way down to Allen Street for the stuffed peppers from Seymour's Parkway, and then came over in the car to heat them up for his dinner. She rushed into the little kitchenette in her red-fox Russian cossack coat and, when she came out with the steaming pot, was wearing only her heels. Gloria was nearly forty, a firm, hefty brunette with protruding circular breasts like targets, and electrifying growths of hair. Her face could have been a Spanish mulatto's: almond eyes, a wide, imposing jaw, and full rounded lips with peculiarly raised edges. There were bruises on her behind. He wasn't the only primitive she babied and he didn't care. He ate the food and he tasted the breasts. He ate the food off the breasts. There was nothing Gloria didn't remember to carry in her bag: nippleless bra, crotchless panties, Polaroid camera, vibrating dildo, K-Y jelly, Gucci blindfold, a length of braided velvet rope—for a treat, on his birthday, a gram of cocaine. "Times have changed," said Zuckerman, "since all you needed was a condom." "A child is sick," she said, "you bring toys." True, and Dionysian rites were once believed to have a therapeutic effect on the physically afflicted. There was also the ancient treatment known as the imposition of hands. Gloria had classical history on her side. His own mother's means for effecting a cure were to play casino on the edge of the bed with him when he was home with a fever. So as not to fall behind in her housework, she'd set her ironing board up in his bedroom while they gossiped about school and his friends. He loved the smell of ironing still. Gloria, lubricating a finger and slipping it in his anus, talked about her marriage to Marvin.

Zuckerman said to her, "Gloria, you're the dirtiest woman I've ever met."

"If I'm the dirtiest woman you've ever met, you're in trouble. I fuck Marvin twice a week. I put down my book, put out my cigarette, turn out the light, and roll over."

"On your back?"

"What else? And then he puts it in and I know just what to do to make him come. And then he mumbles something about tits and love and he comes. Then I put on the light and roll on my side and light up a cigarette and get on with my book. I'm reading the one you told me about. Jean Rhys."

"What do you do to make him come?"

"I make three circles this way, and three circles the other way, and I draw my fingernail down his spine like this—and he comes."

"So you do seven things."

"Right. Seven things. And then he says something about my tits and love, and he comes. And then he falls asleep and I can turn on the light again and read. This Jean Rhys terrifies me. The other night after reading her book about that shit-on woman and no money, I rolled over and kissed him and said, 'I love you, sweetheart.' But it's hard fucking him, Nathan. And getting harder. You always think in a marriage, 'This is as bad as it can be'—and next year it's worse. It's the most odious duty I've ever had to perform. He says to me sometimes when he's straining to come, 'Gloria, Gloria, say something dirty.' I have to think hard, but I do it. He's a wonderful father and a wonderful husband, and he deserves all the help he can get. But still, one night I really thought I couldn't take it anymore. I put down my book and I put out the light and finally I said it to him. I said, 'Marv, something's gone out of our marriage.' But he was almost snoring by then. 'Quiet,' he mumbles. 'Shhhhh, go to sleep.' I don't know what to do. There's nothing I *can* do. The odd thing and the terrible thing and the thing that's most confusing is that without a doubt Marvin was the real love of my life and beyond a doubt I was the love of Marvin's life and although we were never never happy, for about ten years we had a passionate marriage and all the trimmings, health, money, kids, Mercedes, a double sink and summer houses and everything. And so miserable and so attached. It makes no sense. And now I have these night monsters, three enormous night monsters: no money, death, and getting old. I can't leave him. I'd fall apart. He'd fall apart. The kids would go nuts and they're screwy as it is. But I need excitement. I'm thirty-eight. I need extra attention."

"So, have your affairs."

"They're murder too, you know. You can't always control your feelings in those things. You can't control the other person's feelings either. I have one now who wants to run away with me to British Columbia. He says we can live off the land. He's handsome. He's young. Bushy hair. Very savage. He came up to the house to restore some antiques and he started by restoring me. He lives in a terrible loft. He says, 'I can't believe I'm fucking you.' When he's fucking me. That excites me, Nathan. We take baths together. It's fun. But is that any reason to run out on being Adam and Toby's mother and Marvin's wife? When the kids lose something, who's going to find it for them if I'm in British Columbia? 'Mommy, where is my eraser?' 'Just a second, dear, I'm in the bathroom. Wait. I'll look for it.' Somebody's looking for something, I help—that's mothers. You lost something, I *have* to look. 'Mommy, I found it.' 'I'm glad you found it, dear.' And I am—when they find the eraser, Nathan, I'm happy. That's how I fell in love with Marvin. The very first time I was in his apartment, and within five minutes, he looked at me and said, 'Where's my cigarette lighter, Gloria, my good lighter?' And I got up and looked around, and I found it. 'Here it is, Marvin.' 'Oh, good.' I was hooked. That was it. Look, I *live* for the baths I take with my Italian bambino and his bushy hair and his iron biceps—but how can I leave these people and expect that they'll find what they lose on their own? With you it's okay—with you it's like a brother. You need and I need and that's it. Besides, you know what a good girl you've got in Cos Cob's cunning little whore." She'd accidentally met Diana when she stopped by unannounced one afternoon and the chauffeur dragged in a potted palm tree to liven up the sickroom. "She's perfect for you. Underage, upper-class, and really slutty in that little toy skirt—juicy, like when you bite into a fresh apple or a good pear. I like the gun-moll mouth. Clever contrast to the high IQ. While we were debating where to put the tree I saw her down the corridor—in the bathroom, making herself up. A bomb could have gone off in there and she wouldn't have known it. I wouldn't drop her."

"I'm in no position," said Zuckerman, impaled upon Gloria's knuckle, "to drop anyone."

"That's good. Some women might see you as prey. That's all some women want—a suffering male who's otherwise well off. All the slow curing, the taking credit for it, and if God forbid he doesn't survive the cure, owning his life after death. Show me a woman who wouldn't love to be the widow of a famous man. To own it *all*."

"Talking about all the women, or are we talking about you?"

"If it's God's blessing, Nathan, that it happens, I can't think of a single woman who wouldn't put up with it. Luckily this kid's too young and snotty to know the fundamentals yet. Fine. Let her be fresh to you when you start to whine. You're better off. No Jewish mother like me would ever minimize the importance of a morbid affliction. Read this book *Carnovsky* if you don't believe it. Jewish mothers know how to own their suffering boys. If I were in your shoes I'd keep my eye out for that."

Jaga, during his opening hour at Anton's Trichological Clinic, had looked to him first, in white bandanna and long white smock, like a novice in a nursing order; then she spoke, and the Slavic accent—along with the clinician's get-up and the dutiful weary professionalism

with which she worked her fingers across his scalp—
reminded him of the women physicians in *Cancer Ward*,
another of the works from which he'd taken stern in-
struction during his week in traction. His was the last
appointment of the day, and after his second session, as
he was leaving the Commodore and heading home, he
caught sight of her ahead of him out on Vanderbilt Place.
She was in a weatherworn black felt coat whose red em-
broidered hem was coming loose at the back. The shoddy
look of a coat once stylish somewhere else subverted
somewhat that aura of detached superiority that she af-
fected alone in a cubicle with a balding man. The hurried
agitated gait made her look like someone on the run.
Maybe she was: running from more of the questions he'd
begun to ask during the pleasant fingertip massage. She
was small and fragile, with a complexion the color of
skim milk and a tiny, pointed, bony, tired face, a face
a little ratlike until, at the end of the session, she undid
the bandanna and disclosed the corn-silk sheen of her
ash-blond hair, and with it a delicacy otherwise obscured
in that mask so tiny and taut with strain. The undeci-
pherable violet eyes were suddenly startling. Still, he
made no effort on the street to catch up. He couldn't
run because of the pain, and when he remembered the
heavy sarcasm with which she'd spit on his few amiable
questions, he decided against calling her name. "Helping
people," she'd replied, when he asked how she got into
trichology. "I love helping anyone with a problem." Why
had she emigrated to America? "I dreamed all my life of
America." What did she make of it here? "Everybody so
nice. Everybody wishing you to have a good day. We
do not have such nice people in Warsaw."

The next week, to his invitation for a drink, she said
yes—curtly, as though she'd said no. She was in a hurry,
could stay for no more than a quick glass of wine. In

the booth at the bar she drank three quick glasses, and then explained her American sojourn without his having even inquired. "I was bored in Warsaw. I had ennui. I wanted a change." The next week she again said yes as though it were no, and this time she had five glasses of wine. "Hard to believe you left simply because you were bored." "Don't be banal," she told him. "I don't want your sympathy. The client needs sympathy, not the technician with her full head of hair." The following week she came to his apartment, and through the prism glasses he watched as by herself she finished off the bottle he'd given her to open. Because of the pain he could no longer uncork a wine bottle. He was sipping vodka through a bent glass straw.

"Why do you lie on the floor?" she asked.

"Too tedious to go into."

"Were you in an accident?"

"Not that I remember. Were you, Jaga?"

"You must live more through people," she told him.

"How do you know how I should live?"

Drunkenly she tried to pursue her theme. "You must learn to live through other people." Because of the wine and because of her accent, two-thirds of what she was saying was incomprehensible to him.

At the door he helped her into the coat. She had stitched up the hem since he'd first spotted her hurrying along Vanderbilt Place, but what the coat needed was a new lining. Jaga seemed herself to have no lining at all. She looked like something that had been peeled of its rind, exposing a wan semi-transparent whiteness that wasn't even an inner membrane but the bare, pallid pulp of her being. He thought that if he touched her the sensation would make her scream.

"There's something corrupt about both of us," she said.

"What are you talking about?"

"Monomaniacs like you and me. I must never come here again."

Soon she was stopping by every evening on her way home. She began wearing eye shadow and to smell of a peppery perfume, and the face tightened up like a little rat's only when he persisted in asking the stupidest of his questions. She arrived in a new silk blouse the same pale violet as her eyes; though the topmost button was left carelessly undone, she made no move toward the playmat. She stretched instead across the sofa, snuggled cozily there under the afghan and poured out glass after glass of red wine—and then ran off to the Bronx. She climbed the library ladder in her stocking feet and browsed through the shelves. She asked from the topmost rung if she could borrow a book, and then forgot to take it home. Each day another nineteenth-century American classic was added to the stack left behind on his desk. Half contemptuously, satirizing herself, him, his library, his ladder, deriding seemingly every human dream and aspiration, she labeled where she piled the books "My spot."

"Why not take them with you?" Zuckerman asked.

"No, no, not with great novels. I am too old for this form of seduction. Why do you allow me to come here anyway, to the sacred sanctuary of art? I am not an 'interesting character.'"

"What did you do in Warsaw?"

"I did in Warsaw the same as I do here."

"Jaga, why not give me a break? Why not a straight answer to one lousy question?"

"Please, if you are looking for somebody interesting to write about, invite from the clinic one of Anton's other girls. They are younger and prettier and sillier, they will be flattered that you ask lousy questions. They have more adventures to tell than I do. You can get into their pants and they can get into your books. But if you are looking at me for sex, I am not interested. I hate lust. It's a nuisance. I don't like the smells, I don't like the sounds. Once, twice with somebody is fine — beyond that, it's a partnership in dirt."

"Are you married?"

"I am married. I have a daughter of thirteen. She lives with her grandmother in Warsaw. Now do you know everything about me?"

"What does your husband do?"

"What does he 'do'? He is not a graphomaniac like you. Why does an intelligent man ask stupid questions about what people 'do'? Because you are an American or because you are this graphomaniac? If you are writing a book and you want me to help you with my answers, I cannot. I am too dull. I am just Jaga with her upskis and downskis. And if you are trying to write a book by the answers that you get, then you are too dull."

"I ask you questions to pass the time. Is that sufficiently cynical to suit you?"

"I don't know about politics, I am not interested in politics, I don't want to answer questions about Poland. I don't *care* about Poland. To hell with all those things. I came here to get away from all that and I will appreciate it if you will leave me be about things that are the past."

On a windy November evening, with rain and hail blowing up against the windows, and the temperature down below freezing, Zuckerman offered Jaga ten dollars for a cab. She threw the money at him and left. Minutes later she was back, the black felt coat already sopping wet. "When do you want to see me again?"

"Up to you. Whenever you're feeling resentful enough."

As though to bite, she lunged for his lips. The next afternoon she said, "The first time I kissed anyone in two years."

"What about your husband?"

"We don't even do that anymore."

The man with whom she'd defected wasn't her husband. This was revealed to him the first time Jaga undid the remaining buttons of the new silk blouse and knelt beside him on the playmat.

"Why did you defect with him?"

"You see, I should not have told you even that much. I say 'defect' and you are excited. An interesting character. You are more excited by the word 'defect' than you are by my body. My body is too skinny." She removed her blouse and bra and threw them onto the desk, by the pile of unborrowed books. "My breasts are not the right size for an American man. I know that. They are not the right American shape. You did not know that I would look this old."

"On the contrary, it's a child's body."

"Yes, a child. She suffered from the Communists, poor child—I'll put her in a book. Why must you be so banal?"

"Why must you be so difficult?"

"It's you who is difficult. Why don't you just let me come here and drink your wine and pretend with borrowing books and kiss you, if I feel like it. Any man with half of a heart would do this. At moments you should be forgetting about writing books all the time. Here"—and after undoing her skirt and raising her slip, she turned around on her knees and leaned her weight forward onto the palms of her hands. "Here, you can see my ass. Men like that. You can do it to me from behind. The first time and you can do anything you want to me, anything at all that pleases you, *except to ask me more of your questions.*"

"Why do you hate it so much here?"

"Because I am left out here! Stupid man, of course I hate it here! I live with a man who is left out. What can he do here? It's all right that I work in a hair clinic. But

not for a man. He would take a job like that and he
would crumble up in a year. But I begged him to run
away with me, to save me from that madness, and so I
cannot ask him to start to sweep floors in New York
City."

"What did he work at before coming here?"

"You would misunderstand if I told you. You would
think it was 'interesting.'"

"Maybe I misunderstand less than you think."

"He saved me from the people who were poisoning
my life. Now I must save him from exile. He saved me
from my husband. He saved me from my lover. He saved
me from the people destroying everything I love. Here
I am his eyes, his voice, his source of survival. If I left,
it would kill him. It isn't a matter of being loved, it's
a matter of loving somebody—whether you can believe
that or not."

"Nobody asked you to leave him."

Jaga uncorked a second bottle of wine and, seated
naked on the floor beside him, quickly drank half of it
down. "But I want to," she said.

"Who is he?"

"A boy. A boy who did not use his head. That is what
my lover asked him in Warsaw. He saw us in a café and
he came up to him and he was furious. 'Who are you?'
he shouted at the boy."

"What did the boy answer?"

"He answered, 'None of your business.' To you that
does not sound so heroic. But it is, when one man is
half the age of the other."

"He ran away with you to be a hero, and you ran away
with him to run away."

"And now you think you understand why I love my
spot on your desk. Now you think you understand why
I get myself drunk on your expensive claret. 'She is
plotting to trade him for me.' Only that is not so. Even

with my émigré vulnerability, I will not fall in love with you."

"Good."

"I will let you do anything you want to me, but I will not fall in love."

"Fine."

"Only good, only fine? No, in my case it is excellent. Because I am the best woman in the world for falling in love with the wrong man. I have the record in the Communist countries. Either they are married, or they are murderers, or they are like you, men finished with love. Gentle, sympathetic, kind with money and wine, but interested in you mainly as a subject. Warm ice. I know writers."

"I won't ask how. But go on."

"I know writers. Beautiful feelings. They sweep you away with their beautiful feelings. But the feelings disappear quickly once you are no longer posing for them. Once they've got you figured out and written down, you go. All they give is their attention."

"You could do worse."

"Oh yes, all that attention. It's lovely for the model while it lasts."

"What were you in Poland?"

"I told you. Champion woman to fall in love with the wrong man." And again she offered to assume any posture for penetration that would please and excite him. "Come however you like and don't wait for me. That is better for a writer than more questions."

And what is better for you? It was difficult to do her the kindness of not asking. Jaga was right about writers—all along, Zuckerman had been thinking that if only she told him enough, he might find in what she said something to start him writing. She insulted him, she berated him, when it was time to go she sometimes grew so angry that she had all she could do not to reach out and strike him. She wanted to collapse and be rescued, and she wanted to be heroic and prevail, and she seemed to hate him most for reminding her, merely by taking it all in, that she could manage neither. A writer on the wane, Zuckerman did his best to remain unfazed. Mustn't confuse pleasure with work. He was there to listen. Listening was the only treatment he could give. They come, he thought, and tell me things, and I listen, and occasionally I say, "Maybe I understand more than you think," but there's no treatment I can offer to cure the woes of all the outpatients crossing my path, bent beneath their burdens and their separate griefs. Monstrous that all the world's suffering is good to me inasmuch as it's grist to my mill—that all I can do, when confronted with anyone's story, is to wish to turn it into *material*, but if that's the way one is possessed, that is the way one is possessed. There's a demonic side to this business that the Nobel Prize committee doesn't talk much about. It would be nice, particularly in the presence of the needy, to have pure disinterested motives like everybody else, but, alas, that isn't the job. The only patient being treated by the writer is himself.

After she'd gone, and after Gloria had stopped by with his dinner, and some hours before he resumed composing into his tape recorder another rejoinder to Appel, he told himself, "Start tonight. Get on with it tonight," and began by transcribing every word he could still remember of the protracted tirade delivered that afternoon by Jaga while he lay beneath her on the playmat. Her pelvis rose and fell like something ticking, an instrument as automatic as a metronome. Light, regular, tireless thrusts, thrusting distinct as a pulsebeat, thrusting excruciatingly minute, and all the while she spoke without stopping, spoke like she fucked, steady voluptuous coldness, as though he was a man and this was an act that she didn't yet *entirely* despise. He felt like a convict digging a tunnel with a spoon.

"I hate America," she told him. "I hate New York. I hate the Bronx. I hate Bruckner Boulevard. In a village in Poland there are at least two Renaissance buildings. Here it is just ugly houses, one after another, and Americans asking you their direct questions. You cannot have a spiritual conversation with anyone. You cannot be poor here and I hate it." Tick tock. Tick tock. Tick tock. "You think I'm morbid and psychopathic. Crazy Jaga. You think I should be like an American girl—typical American: energetic, positive, talented. Like all these intelligent American girls with their thinking, 'I can be an actress, I can be a poet, I can be a good teacher. I'm positive, I'm growing—I hadn't been growing when I was growing, but now I'm growing.' You think I should be one of those good good boring American girls with their naïveté that goodness does it, that energy does it, that talent does it. 'How can a man like Nathan Zuckerman fall in love with me for two weeks, and then abandon me? I am so good and energetic and positive and talented and growing—how can that be?' But I am not so naïve, so don't worry. I have some darkness to go back to. Whatever darkness was behind them, it was explained to them by the psychiatrist. And now for them it's all recovery. Make my life meaningful. Growth. They buy this. Some of them, the smart ones, they sell it. 'The relationship I had, I learned something from it. It's good for my growth.' If they have a darkness, it's a nice darkness. When you sleep with them, they smile. They make it wonderful." Tick tock. "They make it beautiful." Tick tock. "They make it warm and tender." Tick tock. "They make it *loving*. But I do not have this good American optimism. I cannot stand to lose people. I cannot *stand* it. And I am not smiling. And I am not growing.

I am disappearing!" Tick tock. Tick tock. "Did I tell you, Nathan, that I was raped? When I left here that day in the rain?" "No, you didn't tell me that." "I was walking to the subway in that rain. I was drunk. And I thought I couldn't make it—I was too drunk to walk. And I waved for a taxi, to take me to the station. And this limousine stopped. I don't remember very much. It was the limousine driver. He had a Polish name, too—that's what I remember. I think I had a blackout when I was in the limousine. I don't even know whether I did something provocative. He drove me and drove me and drove me. I thought I was going to the subway, and then he stopped and he said that I owed him twenty dollars. And I didn't have twenty dollars. And I said, 'Well, I can only write you a check.' And he said, 'How can I know the check is good?' And I said, 'You can call my husband.' That was the last thing I wanted to do, but I was so drunk, and so I didn't know what I was doing. And I gave him your number." "Where were you at this point?" "Somewhere. I think on the West Side. So he said, 'Okay, let's call your husband on the telephone. Here's a restaurant and we can go inside and we can call.' And I went inside and it wasn't a restaurant—it was some stairway. And there he pushed me down and raped me. And after that he drove me to the station." "And was it horrible or was it nothing?" "Ah, you want 'material.' It was nothing. I was too drunk to feel anything. He was afraid after I would call the police. Because I told him that I would. I told him, 'You have raped me and I'm going to do something about it. I didn't leave Poland to come to America to be raped by a Pole.' And he said, 'Well, you could have slept with hundreds of men—nobody's going to believe you.' And I didn't even mean to go to the police. He was right—they *wouldn't* believe me. I just wanted to tell him that he had done something dreadful. He was white, he had a

Polish name, he was good-looking, young—why? Why a man feels like raping a drunken woman? What kind of pleasure can that be? He drives me to the station, asking me if I'm okay, if I can make the train. Even walks me down to the platform and buys me a token." "Very generous." "And he never called you?" "No." "I'm sorry I gave him your number, Nathan." "It hardly matters." "That rape itself—it didn't mean anything. I went home and washed myself. And there waiting for me is a postcard. From my lover in Warsaw. And that's when I began to cry. *That* had meaning. Me, a postcard! Finally he writes me—and it's a postcard! I had a vision, after his postcard, of my parents' house before the war—a vision of all that went. Your country is ethically maybe a better country than Poland, but even we, even *we*—you want to come now?" "Even we what?" "Even we deserved a little better than that. I never had a normal life almost from right after I was born. I'm not a very normal person. I once had a little child to tell me that I smell good and that my meatballs are the best in the world. That's gone too. Now I don't even have half-home. Now what I have is no-home. All I'm saying is, after you get tired of fucking me, I'll understand—but, please," she said, just as his body, playing yet another trick, erupted without so much as a warning, "please, don't just drop me as a friend."

Bucking as best he could what he'd had to drink with Jaga and to smoke with Gloria, he got himself upright in his chair and with his notebook open on the lapboard and the collar fixed around his neck, tried to invent what he still didn't know. He thought of his little exile next to hers. Hers next to Dr. Kotler's. Exile like theirs is an illness, too; either it goes away in two or three years or it's chronic and you've got it for good. He tried to imagine a Poland, a past, a daughter, a lover, a postcard, as though his cure would follow if only he began anew as a writer of stories wholly unlike his own. *The Sorrows of Jaga*. But he couldn't get anywhere. Though people are weeping in every corner of the earth from torture and ruin and cruelty and loss, that didn't mean that he could make their stories his, no matter how passionate and powerful they seemed beside his trivialities. One can be overcome by a story the way a reader is, but a reader isn't a writer. Desperation doesn't help either: it takes longer than one night to make a story, even when it's written in a sitting. Besides, if Zuckerman wrote about what he didn't know, who then would write about what he did know?

Only what did he know? The story he could dominate and to which his feelings had been enslaved had ended. Her stories weren't his and his stories were no longer his stories either.

To prepare himself to leave his playmat and travel eight hundred miles to Chicago—when the farthest he'd been in a year was to get a pain suppressor out on Long Island—he first spent fifteen minutes under the new hundred-dollar shower head guaranteed by Hammacher Schlemmer to pummel you into health with hot water. All that came out was a fainthearted drizzle. Some neighbor in the old brownstone running a dishwasher or filling the tub. He emerged looking sufficiently boiled but feeling no better than when he'd gone under. He frequently emerged feeling no better even when the pressure was way up and the water gushed forth as prescribed. He smeared the steam from the medicine-chest mirror and contemplated his reddened physique. No invidious organic enemy visible, no stigmata at all; only the upper torso, once a point of pride, looking just as frail as it had after the regular morning shower, the one to offset the stiffness of sleep. On the advice of the physiotherapist, he stood under scalding showers three times a day.

The heat, coupled with the pounding of the water, was supposed to unglue the spasm and serve as a counter-irritant to the pain. "Hyperstimulation analgesia"—principle of the acupuncture needles, and of the ice packs that he applied between scalding showers, and of jumping off the roof of the Stanhope Hotel.

While drying himself, he probed with his fingertips until he'd located the worst of the muscular soreness midway along the upper left trapezius, the burning tenderness over the processes and to the right of the third cervical vertebra, and the movement pain at the insertion of the long head of the left biceps tendon. The intercostals between the eighth and ninth ribs were only moderately sore, a little improved really since he'd last checked back there two hours before, and the aching heaviness in the left deltoid was manageable, more or less—what a pitcher might feel having thrown nine innings on a cold September night. If it were only the deltoid that hurt, he'd go through life a happy man; if he could somehow contract with the Source of All Pain to take upon himself, even unto death, the trapezial soreness, *or* the cervical rawness—any *one* of his multitude of symptoms in exchange for permanent relief from everything else . . .

He sprayed the base of his neck and the shoulder girdle with the morning's second frosting of ethyl chloride (gift of his last osteopath). He refastened the collar (fitted by the neurologist) to support his neck. At breakfast he'd taken a Percodan (rheumatologist's grudging prescription) and debated with himself—craven sufferer vs. responsible adult—about popping a second so soon. Over the months he'd tried keeping himself to four Percodan pills on alternate days to avoid getting hooked. Codeine constipated him and made him drowsy, while Percodan not only halved the pain but provided a nice gentle invigorating wallop to a woefully enfeebled sense of well-being. Percodan was to Zuckerman what sucking stones were to Molloy—without 'em couldn't go on.

Despite dire warnings about the early hour from his former self, he wouldn't have minded a drag on a joint: eight hundred miles of traveling too nerve-racking to contemplate otherwise. He kept a dozen handy in the egg compartment of the refrigerator, and a loose ounce (obtained by Diana from the Finch pharmacopoeia) in a plastic bag in the butter compartment. One long drag in case he hailed a taxi with no shocks: all he seemed to ride in with his neck brace were cars shipped secondhand from Brazzaville Yellow Cab. Though he couldn't depend upon marijuana to cool things down like Percodan, a few puffs did manage to detach him, sometimes for as long as half an hour, from engrossment with the pain and nothing else. By the time he got to the airport the second Percodan (precipitously swallowed despite all the hemming and hawing) would have begun its percolation, and he'd have the rest of the joint for further assistance on the flight. Two quick puffs—after the first long drag—and then, carefully, he pinched out the joint and dropped it for safekeeping into a matchbox in his jacket pocket.

He packed his bag: gray suit, black shoes, black socks. From inside his closet door he chose one of his sober foulards, then from the dresser one of his blue button-down shirts. Uniform for medical-school interview—for all public outings going on twenty-five years. To fight baldness he packed the hormone drops, the pink No. 7 dressing, a jar of Anton's specially prepared conditioner, and a bottle of his shampoo. To fight pain he packed the electronic suppressor, three brands of pills, a sealed new spray-cap bottle of ethyl chloride, his large ice bag, two electric heating pads (the narrow, nooselike pad that wrapped around his throat, the long, heavy pad that draped over his shoulders), the eleven joints left in the refrigerator, and a monogrammed Tiffany's silver flask (gift of Gloria Galanter) that he filled to the lip with hundred-proof Russian vodka (gift of husband Marvin's firm: case of Stolichnaya and case of champagne for his fortieth birthday). Last he packed Dr. Kotler's pillow. He used to travel to Chicago with a pen and a pad and a book to read.

He wouldn't phone to say where he was going until he got out to LaGuardia. He wouldn't even bother then. It wasn't going to require very much teasing from any of his women to deter him, not if he thought of the Brazzaville taxis and the East River Drive potholes and the inevitable delay at the airport. Suppose he had to stand in a line. Suppose he had to carry his suitcase into the terminal. He had trouble only that morning carrying his toothbrush up to his mouth. And of all he couldn't handle, the suitcase would be just the beginning. Sixteen hours of organic chemistry? twelve of biology? eight of physics? He couldn't follow an article in *Scientific American*. With his math he couldn't even understand the industrial bookkeeping in *Business Week*. A science student? He wasn't serious.

There was also some question as to whether he was sane, or was entering that stage of chronic ailing known as the Hysterical Search for the Miraculous Cure. That might be all that Chicago was about: purifying pilgrimage to a sacred place. If so, beware—astrology lies just around the corner. Worse, Christianity. Yield to the hunger for medical magic and you will be carried to the ultimate limit of human foolishness, to the most preposterous of all the great pipe dreams devised by ailing mankind—to the Gospels, to the pillow of our leading dolorologist, the voodoo healer Dr. Jesus Christ.

To give his muscles a rest from the effort of packing his bag, and to recover the courage to fly to Chicago—

or, alternatively, to undo the grip of the cracked idea
that would really send him flying (off the Stanhope roof)—
he stretched across the unmade sheets in the dark cube
of his bedroom. The room jutted off the parlor-floor
apartment into the enclosed well of the rear courtyard.
In an otherwise handsome, comfortable flat, it was the
one gloomy room, undersized, underheated, only a shade
more sunlight than a crypt. The two unwashable windows were permanently grated against burglars. The side
window was further obscured by the trunk of the courtyard's dying tree, and the rear window half-blinded by
an air conditioner. A tangle of extension cords lay coiled
on the carpet—for the pain suppressor and the heating
pads. Half the kitchen glasses had accumulated on the
bedside table—water to wash down pills—along with
a cigarette-rolling machine and a packet of cigarette papers. On a piece of paper toweling were scattered stray
green flecks of cannabis weed. The two open books, one
atop the other, had been bought secondhand at the Strand:
a 1920 English text on orthopedic medicine, with horrific
surgical photography, and the fourteen hundred pages
of Gray's *Anatomy*, a copy of the 1930 edition. He'd been
studying medical books for months, and not so as to
bone up for any admissions committee. The jailhouse
lawyer stores his well-thumbed library under the bed and
along the cell walls; so does the patient serving a stretch
to which he thinks himself illegally sentenced.

The cassette tape recorder was on the unoccupied half
of the double bed, just where he'd fallen asleep with it
at 4 a.m. So was his file folder on Milton Appel, which
he'd spent his night clutching instead of Diana. He'd
phoned and begged her to stay with him after Gloria
had gone back to Marvin and Jaga had left in tears for
the Bronx, and after he'd flailed about between his chair
and the floor trying to dream up, from Jaga's clues, some

story that was hers and not his. Hopeless—and not only because of the grass and the vodka. If you get out of yourself you can't be a writer because the personal ingredient is what gets you going, and if you hang on to the personal ingredient any longer you'll disappear right up your asshole. Dante got out of hell easier than you'll escape Zuckerman-Carnovsky. You don't want to represent her Warsaw—it's what her Warsaw represents that you want: suffering that isn't semi-comical, the world of massive historical pain instead of this pain in the neck. War, destruction, anti-Semitism, totalitarianism, literature on which the fate of a culture hinges, writing at the very heart of the upheaval, a martyrdom more to the point—some point, *any* point—than bearing the cocktail-party chitchat as a guest on Dick Cavett. Chained to self-consciousness. Chained to retrospection. Chained to my dwarf drama till I die. Stories now about Milton Appel? Fiction about losing my hair? I can't face it. Anybody's hair but mine. "Diana, come over, spend the night." "No." "Why no? Why not?" "Because I'm not going to suck you off for ten consecutive hours on your playmat and then listen to you for ten hours more screaming about this Milton Appel." "But that's all over." But she'd hung up: he'd become another of her terrible men.

He flipped on the tape recorder and rewound the side. Then he pushed "Play." When he heard his voice, spooky and lugubrious because of a defect in the audio mechanism, he thought: I might as well have depressed "Regress." This is where I came in.

"Dear Professor Appel," intoned his warbling ghost, "my friend Ivan Felt sent on to me your odd request for him to ask me to write an Op Ed piece on behalf of Israel. Maybe it wasn't so odd. Maybe you've changed your mind about me and the Jews since you distinguished for Elsa Stromberg between anti-Semites like Goebbels (to whose writings she compared my own in the letters column of *Inquiry*) and those like Zuckerman who just don't like us. It was a most gracious concession."

He pushed "Stop," then "Fast Forward," and then tried "Play" again. He couldn't be so stupid as he sounded. The problem was the speed of the tape.

"You write to Felt that we 'grown-ups' should not kid ourselves (it's okay if we kid students) about 'the differences between characters and authors.' However, would this not seem to contradict—"

He lay there listening till the reel ended. Anybody who says "Would this not seem to contradict" should be shot. You said I said. He said you said. She said I said he said you said. All in this syrupy, pedantic, ghostly drone. My life in art.

No, it wasn't a fight he needed; what he desperately needed was a reconciliation, and not with Milton Appel. He still couldn't imagine having fallen out with his brother. Certainly it happens, yet when you hear about families in which brothers don't speak it's so awful, so stupid, it seems so impossible. He couldn't believe that a book could seem no more to Henry than a murder weapon. It was too dull a point of view for a man of Henry's intelligence to sustain for four years. Perhaps he was only waiting for Nathan, as the elder, to write him a letter or give him a ring. Zuckerman could not believe that Henry, the sweetest and most thoughtful kid, burdened always with too big, too kind a heart, could really continue hating him year after year.

Without any evidence, Zuckerman located his true enemy in Carol. Yes, they were the ones who knew how to hate and keep hating, the mice who couldn't look you straight in the eye. Don't touch him, she'd told Henry, or you'll wind up a caricature in a book—so will I, so will the children. Or maybe it was the money: when families split apart like this, it's usually not literature that does it. Carol resented that Nathan had been left half of Henry's parents' estate, Nathan, who'd made a million by *defaming* his benefactors, left a hundred thousand bucks after taxes. Oh, but that wasn't Carol. Carol was a liberal, responsible, well-meaning woman whose enlightened tolerance was her pride. Yet if nothing was holding Henry back, why no message even on Nathan's birthday? He'd been getting birthday calls from Henry since his first year at college. "Well, how does it feel, Natey, to be seventeen?" To be twenty-five. To be thirty. "Forty?" Zuckerman would have said—"It would feel better, Hesh, if we cut the crap and had lunch." But the biggest of birthdays came and went, and no call or card or telegram from the remaining member of his family; just Marvin's champagne in the morning and Marvin's wife in the afternoon, and in the early evening, drunken Jaga, her cheek crushed to the playmat and her rear raised to face him, and crying out, "Nail me, nail me, crucify me with your Jewish prick!" even while Zuckerman wondered who had been more foolish, Henry for failing to seize the occasion of the milestone to declare a truce or himself for expecting that his turning forty should automatically unburden Henry of what it meant having Nathan Zuckerman as his brother.

He picked up the bedside phone but couldn't dial even a single digit of the area code, so overtaken was he by fatigue. This had happened before on the brink of phoning Henry. As weary of his sentimentality as of their righteousness. He could not have both that brother and that book.

The number he dialed was Jenny's. Somebody to whom, as yet, he owed no explanations.

He let it ring. She would be out back with her pad, drawing snowdrifts in the orchard, or in the shed with her ax, splitting wood. He'd received a long letter from Bearsville only the day before, a long, captivating letter

in which she'd written, "I feel you're on the verge of
something nuts," and he'd kept picking it up and looking
to be sure she'd said on the verge of something nuts and
not already going nuts. Fighting back from a *real* breakdown would be terrible. It could take as long as medical
school. Longer. Even after the dissolution of his marriages—wreckage he still couldn't square with an orderly
personality like his—he'd neither gone nuts nor gone
under. However bad it was, always he'd pushed sanely
on until a new alliance came along to help restore the
old proportions. Only during the last half year had
gloomy, frightening bouts of confusion seriously begun
to erode the talent for steady living, and that wasn't from
the pain alone: it was also from living without nursing
a book that nursed him. In his former life he could never
have imagined lasting a week without writing. He used
to wonder how all the billions who didn't write could
take the daily blizzard—all that beset them, such a
saturation of the brain, and so little of it known or named.
If he wasn't cultivating hypothetical Zuckermans he really
had no more means than a fire hydrant to decipher his
existence. But either there was no existence left to decipher or he was without sufficient imaginative power to
convert into his fiction of seeming self-exposure what
existence had now become. There was no rhetorical over-
lay left: he was bound and gagged by the real raw thing,
ground down to his own unhypothetical nub. He could
no longer pretend to be anyone else, and as a medium
for his books he had ceased to be.

Breathless from running, Jenny answered the phone
on the fifteenth ring and Zuckerman immediately hung
up. If he told her where he was going she'd try like Diana
to stop him. They would all try to stop him, just as
lucidity was breaking through. Jaga in her murky accent
would shower him with Polish despair: "You want to be
like people with real hot ordinary pursuits inside. You

want to have fine feelings like the middle class. You want to be a doctor the way some people admit to uncommitted crimes. Hallo Dostoevsky. Don't be so banal." Gloria would laugh and say something ludicrous: "Maybe you need a child. I'll become a bigamist and we'll have one. Marvin wouldn't mind—he loves you more than I do." But Jenny's real wisdom would stop him. He didn't even understand why she continued to bother with him. Why any of them did. For Gloria, he supposed, coming to his place to loll around in her G-string was something to do a couple afternoons a week; Diana, the budding matador, would try anything once; and Jaga needed a haven somewhere between the home that was no-home and Anton's clinic, and his playmat, alas, was the best she could do. But why did Jenny bother? Jenny was in the long line of levelheaded wives, writers' wives as skillful as explosive experts at defusing a writer's dreadful paranoia and brooding indignation, at regularly hacking back the incompatible desires that burgeon in the study, lovely women not likely to bite your balls off, lovely, clearheaded, dependable women, the dutiful daughters of their own troubled families, perfect women whom in the end he divorced. What do you prove by going it alone when there's Jenny's colossal willingness and her undespairing heart?

Bearsville, N.Y.
Early Pleistocene Epoch

Dear Nathan,

I'm feeling strong and optimistic and whistling marching tunes as I often do when I feel this way, and you are getting more desperate. There is something across your face these days that disappears only after sex and then only for about five minutes. Lately I feel you're on the verge of something nuts. I know this because there is something in me that is bent to your shape (which sounds more obscene than it is). There's a great deal that you don't have to do to please me. My grandmother (who asks me to tell you she wears a size 16 coat) used to say, "All I want is for you to be happy" and it used to gall me. Happiness wasn't all I wanted. How vapid! Eventually I've come to see more depth in that and in simple good nature generally. You have found a girl you could make happy. I am that kind, if that interests you.

I never told you that I went to a psychoanalyst when I came back so confused from France. He told me that men and women whose sexual instincts are particularly unruly are often drawn to styles of extreme repression; with weaker instincts, they might feel free to let the beast in them free. By way of explaining further what I mean about something in me that is bent to your shape. (Erotically speaking, we—women—decide very young that we'll be either priestesses or sacrifices. And we stick to it. And then midway into your career you long to switch and that is just the opportunity you gave me with the grand that I blew at Bergdorf's. By way of explaining still further.)

Snowed in. 10 inches fell atop 12 from the night before. Expected high today on this mountain: zero. There is a nice new ice age on the way. I'm painting it. Strange and lunar. Expect to look in the mirror and see I've grown saber-teeth. Are you alive and well and still living in New York? I didn't think so when we spoke on Monday. I hung up and began thinking of you as someone I used to know. Is Milton Appel's really the final word? Let us name him Tevye and see if you are still upset. He thinks you do what you do for the sadistic joy of it? I thought your book was one genial trick after another. I'm astonished at your doubt. In my view a good novelist is less like a high priest of secular culture than he is like an intelligent dog. Extraordinary sensitivity to some stimuli, like a dog's sense of smell, and selective impoverishment in the communication of them. The combination produces not talking but barking, whining, frantic burrowing, pointing, howling, groveling, anything. Good dog good book. And you are a good dog. Isn't that enough? You once wrote a novel called *Mixed Emotions.* Why don't you read it? At least read the title. In someone who has made his work and his destiny out of mixed emotions, toward his family, toward his country, toward his religion and his education and even his own sex—skip it. To my point. I can't say nothing and saying it to myself isn't the same. There's a little house for rent up here that you would like. Not primitive like mine but warm and cozy. And nearby. I could see that you were all right. I could introduce you to the people around to talk to. I could introduce you to nature. There's no beating nature: *the most abstract art uses colors that occur in nature.* You are forty, the halfway point, and you are exhausted. No punning diagnosis intended, but you are sick of yourself, sick of serving your imagination's purposes, sick of fighting the alien purposes of the Jewish Appels. Up here you can get past all that. If you won't get past your pain, maybe you'll at least lay down the burden of your fiendish dignity and the search for motives, good or bad. I'm not proposing my magic white mountain for the Castorpian seven-year cure. But why not see what happens in seven months? I can't imagine anyone thinking of New York as home. I don't think you do or did, ever. You certainly don't live there that way. You don't live there at all.

You're locked up on a closed ward. Here in the woods it's only rarely crushing isolation. Mostly it's useful solitude. Out here it makes *sense* living apart from people. And I live here. If worst comes to worst, you can talk to me. It's beginning to throw me off balance to have only myself and a cat to care about.

More quotations for your outlook. (Intelligent people are corny too.)

> Nel mezzo del cammin di nostra vita
> mi ritrovai per una selva oscura,
> che la diritta via era smarrita.
> —Dante

It is a good thing in the winter to be deep in the snow, in the autumn deep in the yellow leaves, in the summer among the ripe corn, in spring amid the grass; it is a good thing to be always with the mowers and the peasant girls, in summer with a big sky overhead, in winter by the fireside, and to feel that it always has been and always will be so. One may sleep on straw, eat black bread, well, one will only be the healthier for it.
> —Van Gogh

Love,
A Peasant Girl

P.S. I am sorry that your shoulder is still bad, but I don't think it's going to stop you. If I were a devil, plotting with my minions how to shut Zuckerman up, and some minion said, "How about plaguing shoulder pain?" I would say, "No, sorry, I just don't think that will do it." I hope the pain subsides, and think that if you came up here, in time you'd feel the inner clench loosening. But if it didn't, you would just live with it and write with it. Life really is stronger than death. If you don't believe me, come look at my fat new picture book (32 smackers) of seventeenth-century Dutch realism. Jan Steen couldn't paint an upholstery tack without proclaiming just that.

No, he wouldn't tell her what he was planning and he wouldn't rent the house nearby. It's my vitality I long for, not a deeper retreat; the job is to make sense back among people, not to take a higher degree in surviving alone. Even with you to talk to, winter by the fireside and the big summer sky overhead are not going to produce a potent new man—they're going to give us a little boy. Our son will be *me*. No, I cannot be mothered in that warm cozy house. I will not abet that analyst's inanities about "returning to the infantile mode." Now to renounce renunciation—to reunite with the race!

Yet what if Jenny's black bread is my cure? *There's a great deal that you don't have to do to please me. You have found a girl you could make happy. It's beginning to throw me off balance to have only myself and a cat to care about. You'd feel the inner clench loosening.*

Yes, and after the novelty of healing me wore off? No doubt Gloria is right and the suffering male (who is otherwise well) is to some women the great temptation, but what happens when the slow curing fails to take place and the tender rewards are not forthcoming? Every morning, nine on the button, she's off to the studio and shows up next only for lunch—stained with paint and full of painting problems, anxious to bolt a sandwich and get back to work. I know that absorption. So do my ex-wives. If I were healthy and nailed to a book, I might go ahead and make the move, buy a parka and snow boots and turn peasant with Jennifer. Separate by day for deep concentration, toil alone like slaves of the earth over the obstinate brainchild, then coming uncoiled together at night to share food and wine and talk and feeling and sex. But it's easier to share sex than to share pain. That would dawn on her soon enough, and I'd wind up reading *ARTnews* from under my ice bag and learning to hate Hilton Kramer, while nights as well as days she slugged it out in the studio with Van Gogh. No, he couldn't go from being an artist to being an artist's chick. He had to be rid of all the women. If there wasn't something suspect about someone hanging around somebody like him, it was surely wrong for him to be hanging on to all of them. They all, with their benevolence, with their indulgence, with their compliance to my need, make off with what I most need to climb out of this pit. Diana is smarter, Jenny's the artist, and Jaga *really* suffers. And with Gloria I mostly feel like Gregor Samsa waiting on the floor beneath the cupboard for his sister to bring him his bowl of slops. All these voices, this insistent chorus, reminding me, as though I could forget, how unreasonable I am, how idle and helpless and overprivileged, how fortunate even in my misfortune. If one more woman preaches to me, I'll be ready for the padded cell.

He phoned Dr. Kotler.

"This is Nathan Zuckerman. What do you mean by 'dolorologist'?"

"Hello there, Nathan. So my pillow arrived. You're on your way."

"It's here, yes, thank you. You sign yourself 'dolorologist.' I'm lying on the pillow at this very moment and thought I'd phone for a definition."

But he'd phoned to find out about the hypnotic procedures employed in recalcitrant cases; he'd phoned because the orthodox techniques of the highly esteemed doctors had alleviated nothing, because he could hardly afford to reject the prospect of a cure on account of the age or eccentricity of the physician, or because the physician happened to be a nostalgic exile from the same pile of rubble as himself. Everybody comes from somewhere, reaches an age, and speaks with some accent or other. Cure was not going to come either from God or from Mount Sinai Hospital, that much was clear by now. Hypnosis seemed a terrible comedown after years of making the hypnotic phenomena himself, yet if someone actually could talk to the pain *directly*, without his looking for meaning, without all the interfering ego static . . .

"Is dolorology a coinage of Kotler's or a real medical specialty you can study?"

"It's something every doctor studies every day when the patient walks in and says, 'Doctor, it hurts.' But I happen to consider dolorology my particular specialty because of my approach: anti-prescription, anti-machine. I date back to the stethoscope, the thermometer, and the forceps. For the rest you had two eyes, two ears, two hands, a mouth, and the instrument most important of all, clinical intuition. Pain is like a baby crying. What it wants it can't name. The dolorologist unearths what that is. Chronic pain is a puzzle for which few of my colleagues have time. Most of them are frightened by it. Most doctors are frightened of death and the dying. People need an incredible amount of support when they die. And the doctor who is frightened can't give it to them."

"Are you free this afternoon?"

"For Nathan Zuckerman I am free day and night."

"I'd like to come by, I'd like to talk about what we'll do if the pillow doesn't help."

"You sound distraught, my boy. Come first and have lunch. I overlook the East River. When I moved in I thought I would stand staring at the river four and five hours a day. Now I'm so busy weeks go by and I don't even know the river is here."

"I'm interested in discussing hypnosis. Hypnosis, you say in your note, is sometimes useful for what I have."

"Without minimizing what you have, for far worse than you have. Asthma, migraines, colitis, dermatitis— I have seen a man suicidal from trigeminal neuralgia, a most nightmarish pain that attacks the face, reclaim his life through hypnosis. I've seen the people in my practice that everybody else has written off, and now I can't answer my mail from these patients, given up as incurable, whom I have hypnotized back to health. My secretary needs a secretary, that's how heavy my mail runs."

"I'll be there in an hour."

But an hour later he was on the unmade bed in the little room dialing Cambridge, Mass. Enough cowering before the attack. *But I'm not cowering and it's not the first attack. And will he sit up and listen, no matter how generous the amplitude with which I patiently spell out his hundred mistakes? You expect him to suffer remorse? You figure you'll win his blessing by phoning long distance to tell him he can't read? He expresses the right thoughts about Jews and you express the wrong thoughts about Jews, and nothing you shout is going to change that.* But it's the Appels who've whammied my muscles with their Jewish evil eye. They push in the pins and I yell ouch and swallow a dozen Percodans. But what you do with the evil eye is poke it out with a burning stick! *But he is not my father's deputy, let alone the great warrior chieftain that young Nathan longed to please and couldn't help antagonizing. I am not young Nathan. I am a forty-year-old client at Anton's Trichological Clinic. To be "understood" is no longer necessary once you seriously begin losing your hair. The father who called you a bastard from his deathbed is dead, and the allegiance known as "Jewishness" beyond their moralizing judgment. It's from Milton Appel that*

I found that out, in one of his own incarnations. And you needn't bother to tell him.

Too late for reason: he had Harvard on the phone and was waiting to be connected to the English Department. The real shitside of literature, these inspired exchanges, but into the bitter shit I go if churning up shit is what it takes to get better. Nothing to lose but my pain. *Only Appel has nothing to do with the pain. The pain pre-dates that essay by a year. There are no Jewish evil eyes or double Jewish whammies. Illness is an organic condition. Illness is as natural as health. The motive is not revenge. There is no motive. There are only nerve cells, twelve thousand million nerve cells, any one of which can drive you mad without the help of a book review. Go get hypnotized. Even that's less primitive than this. Let the oracular little dolorologist be your fairy godfather, if it's a regressive solution you're after. Go and let him feed you lunch. Tell Gloria to come over and you can blindfold each other. Move to the mountains. Marry Jenny. But no further appeals to the Court of Appels.*

The English Department secretary rang through to Appel's office, where a graduate student came on the line to tell him that the Distinguished Professor wasn't there.

"Is he home?"

"Can't say."

"Have you his home number?"

"Can't be reached."

Disciple, undoubtedly, holding sacred all the Distinguished Professor's opinions, including those on me.

"This is Nathan Zuckerman."

Zuckerman imagined the smirking disciple passing a cryptic comic note to another smirking disciple. Must have them up there by the dozens. Used to be one myself.

"It's about a piece Appel asked me to write. I'm calling from New York."

"He hasn't been well," the disciple offered. "You'll have to wait till he gets back."

"Can't," Zuckerman told him. "Haven't been well either," and promptly called Boston information. While the operator searched the suburbs for a listing, Zuckerman spread the contents of Appel's file folder on the bed. He pushed his medical books onto the carpet, and arranged on the bedside table all the unfinished draft letters that he'd eked out in longhand. He couldn't trust himself to extemporize, not while worked up like this; yet if he waited till he could think straight and talk sensibly, he wouldn't make the call.

A woman answered at the Appel residence in Newton. The pretty dark wife from the Barnes Hole beach? She must be white-haired by now. *Everybody moving on to wisdom but me. All you do on the phone is document his original insight. All you are doing on the phone is becoming one of the crazies of the kind who phone you. When you saw him strolling by you on the beach, were you that impressed by his narrow shoulders and his soft white waist? Of course he hates your work. All that semen underfoot is no longer to his taste. Never was—not in books at least. You two are a perfect mismatch. You draw stories from your vices, dream up doubles for your demons—he finds criticism a voice for virtue, the pulpit to berate us for our failings. Virtue comes with the franchise. Virtue is the goal. He teaches, he judges, he corrects—rightness is all. And to rightness you are acting out indefensible desires by spurious pseudo-literary means, committing the culture crime of desublimation. There's the quarrel, as banal as that: you shouldn't make a Jewish comedy out of genital life. Leave the spurting hard-on to goyim like Genet. Sublimate, my child, sublimate, like the physicists who gave us the atomic bomb.*

"This is Nathan Zuckerman. May I speak with Milton Appel?"

"He's resting right now."

"It's pretty urgent business." She didn't answer, and so somberly he added, "About Israel."

He was shuffling meanwhile through the letters on the table, looking for an opening shot. He chose (for their adversarial pithiness), then rejected (for lack of tact and want of respect), then reconsidered (for just the sake of those deficiencies) three sentences written the night before, after he'd given up on writing about Jaga; about Jaga he'd been unable to write even three words. *Professor Appel, I am convinced that the quality about a man or a group that most invites the violence of neurotic guilt is public righteousness and innocence. The roots of anti-Semitism are deep and twisted and not easily sterilized. However, to the extent that published statements by Jews have any effect at all, one way or another, on Gentile opinion and prejudice, the words "Jews jerk off daily" on lavatory walls would do us all more good than what you want me to write on the Op Ed page.*

"This is Milton Appel."

"This is Nathan Zuckerman. I'm sorry to bother you when you're resting."

"What is it you want?"

"Do you have a few minutes to talk?"

"Please, what is it?"

How sick is he? Sicker than I am? Sounds strained. Burdened. Maybe he always does, or maybe there's something worse in his kidney than stones. Maybe the evil eye works both ways and I've given him a malignancy. I can't say the hatred hasn't been on that scale.

"My friend Ivan Felt has sent on to me your letter requesting him to ask me to write a piece on Israel."

"Felt sent that letter on to you? He had no right to do that."

"Well, he did it. Xeroxed your paragraph about his friend Nate Zuckerman. I have it in front of me. 'Why don't you ask your friend Nate Zuckerman to write, etc. . . . unless he feels the Jews can stick their historical suffering up their ass.' Odd request. Very odd. To me in that context, infuriatingly odd." Zuckerman had begun to read now from one of his unfinished letters. "Though since you so regularly change your opinion about my 'case,' for all I know you've had yet another flexibility spasm since you distinguished in *Inquiry* between anti-Semites like Goebbels and people like Zuckerman who 'just don't like us.'"

His voice was already out of control, quivering so with rage that he even thought to turn on the tape from the night before and let that double for him over the phone until he recovered the modulations of a mature, confident, reasonable, authoritative adult. But no—purgation requires more turbulence than that, otherwise you might as well lie back on Dr. Kotler's pillow to take your bottle. No—drive pain out with your battering heart the way a clapper knocks sound from a bell. He tried to envision how this would happen. Pain waves springing longitudinally from his silhouetted torso, snaking along the floor, spreading over the furniture, slithering through the blinds, and then throughout his apartment, throughout the whole building, rattling every window in its frame—the roar of his discharged affliction echoing out over all Manhattan, and the evening *Post* hitting the street headlined: ZUCKERMAN PAIN-FREE AT LAST, *18 Month Ordeal Ends with Sonic Boom.* "If I correctly understand your letter to Felt asking him to ask me what apparently you'd rather not ask me directly yourself, you seem to suspect (privately, of course, and not in print or on the lecture circuit) that far from disliking Jews 'for being Jews,' and pathologically reviling them in my work, there's a possibility that I might actually be troubled by their troubles—"

"Look, hold on. You have every right to be angry, but not primarily with me. This paragraph that Felt so kindly sent to you was written in a letter privately addressed to him. He never asked me whether it was okay to forward it. When he did so he must surely have known it could only inflame your feelings, since what I wrote was certainly not civil and obviously represented an eruption of personal feelings. But that seems to me just the sort of thing that would be done by that character in that book he's written with his two club feet. I regard it as hostile, provocative, and nasty—toward both of us. Whatever you may think of my essay on your work or my general opinions, you probably will grant that if I were writing directly to you and asking you to do a piece on Israel for the Op Ed page, I'd be more civil about it and not do it so as to enrage you, rightly or wrongly."

"Because you would be more 'civil' in a letter written directly to me, despite having written about my work as you did in that piece—" Feeble quibbling. Pedantry. Must not extemporize and lose your way.

He looked everywhere on the bed for his three stinging lines from the night before. The page must have slipped to the floor. He reached to retrieve it without bending his neck or turning his head and, only after rushing to resume the attack, discovered that he was reading Appel the wrong page. "It's one thing to think you're pretending to your students when you tell them there's a difference between characters and author, if that's the way you see it these days—but to strip the book of its tone, the plot of its circumstances, the action of its momentum, to disregard totally the context that gives to a theme its spirit, its flavor, its life—"

"Look, I haven't the energy for Literature 101."

"Don't flatter yourself. I was talking about Remedial Reading. And don't hang up—I have more to say."

"I'm sorry but I can't listen to much more. I didn't expect that you'd like what I wrote about your work any more than I like bad reviews of what I write. In these situations, strain is unavoidable. But I really do feel that both of us might have been spared this exacerbation had Felt shown some manners. I wrote him a personal letter in response to a visit he paid. I had a right to assume that a personal letter wouldn't be circulated unless I gave permission. He never asked for it."

"First you scold me, now you scold Felt." And that's why *he's* sick, Zuckerman realized. The addiction to scolding. He's overdosed on scolding. All the verdicts, all the judgments—what's good for the culture, what's bad for the culture—and finally it's poisoning him to death. Let's hope.

"Let me finish," said Appel. "I was given reason by Felt to suppose that you did indeed feel some strong concern about Israel. It won't strike you as any less irritating if you know why I wrote it, but at least you should understand that my suggestion wasn't a mere gratuitous provocation. That I leave to our friend Ivan, whose talent as far as I can tell lies solely in that direction. My letter was for his eyes. If he had behaved decently—"

"Like you. Of course. Mannerly, decently, courteously, decorously, uprightly, civil—oh, what a gorgeous Torah cloth you throw over your meat hooks! How *clean* you are!"

"And your Torah cloth? No more abuse, please. What is this phone call about, except your Torah cloth? If Felt had behaved decently, he'd have written you: 'Appel thinks it would be useful if you did a piece for Op Ed on Israel, since things look black and since he feels you, Zuckerman, would reach kinds of people that he can't.'"

"And what kinds of people are they? People like me who don't like Jews? Or people like Goebbels who gas them? Or the kind of people I pander to by choosing—as you put it so civilly and decently and decorously in *Inquiry*—by choosing an 'audience' instead of choosing readers the way you and Flaubert do. My calculating subliterary shenanigans and your unsullied critical heart!

And you call Felt hostile and nasty! What's disgusting in Felt, in Appel is virtue—in you it's all virtue, even the ascribing of dishonorable motives. Then in that bloodthirsty essay you have the fucking gall to call *my* moral stance 'superior'! You call my sin 'distortion,' then distort my book to show how distorted it is! You pervert my intentions, then call me perverse! You lay hold of my comedy with your ten-ton gravity and turn it into a travesty! My coarse, vindictive fantasies, your honorable, idealistic humanist concerns! I'm a sellout to the pop-porno culture, you're the Defender of the Faith! Western Civilization! The Great Tradition! The Serious Viewpoint! As though seriousness can't be as stupid as anything else! You sententious bastard, have you ever in your life taken a mental position that isn't a moral judgment? I doubt you'd even know how. All you unstained, undegenerate, unselfish, loyal, responsible, high-minded Jews, good responsible citizen Jews, taking on the burdens of the Jewish people and worrying about the future of the State of Israel—and chinning yourselves like muscle-builders on your virtue! Milton Appel, the Charles Atlas of Goodness! Oh, the comforts of that difficult role! And how you play it! Even a mask of modesty to throw us dodos off the track! I'm 'fashionable,' you're for the ages. I fuck around, you *think*. My shitty books are cast in concrete, you make judicious reappraisals. I'm a 'case,' I have a 'career,' you of course have a calling. Oh, I'll tell you your calling—President of the Rabbinical Society for the Suppression of Laughter in the Interest of Loftier Values! Minister of the Official Style for Jewish Books Other than the Manual for Circumcision. Regulation number one: Do not mention your cock. You dumb prick! What if I trotted out your youthful essay about being insufficiently Jewish for Poppa and the Jews—written before you got frozen stiff in your militant grown-upism! I wonder what the kosher butchers over at *Inquisition* would have to say about that. Awfully strange to me that you should no longer care to remember your great *cri de coeur*, written before your self became so legitimate and your heart so pure, while my first stories you can't forget!"

"Mr. Zuckerman, you're entitled to think anything you want of me, and I'll have to try to live with that, as you've managed obviously to live with what I said about your books. What is strange to *me* is that you don't seem to have anything to say about the suggestion itself, regardless of your anger against the person who made it. But what may lie in store for the Jews is a much larger matter than what I think of your books, early or late, or what you think of my thinking."

Oh, if only he were fourteen and Gilbert Carnovsky, he'd tell him to take what may lie in store for the Jews and stick it up his ass. But he was forty and Zuckerman, and so, demonstrating to himself if to no one else the difference between character and author, he hung up the receiver, and found of course that he wasn't anything like pain-free. Standing atop the paper-strewn bed, his hands clutched into fists and raised to the ceiling of that dark tiny room, he cried out, he screamed, to find that from phoning Appel and venting his rage, he was only worse.

// 4 //

Burning

A double vodka on takeoff, then over some waterway in Pennsylvania three drags on a joint in the airplane toilet, and Zuckerman was managing well enough. Not much more pain than he would have felt at home doing nothing but tending pain. And every time his determination began to crumble and he told himself that he was running away on a ridiculous impulse, running away to nothing that made sense or promised relief, running away from what it was impossible to escape, he opened the medical-school catalogue and reread the chart on page 42 that laid out the daily course load for a medical student's first year.

You start at eight-thirty, five mornings a week, with Biology 310/311. From nine-thirty to noon, Clinics 300 and 390. An hour for lunch, and from one to five every afternoon, Anatomy 301. Then the evening's homework. Days and nights, filled not by him with what little he knew but by them with all he didn't. He turned to the description of Clinics 390.

INTRODUCTION TO THE PATIENT. This course is offered in the first year of training . . . Each student will interview a patient before the group, focusing on the present complaint, the illness onset, reaction to the illness and hospitalization, life changes related, personality characteristics, coping styles, etc. . . .

Sounds familiar. Sounds like the art of fiction, except that the coping style and the personality characteristics belong to a patient in off the street. Other people. Somebody should have told me about them a long time ago.

360. FETAL-MATERNAL MEDICINE. The student will work full-time in the labor-delivery floor. He will be required to review the bibliography related to methods and techniques of recording maternal and fetal physiologic parameters during labor and delivery . . .

361. OBSTETRICS: BIRTH ROOMS. This elective will primarily encompass inpatient obstetrics, especially birth-room experience. Some continuity of care can be achieved by post-partum follow-up on selected patients . . .

Not until Michigan did Zuckerman discover that if you take obstetrics as your specialty you specialize in gynecology too. Tumor formations. Infected reproductive organs. Well, it'd bestow a new perspective on an old obsession. What's more, he owed it to women after *Carnovsky*. From what he'd read of the reviews in the feminist press, he could expect a picture of himself up in the post office, alongside the mug shot of the Marquis de Sade, once the militants took Washington and began guillotining the thousand top misogynists in the arts. He came off no better there than with the disapproving Jews. Worse. They had put him on the cover of one of their magazines. WHY DOES THIS MAN HATE WOMEN? Those girls meant business—wanted blood. Well, he'd turn the tables and tend to abnormalities in the discharge of theirs. Relieving menstrual disorders beats he said she said I said you said on anyone's scale of values. In memory of the mother to whom he'd intended no harm. In the name of ex-wives who had done their damnedest. For his ministering harem. Where I have fornicated, there shall I diagnose, prescribe, operate, and cure. Up with colposcopy, down with Carnovsky.

Going to medical school is nuts, a sick man's delusion about healing himself. And Jenny saw it coming: I should have gone to Bearsville.

But he was *not* a sick man—he was *fighting* the idea of himself as sick. Every thought and feeling ensnared by the selfness of pain, pain endlessly circling back on itself, diminishing everything except isolation—first it's the pain that empties the world, then it's the effort to overcome it. He refused to endure one day more.

Other people. So busy diagnosing everybody else there's no time to overdiagnose yourself. The unexamined life— the only one worth living.

The man beside him in the aisle seat was filing into his attaché case the papers that had been absorbing his attention since they'd come on board. As the plane began its descent, he turned to Zuckerman and, in a neighborly way, he asked, "Going out on business?"

"That's right."

"What line you in?"

"Pornography," Zuckerman said.

He looked to be amused by the novel reply. "Selling it or buying it?"

"Publish it. Out to Chicago to see Hefner. Hugh Hefner. *Playboy*."

"Oh, everyone knows who Hefner is. I read the other day in *The Wall Street Journal* where he grosses a hundred and fifty million a year."

"Don't rub it in," Zuckerman said.

The man laughed amiably and seemed ready to leave

it at that. Until curiosity got the better of him. "What exactly do you publish?"

"*Lickety Split*," said Zuckerman.

"That's the publication?"

"You never see *Lickety Split*? On your newsstand?"

"No, afraid I haven't."

"But you see *Playboy*, don't you?"

"I see it occasionally."

"Open it up to look at, right?"

"From time to time."

"Well, personally I find *Playboy* boring. That's why I don't gross a hundred and fifty million: my magazine isn't as boring as his. Okay, I admit it, I'm extremely envious of Hefner's money. He has much more respectability, he has entrée, he has national distribution, and *Lickety Split* is still in the porno ghetto. I'm not surprised you haven't seen it. *Lickety Split* is not a mass-distribution publication because it's too dirty. It doesn't have Jean-Paul Sartre in it to make it kosher for a guy like you to buy at a newsstand and go home and jerk off to the tits. I don't believe in that. Hefner is basically a businessman. I don't think that describes me. Sure it's a high-profit business—but with me money is not the paramount issue."

It wasn't clear how much the "guy like you" had been offended by the allusion. He was dressed in a gray double-breasted chalk-stripe suit and a maroon silk tie, a tall, fit gray-haired man in his fifties who, though perhaps not accustomed to such a casual insult, was not about to take too seriously the provocations of a social inferior. Zuckerman imagined Diana's father looking rather like this. He asked Zuckerman, "What's your name, sir—may I ask?"

"Milton Appel. A-p-p-e-l. Accent on the second syllable. Je m'appelle Appel."

"Well, I'll keep an eye out for your journal."

Putting me down. "You do that," Zuckerman said. His neck was hurting and he got up and went off to the toilet to finish the joint.

They were high over the lake, still way above the rippling gray water and the zigzag slabs of floating ice, when he got back to his seat. Wide stretches of the lake were frozen over completely and strewn with shards of ice, a vast waste of slivers looking like the wreckage of millions of frosted light bulbs jettisoned from the sky. He'd expected that they'd already be passing over the Gold Coast towers and buckling their belts to land. Maybe the descent he'd imagined hadn't been the plane's but his own. Probably he should have tolerated this resurgence of pain instead of piling more grass on top of the pills and the vodka. But his plan wasn't to lie on his back for the rest of the day after they had landed. Flipping through the faculty register in the medical-school catalogue, he'd come upon the name of one of his oldest friends, Bobby Freytag. In their freshman year, they'd been thrown together as roommates just across the Midway in Burton Judson Hall. Now Bobby was a professor of anesthesiology in the School of Medicine and on the staff at Billings Hospital. Knowing Bobby was going to expedite everything. His first lucky break in a year and a half. Nothing now was going to stop him. He'd give up New York and move back to Chicago. It was more than twenty years since his graduation. How he'd loved it out there then! Eight hundred miles between him and home: Pennsylvania, Ohio, Indiana—the best friends a boy ever had. He figured he'd live in Chicago forever, after only his first day. He felt as though he'd come out from the East by covered wagon, a removal that immense, that final. He became a large, hearty American six-footer and a contemptuous bohemian all at once, and returned home twelve pounds heavier for his first Christmas vacation, ready to pick a fight with the nearest philistine. In his first year at Chicago he'd go down to the lake and make noises there alone on starry nights—the Gantian goat cry he'd read about in *Of Time and the River*. He carried *The Waste Land* with him on the El, reading away until Clark Street, where girls no older than himself were taking their clothes off in the striptease bars. If you bought them a drink when they came down off the runway, they did you a favor and put a hand on your cock. He wrote people letters about this. He was seventeen and thought continuously about his courses, his cock, and his pals Pennsylvania, Indiana, and Ohio. Talk to him about medical school in those days and he would have laughed in your face: he wasn't about to spend his life writing out prescriptions. His life was too big for that. Inspiring teachers, impenetrable texts, neurotic classmates, embattled causes, semantic hairsplitting—"What do you *mean* by 'mean'?"—his life was *enormous*. He met people his age who were brilliant but terrifically depressed, couldn't get up in the morning, didn't go to class or finish courses. He met geniuses sixteen years old who'd placed out of the college in two quarters and were already beginning law school. He met girls who never changed their clothes, who wore black makeup around their eyes and the same Left Bank outfit every day, bold, brash, talkative girls with hair halfway down to their black stockings. He had a roommate who wore a cape. He wore a field jacket and khaki trousers, like the last of the ex-GIs. In Stineway's Drugstore he saw people with white hair who'd begun in the college long before the war and were still hanging around contemplating their incompletes and trying to get laid. He joined the Film Society and saw *Bicycle Thief* and *Open City* and *Les Enfants du Paradis*. They were a revelation to him. So was Professor Mackauer's "History of Western

Civilization"—so was the wallowing in ass-wiping throughout Rabelais and all the ripened turds dotting Luther's Table Talk. He'd study from six till ten every night, then head off to Jimmy's, where he waited with his friends for the racier members of the faculty to show up. A sociologist of pop culture who'd once worked in the fallen world for *Fortune* would drink with them some nights until closing time. Even more glamorous was his teacher in Humanities 3, "a published poet" who'd parachuted into occupied Italy for the OSS and still wore a trench coat. He had a broken nose and read Shakespeare aloud in class and all the girls were in love with him, and so was young Zuckerman. He taught them *The Poetics, The Oresteia, Passage to India, The Alchemist, Portrait of the Artist, King Lear, The Autobiography of Benvenuto Cellini*—taught them all like holy books. Enrico Fermi gave a lecture in their physical-science survey course and did the ingratiating number up at the blackboard about needing help with the math. When the students clustered around after to ask the usual dumb celebrity questions, he had dared to inquire of the theoretician of The Bomb what he was doing now. Fermi laughed. "Nothing very important," he told him; "after all, I was trained in pre-Fermi physics." It was the cleverest remark that he had ever heard. He was becoming clever in conversation himself, droll, quick, deliciously self-effacing—and full of disgust for the country and its values. The worst days of the Cold War and they were studying *The Communist Manifesto* in the social-science course. On top of being a Jew in Christian America, he was becoming a member of yet another unloved, suspect minority, the "eggheads" ridiculed by the *Chicago Tribune*, the cultural Fifth Column of the commercial society. For weeks he mooned after a tall blond girl in a plaid flannel shirt who painted abstract pictures. He was floored when he found out she was a lesbian. He was rapidly growing sophisticated—

Manischewitz and Velveeta had by now been superseded by "wine and cheese," Taystee Bread by "French" bread when he could afford to eat out—but a lesbian? It never occurred to him. He did, however, have a girl friend, very briefly, who was mulatto. Fondling madly beneath her sweater in the basement of Ida Noyes Hall, he was still sufficiently analytical to think, "This is real life," though nothing in life had ever seemed stranger. He made a friend a few years older than himself, a Stineway's regular, who was in psychoanalysis, smoked marijuana, knew about jazz, and was a self-proclaimed Trotskyist. To a kid in 1950 this was hot stuff. They went to a jazz club up on Forty-sixth Street, two white Jewish students studiously listening to the music, surrounded on every side by dark, unfriendly, very unstudious faces. One thrilling night he listened to Nelson Algren talk about the prizefights at Jimmy's. Thomas Mann came to Chicago during his first term; *he* spoke at Rockefeller Chapel. Great event: the Goethe Bicentennial. In a German accent Mann spoke the richest English he had ever heard; he spoke *prose*, elegant and powerful and clear—with withering urbanity, pungent phrases intimately describing the genius of Bismarck, Erasmus, and Voltaire as though they were colleagues who'd been to dine at his house the evening before. Goethe was "a miracle," he said, but the real miracle was to be two rows down from the podium, learning from the Good European how to speak your own tongue. Mann said "greatness" fifty times that afternoon: Greatness, Mighty, Sublime. He phoned home that night in ecstasy from all the erudition, but nobody in New Jersey knew who Thomas Mann was, or even Nelson Algren. "Sorry," he said aloud, after hanging up, "sorry it wasn't Sam Levenson." He learned German. He read Galileo, St. Augustine, Freud. He protested the underpaying of the Negroes who worked at the university hospital. The Korean War began and he and his closest friend declared themselves enemies of Syngman Rhee. He read Croce, he ordered onion soup, he put a candle in a Chianti bottle and threw a party. He discovered Charlie Chaplin and W. C. Fields and documentary films and the dirtiest shows in Calumet City. He went up to the Near North Side to look down his nose at the advertising types and the tourists. He swam off the Point with a logical positivist, he savagely reviewed beat novels for *The Maroon*, he bought his first classical records— the Budapest String Quartet—from a homosexual salesman at the co-op whom he called by his first name. He began in conversation to call himself "one." Oh, everything was wonderful, as big and exciting a life as could be imagined, and then he made his first mistake. He published a short story while still an undergraduate, an "Atlantic First"—ten pages about a family of Newark Jews clashing with a family of Syrian Jews in a rooming house at the Jersey shore, the conflict loosely modeled on a battle provoked by a hot-headed uncle and narrated to him (disapprovingly) by his father on a visit home. An Atlantic First. It looked as though life had become bigger yet. Writing would intensify everything even further. Writing, as Mann had testified—not least by his own example—was the only worthwhile attainment, the surpassing experience, the exalted struggle, and there was no way to write other than like a fanatic. Without fanaticism, nothing great in fiction could ever be achieved. He had the highest possible conception of the gigantic capacities of literature to engulf and purify life. He would write more, publish more, and life would become colossal.

But what became colossal was the next page. He thought he had chosen life but what he had chosen was the next page. Stealing time to write stories, he never thought to wonder what time might be stealing from him. Only gradually did the perfecting of a writer's iron will begin to feel like the evasion of experience, and the means to imaginative release, to the exposure, revelation, and invention of life, like the sternest form of incarceration. He thought he'd chosen the intensification of everything and he'd chosen monasticism and retreat instead. Inherent in this choice was a paradox that he had never foreseen. When, some years later, he went to see a production of *Waiting for Godot*, he said afterwards to the woman who was then his lonely wife, "What's so harrowing? It's any writer's ordinary day. Except you don't get Pozzo and Lucky."

Chicago had sprung him from Jewish New Jersey, then fiction took over and boomeranged him right back. He wasn't the first: they fled Newark, New Jersey, and Camden, Ohio, and Sauk Centre, Minnesota, and Asheville, North Carolina; they couldn't stand the ignorance, the feuds, the boredom, the righteousness, the bigotry, the repetitious narrow-minded types; they couldn't endure the smallness; and then they spent the rest of their lives thinking about nothing else. Of all the tens of thousands who flee, those setting the pace for the exodus are the exiles who fail to get away. Not getting away becomes their job—it's what they do all day.

Of course he now wanted to become a doctor instead—to escape not only the never-ending retrospection but all the quarrels he'd provoked by drawing his last novel from the original quarrel. After the popular triumph of his devilish act of aggression, the penitential act of submission. Now that his parents were gone he could go ahead and make them happy: from filial outcast to Jewish internist, concluding the quarrel and the scandal. Five years down the line, he'd take a residency in leprosy and be forgiven by all. Like Nathan Leopold. Like Macbeth, after ordering the last innocent carcass to be dumped in a ditch, joining Amnesty International.

Won't do, thought Zuckerman. No, won't work. A

seriously sentimental illusion. If you kill a king, kill a king—then either break down and ruin yourself or, better still, step up to be crowned. And if it's lay on MacAppel, then so be it.

"You know why I can't get national distribution?" he said, turning to the man in the seat beside him. "Because my magazine isn't as boring as his."

"You mentioned that."

"His is just an obsession with big-titted women. That and Hefner shooting off his mouth about the First Amendment. In *Lickety Split, everything's* in it. I don't believe in censorship anywhere. My magazine is a mirror and we reflect it *all*. I want my readers to know that they shouldn't feel self-hatred if they want to get laid. If they jerk off it doesn't make them beneath contempt. And they don't need Sartre to make it legit. I'm not gay, but we're starting to run a lot of stuff on it. We help out married men who are looking for quick sex. Today most of the blow jobs are being given by guys who are married. You married?"

"Yes, I happen to be married. Happen to have three children."

"And you didn't know that?"

"No, I didn't."

"Well, you wouldn't know it from *Playboy*. Not for Hefner's readers, not that stuff. Not for *The Wall Street Journal* either. But in the back of movie theaters, in the washrooms of bars, outside the diners where the truck drivers stop—most of the blow jobs in America, being given right there. Sex is changing in America—people are swinging, eating pussy, women are fucking more, married men suck cocks, so *Lickety Split* reflects that. What are we supposed to do—lie? I see the statistics. These are real fundamental changes. As a revolutionary it's never enough for me. I feel it's so slow. Still, over the last decade semen production is up in America by at least two hundred percent. Only you're not going to find that out reading *Business Week*. You talk about *Playboy*. The married guy like you who looks at *Playboy*, he looks at those bunnies and the woman is inaccessible, it's the girl you can never get. Fine. Beats off and gets back in bed with his wife. But in *Lickety Split*, if you look at the broads, you know you can have them for a phone call and fifty bucks. It's the difference between infantile fantasy and reality."

"Well," replied the man beside him, turning away again to file the last of his papers, "I'll keep my eye out for it."

"You do that," Zuckerman said. Yet he didn't feel like stopping, not even if this guy had had it. It was starting to be real fun being the pornographer Milton Appel. A little holiday from Zuckerman.

Well, not quite—but why quit? "Know how I began *Lickety Split*?"

No reply. No, he obviously didn't care to know how Appel had begun *Lickety Split*. But Nathan did.

"I used to own a swinging club," Zuckerman said. "Eighty-first Street. Milton's Millennia. You never heard of that either. It was a membership club. No prostitution, no one paying for sex, and there was no law they could bust me on. Consensual sex, and in New York that's legal. They just harassed me to death, that's all. My fire extinguisher is twelve inches off the ground and not six inches off the ground. I lose my liquor license. Suddenly there's a broken main and no running water in the showers. The time wasn't ripe for it, that's all. Well, I had a manager there who's in jail for forgery. He got six years. A very sweet guy named Horowitz. Mortimer Horowitz." Mortimer Horowitz was *Inquiry*'s editor in chief. "Another Jew," said Zuckerman. "There are a lot of Jews in the business. Jews gravitate to pornography like to the rest of the media. You Jewish?" he asked.

"No."

"Well, most of the pornographers who are successful are Jews. And Catholics too. You Catholic?"

"Yes," he said, no longer making the effort to disguise his annoyance. "I am Roman Catholic."

"Well, a lot are Roman Catholics. Who are rebelling. Anyway, Horowitz was sort of fat"—indeed he was, the son of a bitch—"and he sweats, and I liked Horowitz. He's not very deep, but he's a sweet sort of schmuck. A nice man. Well, sexually Horowitz was very boastful, so I bet him a thousand dollars, somebody else bet him two thousand dollars, somebody else bet him five thousand dollars, how many orgasms he could have. He said he could come fifteen times in eighteen hours. He came fifteen times in *fourteen* hours. We had a medical student there who checked the ejaculation. He'd have to pull out so we could check each time. This is in a dark room at the back of Milton's Millennia. 1969. He's fucking a woman, then he'd be yelling I'm coming, the medical student would run over with a flashlight, and we'd see the come. I remember standing there and saying, 'This is my life, and it's not perverse, it's fascinating.' I remember thinking, 'When they do *The Milton Appel Story* this'll be a great scene.' But what really got me was this fascination. I thought, 'We keep records about everything. Assists. Hits. Batting averages. Why not cock? Here's Horowitz and this great record that should be on the front page of *The New York Times*, and nobody knows about it.' That was my cover story in the first issue of *Lickety Split*. Four years ago. Changed my life. Look, I wouldn't *want* a magazine like *Playboy*, not if I was guaranteed five *hundred* million—"

The plane banged down on the runway. Zuckerman

was back. Chicago! But he couldn't stop. What fun this was! And how long since he'd had any. How long before he'd have any again. Back to school for four more years.

"Some guy calls the other day and says, 'Appel, how much would you give to publish pictures of Hugh Hefner fucking?' He says he can get his hands on a dozen pictures of Hefner fucking his bunnies. I told him I wouldn't give him a dime. 'You think it's news that Hugh Hefner fucks? Get me pictures of the Pope fucking—then we can do business.'"

"Look here," said the man beside him, "that is quite enough!" and suddenly he had undone his seat belt and, though the plane was still careening down the runway, jumped across the aisle to an empty seat. "Sir!" called the stewardess. "Remain where you are till we reach the gate, *please*."

Before even waiting for the luggage to appear, Zuckerman found a pay phone and called Billings Hospital. He had to feed a second dime into the phone while waiting for the secretary to find Bobby. Couldn't hang up to be called back later, he told her; he was an old friend just arrived in town and he had to speak to Dr. Freytag right away. "Well, he's stepped down the corridor..." "Try to get him. Tell him it's Nathan Zuckerman. Tell him it's very important."

"Zuck!" said Bobby, when he came to the phone. "Zuck, this is terrific. Where are you?"

"I'm at the airport. O'Hare. Just landed."

"Well, great. You out here to lecture?"

"I'm out here to go back to school. As a student. I'm sick and tired of writing, Bob. I've made a big success and I made a pile of dough and I hate the whole God damn thing. I don't want to do it anymore. I really want to quit. And the only thing I can think of that would satisfy me would be becoming a doctor. I want to go to medical school. I flew out to see if I can enroll in the college for the winter quarter and finish up my science requirements. Bobby, I have to see you right away. I have the applications. I want to sit down and talk to you and see how I can get it done. What do you make of all this? Will they have me, age forty and a scientific ignoramus? On my transcript I'll show nearly straight A's. And they were hard-earned A's, Bob. They're hard-earned 1950s A's—they're like 1950 dollars."

Bobby was laughing—Nathan had been one of their dormitory's big-name late-night entertainers and this must be more of the same, mini-performance over the phone whipped up for old times' sake. Bobby had always been the softest touch. They'd had to live apart in their second year because laughing was murder on Bobby's asthma—out of control, it could bring on an attack. When Bobby saw Nathan heading toward him from across the quadrangle, he'd raise a hand and plead, "Don't, don't. I have a class." Oh, it had been great fun being funny in those days. Everybody had told him he was crazy if he didn't write the stuff down and get it published. So he had. Now he wanted to be a doctor.

"Bob, can I come by to see you this afternoon?"

"I'm tied up till five."

"Driving in will take till five."

"At six I've got a meeting, Zuck."

"Just for the hour then, to say hello. Look, my bag's here—see you soon."

Back in Chicago and feeling exactly as he had the first time around. A new existence. This was the way to do it: defiant, resolute, fearless, instead of tentative, doubt-ridden, and perpetually dismayed. Before leaving the phone booth, rather than hazard a third Percodan in eight hours, he took a swig of vodka from his flask. Aside from the raw stinging line of pain threading down behind the right ear through the base of the neck and into the meat of the upper back, he felt relatively little serious discomfort. But that was the pain he particularly didn't like. If he hadn't been feeling defiant, resolute, and fearless he might even have begun to feel a little dismayed. The muscle soreness he could manage, the tenderness, the tautness, the spasm, all of that he could take, even over the long haul; but not this steadily burning thread of fire that went white-hot with the minutest bob or flick of the head. It didn't always go out overnight. The previous summer he'd had it for nine weeks. After a twelve-day course of Butazolidin it had subsided somewhat, but by then the Butazolidin had so badly irritated his stomach that he couldn't digest anything heavier than rice pudding. Gloria baked rice pudding for him whenever she could stay for two hours. Every thirty minutes, when the timer rang in the kitchen, she'd jump up from the playmat and in garter belt and heels run off to open the oven and stir the rice. After a month of Gloria's rice pudding and little more, when there was still no improvement, he was sent to Mount Sinai for barium X-rays of his digestive tract. They found no hole in the lining anywhere along his gut, but he was warned by the gastroenterologist never again to wash down Butazolidin with champagne. That's how he'd done it: a bottle from the case that Marvin had sent him for his fortieth birthday, whenever Diana came by after school and he tried and failed at dictating a single page—a single paragraph. Didn't see why he shouldn't celebrate, his career was over, Diana's was just beginning, and it was vintage Dom Pérignon.

He hired a limousine. A limousine would be the fastest and smoothest way in, and the driver would be there to carry his suitcase. He'd keep the car till he'd found a hotel for the night.

His driver turned out to be a woman, a very fair young woman, shortish, stocky, about thirty, with fine white teeth, a slender neck, and a snappy, efficient way about her that was gentlemanly in the manner of the gentleman's gentleman. Her dark green worsted uniform was cut like a riding habit, and she wore high black leather boots. A blond braid hung down from the back of her cap.

"The South Side. Billings Hospital. I'll be about an hour. You'll wait."

"Right, sir."

The car began to move. Back! "Shall I comment on the fact that you're not the man I was expecting?"

"Up to you, sir," she said with a lively, bright laugh.

"This a sideline or this your work?"

"Oh, this is it, this is the work, all right. What about you?" Perky girl.

"Pornography. I publish a magazine, I own a swinging club, and I make films. I'm out here to see Hugh Hefner."

"Staying over at the Playboy Mansion?"

"That place makes me sick. I'm not interested in Hefner and his entourage. That to me is like his magazine: cold and boring and elitist."

That he was a pornographer hadn't disturbed her at all.

"My loyalty is to the common man," he told her. "My loyalty is to the guys on the street corner I grew up with and the guys I served with in the merchant marine. That's why I'm in this. It's the hypocrisy I can't stand. The sham. The denial of our cocks. The disparity between life as I lived it on the street corner, which was sexual and jerking off and constantly thinking about pussy, and the people who say it shouldn't be like that. How to get it—that was the question. That was the only question. That was the biggest question there was. It still is. It's frightening it's so big—and yet if you say this out loud you're a monster. There's an anti-humanity there that I can't stand. There's a lie there that makes me sick. You understand what I mean?"

"I think I do, sir."

"I know you do. You wouldn't be driving a limousine if you didn't. You're like me. I don't do well with discipline or authority. I don't want a white line drawn that says that I can't cross it. Because I'll cross it. When I was a kid, whenever I got into a fistfight, most every one was because I didn't want people to say no to me. It makes me crazy. The rebellious part of me says, Fuck 'em, no one's gonna tell me what to do."

"Yes, sir."

"That doesn't mean I've got to oppose every rule just because it's there. Violence I don't do. Children being exploited I find repugnant. Rape is not what I'm in favor of. I'm not into peeing and shit. There are some stories in my magazine I find disgusting. 'Grandma's Lollypop Hour'—I hated that story. It was vulgar and vile and I hated it. But I got a good bright staff, and as long as they're not pissing on the walls and they're doing their job, I let them do what they want. Either they're free or they're not free. I'm not like Sulzberger at *The New York Times*. I don't worry what they think up in the board rooms of corporate America. That's why I can't get national distribution like Hefner. That's why I'm paying him a call. He's a First Amendment absolutist? Then let him put his power where his mouth is in the state of Illinois. With me money is not the paramount issue the way it is with him. You know what is?"

"What?"

"The defiance is. The hatred is. The outrage is. The hatred is endless. The outrage is huge. What's your name?"

"Ricky."

"I'm Appel, Milton Appel. Rhymes with 'lapel' like in zoot suit. Everybody is so fucking serious out there about sex, Ricky—and there are so many fucking lies. *There's* the paramount issue. When I was in school I believed in Civics class that America was special. I couldn't understand the first time I was arrested that I was being arrested for being free. People used to say to me when I first went into sleaze, How long are they going to let you do this? That's crazy. What are they letting me do? They're letting me be an American. I'm breaking the law? I don't want to sound like Hefner but I thought the First Amendment was the law. Didn't you?"

"It is, Mr. Appel."

"And the ACLU, do they help? They think I give freedom a bad name. Freedom's *supposed* to have a bad name. What I do is what freedom's about. Freedom isn't making room for Hefner—it's making room for *me*. For *Lickety Split* and Milton's Millennia and Supercarnal Productions. I admit it, ninety percent of pornography is dull and trivial and boring. But so are the lives of most human beings, and we don't tell them they can't exist. For most people it's real reality that's boring and trivial. Reality is taking a crap. Or waiting for a cab. And being stuck in the rain. Just doing nothing is real reality. Reading *Time* magazine. But when people fuck they close their eyes and fantasize about something else, something that's absent, something that's elusive. Well, I fight for that, and I give them that, and I think what I do is good most of the time. I look in the mirror and I feel that I'm not a shit. I've never sold out my people, never. I like to fly first-class to Honolulu, I like to wear a fourteen-thousand-dollar watch, but I never let my money bulldoze me and manipulate me. I make more money than anybody who works for me because I get the grief and I get the indictments and they don't. They get their rocks off, at my office, calling me an acquisitive capitalist dog—they're all pro-Fidel and anti-Appel, and write graffiti on my door that their professors taught them at Harvard. 'The Management Sucks.' '*Lickety Split* is too intellectual.' Anarchists from nine to five, with me footing the bill. But I don't live in an anarchy. I live in a corrupt society. I've got a world of John Mitchells and Richard Nixons to face out there, plus an analyst, plus death, plus a fourth wife who's talking divorce, plus a seven-year-old kid I don't want to lay my trip on because that isn't the way I want it. That's not freedom for him. You follow me?"

"Yes, sir."

"About a year ago, when my wife started talking divorce, before I agreed to analysis, she took on a lover, the first in her life, and I felt myself destroyed. Couldn't handle it. I got crazed. Very insecure. I fuck hundreds of women and she fucked one guy, and I was wigged out. And he was nothing. She picked a guy who was older than me, who was impotent—I mean she didn't pick a twenty-five-year-old stud, and still I was wigged out. The guy was a checkers champion. Mortimer Horowitz. Always sitting there looking at his board. 'King me.' That's what she wanted. We had a reconciliation and I told her, 'Sweetheart, at least pick a guy next time who's a threat to me, pick a California surfer.' But she picks a Jewish nebbish—the checkers champion of Washington Square Park. But that's the pressure I'm under, Ricky: to play games, to sit still, to talk soft, to be nice. But I have never softened my stand so as to be nice and get the rewards that the nice boys get, like staying out of jail and owning legal guns and not having to wear a bulletproof vest every time I go out for a meal. I have never softened my stand to protect my money. There's a part of me that says, Fuck all that money. I like that part of me. When Nixon came in, I could have softened the magazine and avoided a lot. After they closed down Milton's Millennia, I could have got the message and quit. But I came back with Millennia Two, bigger and better and swankier than the old place, with its own fifty-foot swimming pool and a transvestite stripper for entertainment, a beautiful girl with a big dong, and let

Nixon go fuck himself. I see the way blacks are treated in this country. I see the inequities and it makes me sick. But do they fight the inequities? No. They fight kike-pornographer. Well, kike-pornographer is gonna fight back. Because I believe deep down in what I'm doing, Ricky. My staff laughs: it's become a polemic in my life that Milton Appel believes what he's doing. It's like Marilyn Monroe saying, 'I'm an actress I'm an actress.' She was also tits. I can tell people a thousand times that I'm a serious person, but it's hard for them to take at face value when the prosecution holds up *Lickety Split* and on the cover is a white girl sucking a big black cock and simultaneously fucking a broom. It's an unforgiving world we live in, Ricky. Those who transgress are truly hated as scum. Well, that's fine with me. But don't tell me scum has no right to exist along with everybody who's nice. Nobody should tell me that *ever*. Because scum is human too. *That's* what's paramount to me: not the money but the anti-humanity that calls itself nice. Nice. I don't care what my kid grows up to be, I don't care if he grows up wearing pantyhose as long as he doesn't turn out *nice*. You know what terrifies me more than jail? That he'll rebel against a father like me, and that's what I'll get. Decent society's fucking revenge: a kid who's very very very nice—another frightened soul, tamed by inhibition, suppressing madness, and wanting only to live with the rulers in harmonious peace."

"I want a second life. It's as ordinary as that."

"But what are you assuming?" Bobby asked. "That you're somehow going to be a completely erased tablet too? I don't believe in that, Zuck. If you're really going to do it, why pick a profession that's the most difficult and tedious to prepare for? At least choose an easier one so you don't lose so much."

"What's easier doesn't answer the need for something difficult."

"Go climb Mount Everest."

"That's like writing. You're alone with the mountain and an ax. You're all by yourself and it's practically undoable. It *is* writing."

"You're by yourself when you're a doctor too. When you're leaning over a patient in a bed, you've entered into a highly complicated, specialized relationship that you develop over the years through training and experience, but you're still back there somewhere by yourself, you know."

"That's not what 'by yourself' means to me. Any skilled worker's by himself like that. When I'm by myself what I'm examining isn't the patient in the bed. I'm leaning over a bed, all right, but I'm in it. There are writers who start from the other direction, but the thing that I grow grows on me. I listen, I listen carefully, but all I've got to go on, really, is my inner life—and I can't take any more of my inner life. Not even that little that's left. Subjectivity's the subject, and I've had it."

"That's all you're running out on?"

Do I tell him? Can Bobby cure me? I didn't come here to be treated but to learn to give the treatment, not to be reabsorbed in the pain but to make a new world to absorb myself in, not passively to receive somebody's care and attention but to master the profession that provides it. He'll put me in the hospital if I tell him, and I came out for the school.

"My life as cud, that's what I'm running out on. Swallow as experience, then up from the gut for a second go as art. Chewing on everything, seeking connections— too much inward-dwelling, Bob, too much burrowing back. Too much doubt if it's even worth the effort. Am I wrong to assume that in anesthesiology doubt isn't half of your life? I look at you and I see a big, confident, bearded fellow without the slightest doubt that what he's doing is worthwhile and that he does it well. That yours is a valuable service is undebatable fact. The surgeon hacks open his patient to remove something rotten and the patient doesn't feel a thing—because of you. It's clear, it's straightforward, it's unarguably useful and right to the point. I envy that."

"Yes? You want to be an anesthesiologist? Since when?"

"Since I laid eyes on you. You look like a million bucks. It must be great. You go up to them the night before the operation, you say, 'I'm Bobby Freytag and I'm going to put you to sleep tomorrow with a little sodium pentothal. I'm going to stay with you throughout the operation to be sure all your systems are okay, and when you come out of it, I'll be right there to hold your hand and see that you're comfortable. Here, swallow one of these and you'll sleep like a baby. I'm Bobby Freytag and I've been studying and training and working all my life just to be sure you're all right.' Yes, absolutely—I want to be an anesthesiologist like you."

"Come on, what's this all about, Zuck? You look like hell. You stink of gin."

"Vodka. On the plane. Fear of flying."

"You look worse than that. Your eyes. Your color. What the hell is going on?"

No. He would not let this pain poison another connection. Hadn't even worn the collar, fearing they wouldn't begin to consider him for medical school if they were to discover that he was not only forty and a scientific ignoramus but sick besides. Repetitious pain's clamorous needs were back on the playmat with his prism glasses. No more looking from the floor at everybody gigantically up on their feet. Percodan if required, Kotler's pillow for that chance in a million, but otherwise, to all he met in Chicago—to Bobby and the admissions committee certainly—another indestructible mortal, happy and healthy as the day he was born. Must suppress every temptation to describe it (from the meaningless first twinge through the disabling affliction) to your enviable old roommate, dedicated pain-killer though he may be. No more to be done for my pain, no more to be said. Either the medicines are still too primitive or the doctors aren't yet up to it or I'm incurable. When he felt pain, he'd pretend instead that it was pleasure. Every time the fire flares up, just say to yourself, "Ah, that's good—makes me glad to be alive." Think of it not as unreasonable punishment but as gratuitous reward. Think of it as chronic rapture, irksome only inasmuch as one can have too much even of a good thing. Think of it as the ticket to a second life. Imagine you owe it everything. Imagine anything you like. Forget those fictionalized book-bound Zuckermans and invent a real one now for the world. That's how the others do it. Your next work of art—*you*.

"Tell me about anesthesiology. I'll bet it's beautifully clear. You give them something to sleep, they sleep. You want to raise their blood pressure—you give them a drug, you raise their blood pressure. You want to raise it this much, you get this much—you want that much, you get that much. Isn't that true? You wouldn't look like you look if it wasn't. A leads to B and B leads to C. You know when you're right and you know when you're wrong. Am I idealizing it? You don't even have to answer. I see it on you, in you, all over you."

It was the Percodan he'd swallowed on the hospital steps, his third of the day (at least he was hoping it was his third and not his fourth), that had him talking away like this. Percodan could do that: first that lovely opening wallop and then for two hours you didn't shut up. In addition there was the excitement of seeing earnest, shy, amiable Bobby as a large full-grown physician: a pitch-black chin beard to cover his acne scars, a corner office in Billings overlooking the Midway lawn where once they'd played their Sunday softball, and rows of shelves bearing hundreds of books not one of which the novelist could recognize. It was thrilling just seeing Bobby weigh two hundred pounds. Bobby had been even skinnier than Nathan, a studious bean-pole with asthma, bad skin, and the kindest disposition in the history of adolescence. He was the only grateful seventeen-year-old that Nathan had ever met. Zuckerman was suddenly so proud of him he felt like his father, like Bobby's father, like the owner of the ladies' handbag store on Seventy-first Street where Bobby used to go to help on Wednesday nights and Saturday afternoons. A strong weepy feeling started to heat up his eyes, but no, he'd never get Bobby's backing by lowering his head to the desk and sobbing his heart out. This wasn't the place or the moment, even if both were urging everything so long held back to come forth in one big purgative gush. Look, it would be nice to shoot somebody too. Whoever had disabled him like this. Only no one was responsible—and unlike the pornographer he didn't own a gun.

The tears he suppressed, but he couldn't stop talking. Aside from the Percodan buoying him up, there was the decisive landmark decision made only the minute before—to have no pain even when he had it, to treat it like pleasure instead. He didn't mean masochistic pleasure either. It was bunk, at least in his case, that the payoff for being in pain was morbid secret gratifications. Everybody wants to make pain interesting—first the religions, then the poets, then, not to be left behind, even the doctors getting in on the act with their psychosomatic obsession. They want to give it *significance*. What does it mean? What are you hiding? What are you showing? What are you betraying? It's impossible just to suffer the pain, you have to suffer its meaning. But it's not interesting and it has no meaning—it's just plain stupid pain, it's the *opposite* of interesting, and nothing, *nothing* made it worth it unless you were mad to begin with. Nothing made it worth the doctors' offices and the hospitals and the drugstores and the clinics and the contradictory diagnoses. Nothing made it worth the depression and the humiliation and the helplessness, being robbed of work and walks and exercise and every last shred of independence. Nothing made it worth not being able to make your own bed in the morning without crawling back in immediately afterwards, nothing, not even a harem of a hundred in only their garter belts cooking rice pudding all at the same time. Nobody could make him believe that he'd had this pain for a year and a half because he believed he deserved it. What made him so resentful was that he didn't. He wasn't relieving guilt feelings—he didn't *have* guilt feelings. If he agreed with the Appels and their admonitions, he wouldn't have written those books in the first place. He wouldn't have been able to. He wouldn't have wanted to. Sure he was weary of the fight, but it didn't follow that his illness represented capitulation to their verdict. It wasn't punishment or guilt that he was expiating. He had not been four years to this great university having rational humanism drummed into his skull in order to wind up expiating irrational guilt through organic pain. He hadn't been writing for twenty years, writing principally *about* irrational guilt, to wind up irrationally guilty. Nor was he in need of a sickness to gain attention. Losing attention was what he was after—masked and gowned in the operating room, *that* was the objective. He did not wish to be a suffering person for any banal, romantic, ingenious, poetical, theological, or psychoanalytical reason, and certainly not to satisfy Mortimer Horowitz. Mortimer Horowitz was the best reason in the world to stay well. There was nothing in it and he wouldn't do it. He refused.

Three (or four) Percodan, two-thirds of a gram of marijuana, six ounces of vodka, and he saw everything clearly and couldn't stop talking. It was over. The eighteen months were over. He'd made up his mind and that was that. *I am well*.

"I can't get over it. I was the great performer, glib and satiric and worldly, and you were this earnest, dutiful, asthmatic kid helping his father in the handbag shop. I saw your name in the catalogue and I thought, 'So that's where Bobby's found to hide. Behind the surgeon.' But what I see is somebody hiding from nothing. Somebody who knows when he's right and knows when he's wrong. Somebody who doesn't have time in the operating room to sit around wondering what to do next and whether it'll work or not. Somebody who knows *how* to be right—how to be right *quickly*. No errors allowed. The stakes never in doubt. Life vs. Death. Health vs. Disease. Anesthesia vs. Pain. What that must do for a man!"

Bobby leaned back and laughed. Big hearty laugh, no oxygen shortage in those lungs anymore. He's the size of Falstaff. And not from booze but from this usefulness. He's the size of his worth.

"When you know how to do it, Zuck, it's very easy. It's like riding a bike."

"No, no, people tend to devalue the sophistication of their own special field. It's easy only because of all you know."

"Speaking of specialties, in *Time* they say you've had four wives."

"In life only three. And you?"

"One. One wife," said Bobby, "one child, one divorce."

"How's your father?"

"Not so good. My mom just died. Forty-five years of marriage. He's in a bad way. In the best of times he's not your most unemotional Jew—he can't even tell you it's Wednesday without tears coming to his eyes. So it's pretty rough right now. He's staying at my place for the time being. And your folks?"

"My father died in '69. Half out of it with a stroke, and then a coronary. My mother went a year later. Brain tumor. Very sudden."

"So you're orphaned. And right now no wife. Is that the problem? Abandonment?"

"I've got some girls looking after me."

"What drug you on, Zuck?"

"None, nothing. Just beat, that's all. The wives, the books, the girls, the funerals. The death of my folks was strong medicine. I'd been rehearsing it for years in my fiction, but I still never got the idea. But mostly I'm dead tired of the job. It's not the elevating experience they promised in Humanities 3. Starving myself of experience and eating only words. It brought out the drudge in me, Bob, this ritual that it takes to write. It may look to outsiders like the life of freedom—not on a schedule, in command of yourself, singled out for glory, the choice apparently to write about anything. But once one's writing, it's *all* limits. Bound to a subject. Bound to make sense of it. Bound to make a book of it. If you want to be reminded of your limitations virtually every minute, there's no better occupation to choose. Your memory, your diction, your intelligence, your sympathies, your observations, your sensations, your understanding—never enough. You find out more about what's missing in you than you really ought to know. All of you an enclosure you keep trying to break out of. And all the obligations more ferocious for being self-imposed."

"Every construction that helps anybody is also a boundary. I hate to tell you, but that's true even in medicine. Everybody's trapped in the thing he does best."

"Look, it's simple: I'm sick of raiding my memory and feeding on the past. There's nothing more to see from my angle; if it ever was the thing I did best, it isn't anymore. I want an active connection to life and I want it now. I want an active connection to *myself*. I'm sick of channeling everything into writing. I want the real thing, the thing *in the raw*, and not for the writing but for itself. Too long living out of the suitcase of myself. I want to start again for ten hundred different reasons."

But Bobby shook his bearded head: didn't get it, wouldn't buy it. "If you were a penniless failure as a writer, and nothing you wrote got published, and nobody knew your name, and if you were going into social work, say, which only took two years more of study, well, okay. If during all these years as the writer you are you'd been hanging around hospitals and doctors, if for the last twenty years you'd been reading medical books and the medical journals on the side—but as you say yourself, you're just as stupid about science as you were in 1950. If you really had been living some kind of secret life all these years—but have you? When did you get this great idea?"

"Two, three months ago."

"I think you've got another problem."

"What's that?"

"I don't know. Maybe you *are* just tired. Maybe you want to hang a sign on your door, 'Gone Fishin,' and take off to Tahiti for a year. Maybe you just need your second wind as a writer. You tell me. Maybe you've got to get screwed more or something."

"No help. Tried it. All the outward trappings of pleasure, but the result is the inverse of pleasure. Getting screwed, climbing Mount Everest, writing books—not enough companionship. Mailer ran for Mayor of New York. Kafka talked about becoming a waiter in a Tel Aviv café. I want to be a doctor. The dream of breaking out isn't that rare. It happens to the most hardened writers. The work draws on you and draws on you and you begin to wonder how much of you there is to draw on. Some turn to the bottle, others the shotgun. I prefer medical school."

"Except, whatever problems are plaguing you in writing, they're going to be right there, you know, when you're a doctor. You can grow sick and tired of the real thing too. Tired of the cancers, tired of the strokes, tired of the families taking the bad news. You can get just as tired of malignant tumors as you can of anything else. Look, I've had experience right up to here, and it doesn't pay off as greatly as you might think. You get so involved in experience, you lose the opportunity to grasp what you're going through. You pay your money, Zuck, and you take your choice. I happen to think you're going to be Zuckerman the doctor just the way you're Zuckerman the writer, no different."

"But the isolation won't be there, the solitude won't be there—it *can't* be there. The physical differences are too great. There are a thousand people walking around this hospital. Know who walks around my study, who I palpate and tell to say 'Ahhh'? Writing is not a very sociable business."

"I don't even agree with that. Your solitude is of your own making. Working with people is obviously alien to your nature. Your temperament's your temperament, and it'll still be yourself you're telling to say 'Ahhh.'"

"Bob, remember me out here? You don't remember an isolate, damn it. I was a lively, gregarious, outgoing kid. Laughing. Self-confident. I was practically crazy with intellectual excitement. Your old pal Zuck was not a remote personality. I was somebody burning to begin."

"And now you're burning to end. That's the impression I get anyway, underneath what you say."

"No, no, no—burning to begin *again*. Look, I want to take a crack at med school. What the hell is so wrong with that?"

"Because it isn't like you're taking a six-month sabbatical. It's a big investment of time and money. For a man of forty without real demonstrable qualifications, with an unscientific mind, it's just going to be too arduous."

"I can do it."

"Okay—let's say you even manage to, which I doubt. By the time you're worth anything you're going to be damn near fifty. You'll have plenty of companionship, but you'll have no recognition, and how the hell are you going to like that when you're fifty?"

"I'll love it."

"Bullshit."

"You're wrong. I had the recognition. I had the public. In the end it doesn't do anything to the public, but to me it did plenty. I sentenced myself to house arrest. Bobby, I have no desire to confess or to be taken for a confessor, and that was mostly where their interest got stuck. It wasn't literary fame, it was sexual fame, and sexual fame stinks. No, I'll be content to give that up. The most enviable genius in literary history is the guy who invented alphabet soup: nobody knows who he is. There's nothing more wearing than having to go around pretending to be the author of one's own books—except pretending not to be."

"What about money, if you think you don't need recognition?"

"I made money. Plenty of money. A lot of money and

a lot of embarrassment, and I don't need any more of either."

"Well, you'll have plenty of money, minus what it's going to cost you to go to medical school and to live for ten years. You haven't sold me on the idea that you want to be a doctor or ought to be a doctor, and you're not going to sell the admissions committee."

"What about my grades? All those A's, damn it. Nineteen-fifties A's!"

"Zuck, as a faculty member of this institution I'm quite touched to learn that you're still hung up on bringing home all those A's. But I have to tell you, we don't even look at anything that isn't an A. The problem is which A we take. And we're not going to take an A just because we've got a writer who doesn't want to be alone anymore with his typewriter and is sick of screwing his girlfriends. This might be a nice out for you from what you're doing, but we've got a doctor shortage in this country and only so many medical-school openings, et cetera and so forth. If I were the dean that's what I'd tell you. I wouldn't want to have to be the one to explain your case to the board of trustees. Not the way you've explained it, and not with you looking like this. Have you had a good physical lately?"

"I've been traveling, that's all."

"For more than three hours, from the sound of it."

Bobby's phone rang. "Dr. Freytag . . . What's the matter? . . . Come on, pull yourself together. Calm down. Nothing has happened to him . . . Dad, I don't know where he is either . . . He's not dead—he's out . . . Look, come to the hospital and wait in my office. We can go to the Chinese place . . . Then watch TV and I'll be home at eight and make us some spaghetti . . . I don't care what Gregory eats . . . I know he's a beautiful, wonderful boy, but I happen not to care any longer whether he eats or not. Don't sit there waiting for Gregory. You're driving yourself nuts with Gregory. Look, you know who's here, sitting across from my desk? My old roommate Zuck...Nathan. Nathan Zuckerman...Here, I'll put him on." He handed the phone across the desk. "My old man. Say hello."

"Mr. Freytag—it's Nathan Zuckerman. How are you?"

"Oh, not so good today. Not good at all. I lost my wife. I lost my Julie." He began to cry.

"I heard that. I'm terribly sorry. Bobby told me."

"Forty-five years, wonderful years, and now my Julie's gone. She's in the cemetery. How can that be? A cemetery where you can't even leave a flower or someone will steal it. Look, tell Bobby—is he still there? Did he go out?"

"He's here."

"Tell him, please, I forgot to tell him—I have to go there tomorrow. I must go out to the cemetery before it snows."

Zuckerman passed the phone over to Bobby.

"What is it?...No, Gregory can't take you out. Dad, Gregory can't take the garbage out. We're lucky we got him to give up a morning for the funeral...I know he's a wonderful boy, but you can't...What?...Sure, just a minute." To Zuckerman he said, "He wants to say something to you."

"Yes? Mr. Freytag?"

"Zuck, Zuck—it just now dawned on me. I'm sorry, I'm in a terrible state of confusion. Joel Kupperman—remember? I used to call you Joel Kupperman, the Quiz Kid."

"That's right."

"Sure, you had all the answers."

"I'll bet I did."

"Sure, you and Bobby with your studies. What students you boys were! I was telling Gregory just this morning how his father used to sit at that table and study. He's a good boy, Zuck. He just needs direction. We are not losing that boy! We made a Bobby, we can make another Bobby. And if I have to do it singlehanded I will. Zuck, quick, Bob again, before I forget."

The phone back over to Bobby.

"Yes, Dad . . . Dad, tell him one more time how much I loved my homework and the kid'll knife us both . . . You'll get to the cemetery . . . I understand that. I'll take care of it . . . I'll be home around eight . . . Dad, live with it—he is not coming home for dinner just because you'd like him to . . . Because he *often* doesn't come home for dinner . . . I don't know where, but he'll eat something, I'm sure. I'll be home at eight. Just watch the TV till I get there. I'll see you in a few hours . . ."

Bobby had been through it lately. Divorce from a depressive wife, contempt from a recalcitrant eighteen-year-old son, responsibility for a bereaved seventy-two-year-old father who filled him with infinite tenderness and infinite exasperation; also, since the divorce, sole responsibility for the son. Because of a severe case of mumps in late adolescence, Bobby could father no children, and Gregory had been adopted while Bobby was still a medical student. To raise an infant then had been an enormous burden, but his young wife was impatient to begin a family, and Bobby had been an earnest and dutiful young man. Of course his parents doted on Gregory from the moment the newborn child arrived. "Everybody doted on him—and what's come of him? Nothing."

The voice, weary with loathing, attested more to Bobby's suffering than to the hardening of his heart. It clearly wasn't easy to kill the last of his love for the thoughtless brat. Zuckerman's own father had had to feel himself leaving life before *he* could finally face disowning a son. "He's ignorant, he's lazy, he's selfish. A shitty little American consumer. His friends are nobodies, nothings, the kids they make the car commercials for. All they talk about is how to be millionaires before they're twenty-five—without working, of course. Imagine, when we were in the college, somebody saying 'millionaire' with awe. I hear him rattling off the names of the titans in the rock business and I want to wring his neck. I didn't think it could happen, but with his feet up and his bottle of Bud, watching a doubleheader on TV, he's even made me hate the White Sox. If I didn't see Gregory for another twenty years I'd be perfectly happy. But he's a fucking freeloader and it looks like I'll have him forever. He's supposed to be enrolled at some college downtown and I don't even think he knows which one. He tells me he doesn't go because he can't find a place to park. I ask him to do something and he tells me to eat shit and that he's leaving to live with his mother and never coming back because I'm such a demanding prick. 'Go, Greg,' I say, 'drive up tonight and I'll pay for the gas.' But she's in freezing Wisconsin and sort of screwy, and the louts he knows all hang out down here, and so next thing I know is that instead of leaving home and never coming back he's screwing some little twat in his room. He's a honey, Gregory. The morning after my mother died, when I told him his grandfather was coming to stay with us until he was better, he hit the ceiling. 'Grandpa *here*? How can Grandpa come here? If Grandpa moves in here, where am I going to fuck Marie? I'm asking a serious question. *Tell* me. Her house? With her whole family watching?' This is twelve hours after my mother had dropped dead. I'd been at their place all night with my old man. They'd set up the card table in the living room and were starting their game of gin, just the two of them. Suddenly my mother puts down her hand. 'I don't want to play anymore,' she says. Her head goes back, and that's it. Massive coronary. Now he's with us until the worst is over. Gregory goes out to start the night just when my father's in his pajamas watching the ten o'clock news. 'Where's he going at this hour? Where are you going, bubeleh, at ten o'clock at night?' The kid thinks he's hearing Swahili. I say, 'Dad, forget it.' 'But if he's first going out ten at night, what time is he coming home?' I tell him that those are questions that exceed all understanding—you have to have the brain of an Ann Landers to answer those questions. Sad business. He's facing the truth about bubeleh, and just when he's least prepared. Bubeleh turns out to be a con man and a bullshit artist who can't even be bothered to go out to the corner to get a quart of milk for Grandpa's cornflakes. It's been rough to watch. We've been together these last three weeks the way we were when I was a kid working in the store. Only now he's the kid. The mother dies, the old father becomes the son's son. We watch the Watergate news together. We eat dinner together. I make breakfast for him in the morning before I go to the hospital. I stop on the way home to get the chocolate-covered cookies that he likes. Before he goes to bed, I give him two with a Valium and a warm glass of milk. The night my mother died I stayed there and slept with him in their bed. During the day, during the first week, he came and sat at my desk while I was down in surgery. He told my secretary about the handbag business. Every day he sat in my office and read the paper for four hours until I came up from the operating room and took him down to the cafeteria for lunch. Nothing like a father's defenselessness to bring you to your knees. It's why I can't forgive that fucking kid. The vulnerability of this old guy and it leaves him absolutely cold. I know he's only eighteen. But *so* callous? *So* blind? Even at eight it would stink. But that's how it worked out, and there we are. I've been so busy with my old man I haven't even had time to think about my mother. That'll come later, I suppose. What's it like for you, without them?

I still remember your folks and your kid brother when they all came out to visit on the train."

The differences in their family predicament Zuckerman preferred not discussing right then—it could only promote further dismissive interpretations of his motives. Zuckerman was still stunned by how matter-of-factly Bobby had opposed him. His plan to change his life had seemed as absurd to Bobby as it had to Diana when he'd invited her to come out with him to Chicago and go to school.

"What's it like," Bobby asked him, "three, four years after they're gone?"

"I miss them." To miss. To feel the absence of. Also, to fail to do, as to miss an opportunity.

"What'd they make of *Carnovsky*?"

In the old days he would have told him the truth— back then Zuckerman would have kept Bobby up half the night telling him the truth. But to explain that his father had never forgiven the mockery that he saw in *Carnovsky*, of both the Zuckermans and the Jews; to describe his acquiescent mother's discomposure, the wounded pride, the confused emotions, the social embarrassment during the last year of her life, all because of the mother in *Carnovsky*; to tell him that his brother had gone so far as to claim that what he'd committed wasn't mockery but murder...well, he didn't consider it seemly, twenty years on, still to be complaining to his roommate that nobody from New Jersey knew how to read.

Up the Outer Drive with Ricky at the wheel. Chicago by night, said the Percodan, visit the new Picasso, the old El, see how the dingy bars you wrote up in your diary as "real" have now become far-out boutiques— "First a room where I can lie down. My neck. Must get my collar out of the suitcase." But the Percodan wouldn't hear of it: Your collar's a crutch. You're not going to medical school in that collar. "What's Percodan then?" True, but one crutch to be discarded at a time. You're back, but it's only Chicago, not Lourdes.

On the Outer Drive it seemed more like Chartres he'd returned to: away while they were hauling up the spires, he was seeing a wonder and an era all complete, a legend knocked together in twenty years. They'd built Rome, Athens, Angkor Wat, and Machu Picchu all while he was writing (and defending—stupidly defending!) his four books. He could have been seeing electric lighting for the first time too. Broken bands of illumination, starred, squared, braided, climbing light, then a ghost wall of lakeshore, and of this day and age, nothing more. And to confound the enigma of all that light encoding all that black—and of the four books, the thousand pages, the three hundred thousand words that had made him what he was today—there was all the synthetic opium lacing his blood and steeping his brain.

Oxycodone. That was the ingredient doing the confounding. What egg whites had been to his mother's angel-food cake, oxycodone was to Percodan. He'd learned about oxycodone from the *Physicians' Desk Reference to Pharmaceuticals and Biologicals*, the big blue 25th edition, a full fifteen hundred pages to select from at bedtime, three hundred more even than his bedside copy of Gray's *Anatomy*. Thirty pages showed color photographs, in actual size, of a thousand prescription drugs. He would swallow 500 milligrams of Placidyl—a rubbery reddish sleeping capsule exuding a faintly stinging aftertaste and odor—and, while waiting to discover if just one would work, lay alone in the lamplight with his PDR, boning up on side effects and contraindications, and feeling (if he could manage to) like the sleepy boy who used to take his stamp album into his bed with him back when inspecting watermarks under his magnifying lens was all it took to put him out—and not for thirty minutes, but ten hours.

Most of the pills looked banal enough, like M&Ms, like the pharmacopoeia's counterpart of the multicolored sets of boring stamps portraying impregnable monarchs and founding fathers. But waiting on sleep he had all the time in the world, and like the young philatelist of years ago scanned the thousand pictures to find the most delicately decorated, the whimsical, the inspired: to sub-due nausea, Wans, suppositories looking like pastel tor-pedoes out of a toy war game; a pill called Naqua, to treat edema, fashioned like a fragile snowflake; Quaalude pills, marketed for sedation, initialed like a signet ring. For steroid therapy, Decadron, modeled after the party hat, and to soften the stool, Colace capsules as radiant as rubies. Paral capsules, another sedative, looked like garnet-shaped bottles of burgundy wine, and to combat severe infection, V-Cillin K, tiny white ostrich eggs stamped, as though for a birthday child, "Lilly." Antivert they marked with a fossil arrowhead, Ethaquin with a fossil insect, and scratched upon the Theokin was a char-acter identified by Zuckerman as runic. To alleviate pain there were dollhouse lipsticks called Darvon capsules, Phenaphen pills disguised as raspberry mints, and the die from which they cast the Ur-placebo, the little pink Talwin pill. But none of these—and he'd tried enormous doses of all three—alleviated Zuckerman's pain like the oxycodone that the master chef at Endo Laboratories, Inc., mixed with a little aspirin, a little caffeine, a little phenacetin, then lightly sprinkled with a dash of hom-atropine terephthalate, to make mellow, soft, and cheer-ing Percodan. Where would he be without it? Praying at the pillow of Dr. Kotler, instead of out on the town with midnight still hours away.

To cease upon the midnight with no pain. Keats studied medicine (was also said to have died of a review). Keats, Conan Doyle, Smollett, Rabelais, Walker Percy, Sir Thomas Browne. The affinity between vocations was real—and that wasn't Percodan sweet talk, that was weighty biographical fact. Chekhov. Céline. A. J. Cronin. Carlo Levi. W. C. Williams of Rutherford, N.J. . . .

He should have recited that list for Bobby. But they were all doctors first, Bobby would have replied. No, other doctors won't trust me because I chose first to be an artiste. Nobody'll believe I can do it. Or mean it. I'll be as suspect a physician as I was a writer. And what about the poor patients? This new doctor wrote *Carnovsky*—he doesn't want to cure me, he just wants to get my story and put it in a book.

"You a feminist, Ricky?"

"I just drive a car, sir."

"Don't get me wrong. I like the feminists actually because they're so fucking stupid. They talk about exploitation. To them exploitation in most cases is if a guy has sex with a woman. When I do the TV shows, when they invite me there to fight the feminists and those women start carrying on, I say to them, 'You know, I've got the place for you: no pornography, no prostitution, no perversion. It's called the Soviet Union. Why don't you go?' It generally shuts them up for a while. Wherever I am, there seems to be controversy. Always suing and fighting. It's a constant being at war. I am an endangered species, under attack. That's because I'm threatening. The most threatening. Physically I'm constantly aware of being hurt. That's not just dramatizing. There are people who can hurt me. I get death threats, Ricky. If I showed you some of my death mail, half of it deals with 'Only a Jew could do this. Only a kike could crawl so low.' It's like the body count in Vietnam. If you're defined as not being human, somebody can justify your execution. One guy with a bullet can end it all. He can do it to me tomorrow. He can do it tonight. I want a gun permit. I want it now. I have many guns, but I'd like to have them legal, you know. In New York the Mayor still makes me fight to get a gun permit, and then he asks me to endorse his opponent. Never directly, no, not like that—but somebody comes down to the club and says, 'The Mayor would appreciate blah blah blah,' and so I do it. Otherwise City Hall would make it even worse than it is. I'm very frightened of kidnapping. In all my interviews and public statements I never touch on my wife and my son. I've got kidnapping insurance with Lloyds of London. But that doesn't mean they're going to get me to stop. I'll never be the good acceptable pornographer like Hefner, with an acceptable bullshit 'philosophy.' I'll never be the good acceptable Jew, never. What's your religion?"

"Lutheran."

"I never wanted to be Protestant. Jews do, plenty of them. Not me. To be assimilated, to be respectable, to be detached like the Wasps, I understand the desire, but I knew never to try. I see all those distinguished Wasps with the beautiful gray hair and the pinstripe suits who don't have pimples on their ass. They're my lawyers. That's who I send into court for me. I don't send in Jews. Jews are too crazy. They're like me. Volatile extremes. Jews sweat. These guys are in control, there's a coolness there that I respect. These guys are *quiet*. I don't want to be that way. I couldn't begin to be that way. I'm the wild Jew of the pampas. I am the Golem of the U.S.A. But I love these guys—they keep me out of prison. Though a lot of them are crazy too, you know. They're alcoholics, their wives stick their heads in ovens, their kids drop LSD and jump out of windows to see if they can fly. Wasps have troubles, I know that. What they don't have is my enemies. I've cornered the market. Everybody hates me. Everybody. There's a theatrical club in New York where I'd love to be a member. The Inquiry Club. I love show business, slapstick, the old comics. But they won't let me in. They'll take Mafia hit men, they'll accept Shylocks, but the Jewish businessmen who run it won't let me in. I've got more enemies than Nixon. The police. The mob. Crazy, fucking, paranoid Nixon himself. I've got Chief Justice Warren Burger. Justice Lewis Powell. Justice Harry Blackmun. Justice William Rehnquist. Justice 'Whizzer' All-American White. My *wife* is my enemy. My *child* is my enemy. I've got an analyst who gets *paid* to be my enemy. Either they're out to bust me, to indict me, to usurp me, or they want to change me into somebody else. I started psychoanalysis three months ago. You ever been in psychoanalysis?"

"No, sir."

"It's very scary, Ricky. There's no product. I was just complaining to the shrink this morning that it's an endless process. Sometimes I don't know from one session to another if I'm getting my money's worth. It's a hundred bucks a session. It's over sixteen hundred dollars a month. It's expensive. But my wife is a very conservative woman and she wants it and I'm doing it. This is my fourth wife. She's conservative and we fight all the time. She thinks pornography is juvenile. I tell her, 'Yes, it's true, so what?' She thinks it's beneath me. She tells me that I'm boxed in with a persona that doesn't fit. What a grand human being I would be if only I would be somebody else. That's what she and the analyst have in mind. I can't say I'm not a little sick of pornography. There's a lot of compulsivity in all this—I know that. I'm to some degree bored with talking about eating pussy and sucking cock and whose dick is larger than whose. A lot of times I'm tired of the lawsuits. I'm tired of the debates. It's getting harder for me to wage a fervent battle about letting people watch other people fuck—but for those who want it, why 'no'? Every other kind of shit is accessible, why not this? The analyst says to me, 'Why do you go to such lengths to be unacceptable?' Do I? I'm not unacceptable to the readers of *Lickety Split*. I'm not unacceptable to the poor bastards who want to go to a good porno film and jerk off. I'm not unacceptable to the people who come to Milton's Millennia Two. I'm not saying you can come to my place and throw the women down on the floor and fuck them. I never said you can fuck everybody you want. Those are words that have been put into my mouth by all those fucking fascistic feminists who hated their fathers and now hate me. But that is not my position. Everything's by mutual consent and every woman comes with a man to escort her inside. But immediately you eliminate the ninety percent of the people who say, 'Oh, I don't do that.' You're immediately in the ball park. Whoever *wants* you to fuck 'em, you fuck 'em. It's the best buy in New York. For a couple it's thirty-five dollars. That includes dinner, dancing, and staying till 4 a.m. You go to a disco in New York, you pay twenty-five dollars just to get in. At Milton's for thirty-five bucks you've got your hotel room, you got your food, and you got your whole evening. And you're *safe*. I reopened a year and a half ago and there hasn't been a fight yet. Name a bar in Chicago without a fight in the last eighteen months. To fight over a woman there, you have to be off the fucking wall to do it. You fight when there's repression, when you're denied. At Milton's, you're obviously with a woman, you're in there *because* you're with a woman— so you can either watch and jerk off, or you fuck the woman you brought, or you can swing with another couple, if each person finds the other one compatible. We've got small rooms if you want to fuck alone and we've got a big orgy room with mirrors and a bar. Sure, to some degree it's boring—a hundred people fucking, so what? I'm not saying it's classy. These are people who live in Jersey and Queens. The pretty people aren't going to Milton's, other than to look. The real swingers who are very attractive swing privately at parties, California-style. At Milton's it's nice people, schleppy people—it's sort of middle-class. You know how many come there who actually fuck?"

"No, sir."

"Take a guess."

"Better if I concentrate on my driving, sir. Heavy traffic."

"Twenty percent. Tops. Eighty percent watch. Like television. Spectator stuff. But it's not like Hefner's mansion and the champagne parties for his entourage. I see him and Barbi on television and I want to throw up. I provide a service for the common man. I give entertainment, information—I legitimize feelings in people as real as anybody else. They need it dirty to get turned on? So what? They're still human beings, you know, and there are millions of them out there. All the men's magazines taken together have thirty million readers. That's more people than voted for McGovern. If the men's magazines had got together and held a convention and put up a candidate, he would have beaten George McGovern. That's more men buying magazines to jerk off with than there are people living in Holland, Belgium, Sweden, Finland, and Norway combined. Still, the analyst tells me that all I've done is institutionalized my neurosis. So did Napoleon. So did Sigmund Freud! This is the problem with analysis for me. Sure I want to be a better father. I have to deal with a seven-year-old son who is very bright, very precious to me, and very difficult. He's a ball-breaking, bright kid, who's constantly interrogating everything I do. Do I give my little Nathan values where he's to challenge authority or to accept authority? I don't have a glimmer. I don't like the job of forbidding something—it's not my way. But here I am, grossing seven million a year, the most wanted terrorist of the sexual revolution, and I don't have a fucking glimmer what to teach him. I want to learn to share with him. I want him to feel my strength and who I am, and to enjoy him. I'm concerned about Nathan. In some ways people are going to treat him badly because of me. But must I change my entire life for him? Right now he's only seven and he doesn't quite know who I am. He knows that sometimes people ask me for my autograph, but he doesn't know what the business is. I tell him I make movies and I own a nightclub and I publish a magazine. He once wanted to look at *Lickety Split*. I tell him, 'It's not for you, it's for grown-ups.' He says, 'Well, what's in it?' I say, 'People making love.' He says, 'Oh.' 'What do you think making love is?' I ask him. So he says, 'How should I know?'—very indignant. But when he knows, it's going to be difficult for him. When I pick him up at school, the twelve-year-olds know who I am— and I'm concerned about that. But analysis is complicated for someone like me. I've gotten such payoffs from being repulsive. I hear the analyst talking about monogamy and making a commitment to marriage, and these ideas are sort of goofy to me. That's what he holds up to me as health. I don't know—am I defending a stupid entrenched neurosis, or am I paying a hundred dollars an hour to get myself brainwashed by a professional bourgeois? I have a lot of girl friends. I'm supposed to get rid of them. I do group sex. I'm supposed to cut it out. I get blow jobs from my receptionist. I'm supposed to stop. My wife is sort of tuned-out—she's detached and innocent and good, and she doesn't know. People can't believe she doesn't know, but that's the kind of woman she is, and I'm careful. So there's *The Milton Appel Story*: the most notorious pornographer in America, and I live the dishonest life of most Americans about my sexuality. Ridiculous. The wildest antisocial desperado of them all, the embodiment of crudity, the Castro of cock, the personification of orgasmic mania, commander in chief of the American pornocracy—"

He couldn't have stopped if he'd wanted to. *Let him speak.*

// 5 //

The Corpus

He had registered as a man grossing seven million a year. He remembered, some time earlier, trying a sentimental walk around the Loop as himself. When that didn't work he got back in the car, and they drove on to the Ambassador East. They drank in the bar. As best he remembered, he'd brought tremendous pressure on her to come back with him to New York to drive his Rolls. When men like that want something, they don't stop till they get it. He'd offered an enormous future as chauffeur to Milton Appel. She laughed, a good-natured girl of twenty-seven, only a few years out of rural Minnesota, cheery, polite, not at all so simple as she'd first sounded, with remarkable turquoise eyes and a blond braid and the chunky arms of a healthy child. She laughed and said no, but he wouldn't let up. The well-known pornographical paradox: one has to esteem innocence highly to enjoy its violation. He was taking her to the Pump Room, he told her, to negotiate further over dinner, but when he came up to his room to wash and to change, he'd dropped onto the bed to assuage the flesh, and now it was a dim winter morning.

Back in 1949, when the dangers of night stalking were still all metaphorical, he'd circle the Loop three and four times after dark. Starting at Orchestra Hall, where the unmusical boy raised on "Make-Believe Ballroom"

and "Your Hit Parade" had first heard Beethoven's Fifth,
he would cut across to LaSalle (seething with hatred for
the Stock Exchange) and on up to Randolph and the
garish downtown that reminded him always of home, of
Market Street back in Newark, of the chop-suey joints
and cheap specialty shops, the saloon grills, the shoe
stores, the penny arcades, all battened down beneath
rooftop billboards and fastened in by the movie palaces.
At State and Lake he'd pass under the El and, resting
against a pillar, wait for the thrill of the first vibrations.
That he who had been born in New Jersey should hear
an elevated train pounding overhead in Illinois seemed
to him as dark and exalting as any of the impenetrable
mysteries tormenting Eugene Gant in *Of Time and the
River*. *If this can happen, anything can happen.* Meaning by
"anything" nothing at all like the pain in the neck that
in 1973 forced him back to the limousine after just a
few blocks, and on to the hotel where he'd slept for ten
hours in his clothes.

He'd dreamed all night. There was a nude woman.
She was short and firm, her face obscure, her age inde-
cipherable except for the youthful breasts, grotesquely
high and spherical and hard. She was posing on a platform
for an art class. It was his mother. Drenched in yearning,
he dreamed again. She flew into his room, this time
clearly his mother and no one else—only she flew in as
a dove, a white dove with a large round white disc,
toothed like a circular saw, whirling between her wings
to keep her aloft. "Strife," she said, and flew out through
an open window. He called after her from where he was
pinned to his bed. Never had he felt so wretched. He
was six and calling, "Mama, I didn't mean it, please
come back."

She's with me here. At 3 a.m., in the Ambassador East,
where he was doubly disguised—falsely registered under
his worst enemy's name, and passing himself off as a

social menace——his mother's ghost had tracked him down. He wasn't being poetic or mad. Some power of his mother's spirit had survived her body. Always he had tended to think rationally, as a rationalist, that life ends with the death of the human body. But at three that night, wide awake in the dark, he understood that this is not so. It ends and it doesn't. There is some spiritual power, some mental power, that lives after the body is dead, and that clings to those who think about the dead one, and my mother has revealed hers here in Chicago. People would say this is only more subjectivity. I would have said so myself. But subjectivity is a mystery too. Do birds have subjectivity? Subjectivity is just the name for the route she takes to reach me. It's not that I want to have this contact or that she wants to have this contact, and it's not that the contact will continue forever. It is also dying like the body is dying, this remnant of her spirit is dying too, but it's not quite gone yet. It's in this room. It's beside this bed.

"Close," he said to her, very softly, ". . . but not too close."

When she was alive she didn't want to risk antagonizing me. She wanted me to love her. She didn't want to lose my love and would never be critical or argue. Now she doesn't care if I love her or not. She doesn't need love, she doesn't need support, she is beyond all these encumbrances. All that is left is the wound I inflicted. And it was a terrible wound. "You were intelligent enough to know that literature is literature, but still, there were things that were real that Nathan had used, and you loved Nathan more than anything else in the world . . ."

He didn't know if the sound of her voice would be wonderful or terrifying. He didn't find out. He waited for what she would say, but she wasn't speaking: simply purely present.

"Mother, what do you want?"

But she was dead. She wanted nothing.

He awakened in a large penthouse suite looking out over the lake. Before even removing his clothes to shower, he called Bobby's house. But by eight Bobby's hospital day had already begun. Eight to eight, thought Zuckerman, and at night the emergency calls.

Mr. Freytag answered the phone. The old man was vacuuming carpets and had to turn off the machine in order to hear him. He said that Bobby was gone.

"The mornings aren't good," he told Zuckerman. "I cleaned out the oven, I defrosted the freezer—but my Julie, I want her back. Is that wrong, is that only selfish, to want my Julie back for myself?"

"No, it isn't."

"I've been up since five. Gregory never came home. I don't understand how Bobby accepts it. He hasn't even called to tell his father where he is. It's morning. It's starting to snow. We're going to have that storm, and big. Everybody in the world knows. The 'Today Show' says so. The papers say so. Only Gregory hasn't heard. I'm supposed to go out this morning before it really starts up, but where is Gregory?" He was beginning to sob. "To snow—to snow so soon. Zuck, I can't stand it. Two feet of snow."

"Suppose I take you. Suppose we go out in a taxi together."

"I've got my car, it runs beautiful—only Bobby would be furious if I went alone, especially in this weather. How she loved to look out the window when it snowed. Like a little girl, whenever she saw the first snow."

"I'll take you in your car."

"Out of the question. You have a life to live. I wouldn't hear of it."

"I'll be by at ten."

"But if Gregory comes back—"

"If he's back, go. If no one's home, I'll understand that you went with him."

Under the shower he tested his torso. Nothing encouraging there. The change was that for a second consecutive day it would be him taking charge, not the pain. The best adaptation to make to pain is to make no adaptation. A year and a half to learn but now he knew. First, he would take Mr. Freytag to visit the grave before the snow buried his wife a second time. His own son was busy, his grandson still missing, but Zuckerman was free and fit enough. To so easily answer a father's need! It was a job for which he'd received an excellent education—for which he'd displayed prodigious talent even as a very small boy. Only when he was fully grown did the task for which his other talents equipped him keep getting in the way. How he went about *that* estranged him from father, mother, brother, and then from three wives—rooted more in the writing than in them, the sacrificial relationship with the books and not with the people who'd helped to inspire them. As the years passed, along with the charge of being out of reach, there were sexual complaints from the wives. Then the pain, so persistent as to estrange him even from the writing. On the playmat every other predicament, large or small, was inconceivable: no character imaginable other than the one in pain. What prevents my recovery, what I do or what I don't do? What does this illness want with me anyway? Or is it I who want something from it? The interrogation had no useful purpose, yet the sole motif of his existence was this hourly search for the missing meaning. Had he kept a pain diary, the only entry would have been one word: Myself.

Back when he'd still been hunting for a hidden cause, he'd even come to wonder if the aim of the affliction mightn't be to provide a fresh subject, the anatomy's gift to the vanishing muse. Some gift. To pay not only a patient's fixated attention to a mystifying infirmity but an obsessional writer's as well! God only knew what his body would come up with, if physical suffering turned out to be good for his work.

No, divorce number four from the flesh and its incessant wailing. Once and for all to dissolve that misalliance and resume life as your own man. First, out to the cemetery as a stand-in son, then lunch with Bobby and, if he'll arrange it (and he will, if at lunch I insist), fifteen minutes with the medical-school dean. Didn't Bobby see how the dean could make a big thing out of this? "We believe in diversity in this medical school. We brought in this writer, and we put him here with these other students, and it's going to be a new and broadening experience for him, it's going to be a new and broadening experience for all of us. We are going to benefit by this ingenious alchemy that I, Dr. Innovative, have wrought." Why the hell not? At least let me have my crack at him. And after lunch, the registrar, to sign on for the first quarter back in the college. By nightfall his career as a writer would be officially over and the future as a physician underway. As of yesterday, he'd officially signed off as a patient. This was as far as he'd be pushed by mindless matter. Now for the spirit to speak out. I have longings and they must be met.

He washed down a Percodan with a mouthful of vodka and from a phone beside the toilet rang for coffee to be sent up while he shaved. He'd have to watch the booze and the pills. And enough of Milton Appel. All that raw force pouring out over his life. More squeezed out of him in that limousine than in the last four years at his desk. He'd felt like some enormous tube of linguistic paste. Diatribe, alibi, anecdote, confession, expostulation, promotion, pedagogy, philosophy, assault, apologia, denunciation, a foaming confluence of passion and language, and all for an audience of one. Into his parched-out desert,

that oasis of words! The more energy he spends, the more
he gains. They are hypnotic, these talking nuts. They
go all the way out, and not just on paper. They say it
all. His humanity. His depravity. His ideals. Is this guy
a charlatan, Zuckerman wondered. Doesn't seem to know
himself, doesn't know whether to make himself sound
worse than he is or better. Though had he really said
much that we haven't already heard in *Mrs. Warren's
Profession?* The language may have ripened since Shaw,
but nothing much had happened to the wisdom: the
madam is more moral than the sick and hypocritical
society. It was still Sade, and not the publisher of *Lickety
Split*, who could carry that argument to the bottom of
the bottom and dispense with every moral pretext—no
other claim than that pleasure justifies everything. Perhaps it was only the wife and the analyst and the kid—
and you make his life much easier by giving him a son
instead of a daughter—but he still couldn't get himself
to go that far. Of course, he was a Jew, and anti-Sem-
itically speaking, if a Jew wants to make money running
a brothel, he'll make it sound like an adult day-care
center. Philo-Semitically speaking, what poor Ricky had
endured in that bar was a saint in the line of the great
healer Jews going back to Freud and his circle: crusading,
do-gooding Dr. Appel, easing suffering mankind of its
psychic tensions. The noble cause of Milton's Millennia.
Not a fistfight there in eighteen months—if the place
catches on like McDonald's, it might mean the end of
war. Yet, the moral stubbornness, the passionate oth-
erness—maybe he is what makes one secretly proudest
of being a Jew after all. The more he sits with me, the
more I find to like.

"I'm *serious*," said Zuckerman aloud, in the bedroom
now dressing for the big day ahead, "—why is it so hard
for people to take that at face value? I had to apply to
four private schools to get Nathan accepted. A kid with

an IQ of 167 and the first three schools turned him down.
Because of me. I went with him for interviews. Why
shouldn't I? I asked them questions about the curricu-
lum. I'm a dignified man. I feel myself to be a very
dignified man. I have deep respect for education. I want
him to have the best. I remember reading Henry Miller
when I was fifteen. Pages and pages of eating pussy. I
would read his description of pussies and think how
limited I was. I couldn't describe a pussy in longer than
six words. That's the first time in my life that it occurred
to me to be ashamed of my vocabulary. If the teachers
at school had told me that by building up my vocabulary
I could write descriptions of pussy like Henry Miller, I
would never have been left back. I would have had the
motivation. That's what I want to give my son. I would
do anything in the world for him. I took a bath with
him just last week. It was wonderful. You can't imagine
it. Then I go to Dr. Horowitz and he tells me don't do
that, the male cock is threatening to a young child. The
child feels inadequate. I feel terrible. Horowitz tells me
I got that wrong too. But I want to share a *closeness* with
Nathan. And I did. Man to man. My father was never
behind me, never. I was going to change all that. My
father gave me nothing. I'm a success so now he's impressed. He sees the Rolls, he sees that people work for
me, that I live in a multimillion-dollar house, he sees
the way my wife dresses, the school the kid goes to, and
that keeps his fucking mouth shut. But the kid has got
an IQ of 167, and when he starts asking me what I do,
what am I supposed to tell him? You're the writer, you're
the genius who has the great ideas—you tell me what
it is to be a father without having the answers. I have
to get through the day *without having the answers*. And
you don't know them any more than I do. You don't
have kids so you don't know *anything*. You would abolish,
for all future Zuckermans, the maximum security of that

crazy love. You would abolish all future Zuckermans! Zuckerman the Great Emancipator brings all that begetting to a stop . . . But you don't know suffering until you have children. You don't know joy. You don't know boredom, you don't know—*period*. When he's twelve, when he starts to jerk off, then I can get through to him what the business is about. But at seven? How do you explain to a child of seven the irrepressible urge to spurt?"

Well, however much pleasure was to be had from that mischief, it was time now to go. As a character he is still far from complete, but who isn't? So Zuckerman thought until down in the lobby he was told by the doorman that the car and driver were waiting. The pornographer with the protesting mouth had apparently hired her for the length of his stay.

Big white snowflakes swept lightly across the hood of the limousine as they headed back onto the Drive. The distant sky looked just about ready to bring on in from the northern plains the season's first big show. Mr. Freytag's ordeal was now to begin: a Midwestern winter— blizzards to bury her anew every night. Zuckerman's mother was stored in the sunny South, where they buried you only once. After her funeral, a muscular man in a soiled T-shirt, his bicep tattooed "USMC," had taken Zuckerman aside to say that he was Mike, the cemetery caretaker, and to ask how deep the family wanted her letters chiseled. Mike understood that both sons would be returning to New Jersey and wanted to be sure he had his instructions right. Zuckerman told him, "The same as my father's letters." "That's a half inch deep," Mike warned; "not everybody knows how to do it that deep." Zuckerman, stunned by the murderous speed of the tumor and then the swiftness of the interment, still couldn't follow. The burial had taken no time at all. He was thinking that they *ought* to do these things twice:

the first time you could just stand there not knowing what's happening, while the second time you could look around, see who was in tears, hear the words being said, understand at least a little of what was going on; sentiments uttered over a grave can sometimes alter a life, and he'd heard nothing. He didn't feel like a son who'd just witnessed his mother's burial, but like an actor's understudy, the one they use in rehearsals to see how the costumes look under the lights. "Look," said Mike, "just leave it to me. I'll get somebody who won't damage the stone. I'll see you don't get rooked. I know you want your mother looked after right." Zuckerman got the message. He handed Mike all the loose bills in his pocket, and assured him he would see him the following year. But once the apartment had been emptied and sold, he never visited Florida again. Cousin Essie saw to the stone, and wrote the two boys to assure them that the cemetery sprinkled the grass daily to keep the grave site green. But that was like sprinkling Antarctica for the good it did the astonishingly intractable grief. Mother's gone. Mother is matter, too. Almost three years, yet that idea had lost no force. It could still pop up out of nowhere to shut down all other thinking. A life previously subdivided by the dates of his marriages, his divorces, and his publications had fallen into two clean-cut historical epochs: before those words and after. Mother's gone. The theme of his tortured night-long dreaming, the words that had moved his little double to cry, "Come back, I didn't mean it."

This longing for a mother he'd left behind at sixteen—would he be suffering it so if he were working and well? Would he be feeling *any* of this so keenly? All a consequence of being mysteriously ill! But if not for the longing would he have fallen ill? Of course a large, unexpected loss can undermine anyone's health—so will controversy and angry opposition. But undermining it still, three and four years on? How deep can a shock go? And how delicate can I be?

Oh, too delicate, too delicate by far for even your own contradictions. The experience of contradiction *is* the human experience; everybody's balancing that baggage— how can you knuckle under to that? A novelist without his irreconcilable halves, quarters, eighths, and sixteenths? Someone who hasn't the means to make novels. Nor the right. He wasn't leaving voluntarily, he was being drummed out of the corps. Physically unfit for being torn apart. Hasn't the muscle for it. Hasn't the soul.

Equally pointless, he thought: trying to defend your work and trying to explain your pain. Once I've recovered, won't indulge in either ever again. *Once I've recovered.* Terrific tribute to the indomitable will to have so bracing a thought only the morning after—and about as likely as a dead woman returning to life because of a child in a dream crying out that he's sorry.

Zuckerman finally realized that his mother had been his only love. And returning to school? The dream of at least being loved again by his teachers, now that she was gone. Gone and yet more present than she'd been in thirty years. Back to school and the days of effortlessly satisfying the powers that be—and of the most passionate bond of a lifetime.

He popped a second Percodan and pushed the button lowering the partition window between the front and back seats.

"Why am I unacceptable to you, Ricky?"

"You're not. You're interesting to me."

Since their negotiating session in the bar she'd dropped the "sir."

"What interests you about me?"

"The way you see things. That would interest anyone."

"But you wouldn't work for me in New York."

"No."

"You think I exploit women, don't you? You think I debase them. A girl works at the Merchandise Mart making a hundred a week and she's not being exploited, but a girl works in a Supercarnal flick, makes five hundred in a day—in a *day*, Rick—and she's being exploited. Is that what you think?"

"I don't get paid to think."

"Oh, you know how to think, all right. Who do you fuck out here, a good-looking independent young woman like you? In your position you must get a lot of cock."

"Look, I don't understand what you mean."

"You got a boyfriend?"

"I'm just divorced."

"You a parent?"

"No."

"Why not? You don't want to bring children into the world? Why, because you feminists find motherhood a nuisance or is it because of The Bomb? I'm asking why you don't have kids, Ricky. What are you afraid of?"

"Is a childless home a sign of fear to the owner of *Lickety Split*?"

"Very sharp. But what are you sparring with me for? I'm asking you a serious question about life. I'm a serious person. Why won't you buy that? I'm not saying I'm sinless—but I am a man of values, I am a crusading person, and so I talk about what I'm crusading for. Why is it hard for people to take that at face value? I have been crucified on the sexual cross—I am a martyr on the sexual cross, and don't give me that look, it's true. Religion interests me. Not their fucking prohibitions, but *religion*. Jesus interests me. Why shouldn't he? His suffering is something that I can sympathize with. I tell that to people and they look at me just like you. Egomania. Ignorance. Blasphemy. I say that on a talk show and the death threats start rolling in. But he never referred to himself, you know, as the Son of God. He insisted that he was just the Son of Man, a member of the human race, with all that goes with it. But the Christians made him into the Son of God anyway, and became everything he preached against, a new Israel in just the wrong way. But the new Israel is me, Ricky—Milton Appel."

That got her.

"You and Jesus. My God," she said, "there really are people who think they can get away with anything."

"Why not Jesus? They hated him too. Men of sorrows acquainted with grief. Appel Dolorosus."

"'Grief'? What about pleasure? Power? What about wealth?"

"That's true. I admit it. I love pleasure. I love to ejaculate. To ejaculate is a deep, wonderful feeling. My wife and I had sex the night before I left. She had her period, I was horny, and so she gave me a blow job. It felt great. It felt so great that I couldn't sleep. Two hours later I jerked off. I didn't want to let go of the feeling. I wanted to feel it again. But she woke up and saw me coming, and she started to cry. She doesn't understand. But you do, don't you, a woman of the world like you?"

She did not bother to answer. Did what she was paid to do and drove. Superhuman restraint, Zuckerman thought. Make some novelist a wonderful wife.

"So you do think I debase women. That's why whatever I would offer you, you still wouldn't come with me back to New York."

When she did not reply, Zuckerman leaned forward in his seat, the better to drop each word in her ear. "Because you are a God damn feminist."

"Look, Mr. Dolorosus, I drive who pays me. This is my car and I do what I like. I work for myself. I'm not under contract to Hefner out here—I don't want to be under contract to you there."

"Because your are a God damn feminist."

"No, because that partition between you and me in this car is there for me as well. Because the truth is I'm not interested *at all* in your life, and I certainly wouldn't go to New York and become involved in that kind of setup. It smells bad, if you want to know my opinion. And it's your honesty that stinks the most. You think because you're honest and open about it, that it's acceptable. But that doesn't make it acceptable. It only makes it worse. Even your honesty is a way of debasing things."

"Am I worse than the executives you drive around who are screwing the American worker? Am I worse than the politicians you drive around who are screwing the American nigger?"

"I don't know. Most of them are quiet in the back. They've got their briefcases and they're writing out their little notes, and I don't know how awful they are, or if they're awful at all. But I do know about you."

"And I'm the worst person you ever met."

"Probably. I don't know you intimately. I'm sure your wife would say you were."

"The worst."

"I would think so."

"You feel sorry for my wife, do you?"

"Oh God, yes. To try to have an ordinary life, to try to bring up a child and to have a fairly decent life—and with a man like you? With a man whose life is devoted to 'cunts' and 'cocks' and 'coming,' to 'pussy' or whatever you like to call it—?"

"You feel sorry for me too, Ricky?"

"You? No. *You* want it. But *she* doesn't want that kind of life. I feel sorry for your child."

"The poor child too."

"Personally I would think your child's chances are nil, Mr. Appel. Oh, I'm sure you do love him in your egomaniacal way—but to grow up and know that that was what your father did for a living, and that he was pretty famous for it, well, that's a tough start in life, isn't it? Of course if you want him to run your empire, he's set. But is that what you're sending him to the best private schools for? To run *Lickety Split*? I feel sorry for your wife, I feel sorry for your child, and I feel sorry for all the people who sit in the movie theaters to watch your Supercarnal productions. I'm sorry for them if that's what it takes to get them turned on. And I'm sorry for the girls in those films, if that's how they have to make a living. I wasn't trained for anything, either. I was trained to get married, and that didn't work out very well. So now I'm a chauffeur. And a good one. I wouldn't do the kind of work they do, never—and not because I'm feminist: because it would ruin my sex life, and I like sex too much to have it ruined. I'd have the scars forever. Privacy is as good a cause as pornography, you know. No, I don't find you unacceptable because I'm a God damn feminist. It's because I'm a human being. You don't just debase women. Only part of it's the exploitation of these dumb women. You debase everything. Your life is filth. On every level. And you make it all the more awful because you won't even shut up."

"Oh, but let's just stick to women, my dear human being—to those girls you feel so sorry for, who don't happen to run their own limousines. There are girls, some of them, in my pictures, that are such bubbleheads they don't even know how to brush their teeth—and I pay 'em a hundred bucks an hour. Is this debasing women? Is this scarring them for life, giving them money to pay the rent? I've been on the set where I've taken girls to the bathroom and washed their *feet* for them because they were so dirty. Is this debasing women? If someone smells bad, we show her feminine hygiene. Because some of these girls, my dear human being, some of them come in off the street stinking even worse than I do. But we go out and buy the whole kit for them and show them how to use it. Most of these girls, when they work for me, they enter idiots and leave at least *resembling* what I take to be people. Shirley Temper happens to be as bright as any actress working in the legitimate theater. Why is she doing it? She's doing it because she is pulling in *a thousand dollars a day*. *My money.* Is that debasing women? She's doing it because a Broadway play opens and closes in a week and she's back with the unemployed, while with me she works all the time, has the dignity of a working person, and gets the chance to play a whole variety of roles. Sure, some of them are the classic woman who is looking for a strong pimp to rob them blind. Some people are always going to be exploited and not take responsibility for their own lives. Exploiting goes on everywhere there are people willing to be exploited. But Shirley says fuck that. And she didn't belong to the college sorority with Jane Fonda and Gloria Steinem. Scranton PA, that was her college. Fuck that, she said, age sixteen, and got out from behind a checkout counter at the A&P—out of the Scranton slums to make fifty grand her first year in the business. At *sixteen*. The girls who are in porno films, most of them take *pride* in what they do. It turns you on to drive the big limo and dress yourself up in a man's uniform? Well, it turns them on to show their pussies. They enjoy the exhibitionism, and who are you in your Gestapo boots to tell them that they shouldn't? There are guys out there jerking off over them. They love that. That's exploitation? That's debasement? That's *power*, sister. What you have got behind this wheel. Marilyn Monroe is dead, but kids all over America are still flogging their dum-dums over those tits. That's exploitation of Marilyn Monroe? That's her immortality! She's nothing in the ground, but to kids who haven't even been born yet, she'll always be this great piece of ass. These are women who feel no shame about fucking in public. They love it. Nobody's forcing anybody to do anything. If the ribbon counter at Woolworth's makes them feel liberated, let 'em work there for two bucks an hour. There are enough bodies you can get, enough women who want to do it for money or kicks, for catharsis, that you don't have to force people. The fact is that the women have it easier than anybody. They can fake orgasm, but for the poor guy up in front of the lights, it's no picnic. The guy who exhibits the greatest bravado, who says, Hey, I'd like to do that, I got a big cock—he can't get it up at all. Exploited? If anybody's exploited it's the God damn *men*. Most of these girls are on a total ego trip in front of the cameras. Sure I had animals in my last film, but nobody there forced anybody to fuck them. Chuck Raw, my star, walked off the picture because of the dog. He says, 'I love dogs and I won't be a party to this, Milton. Banging women fucks up their minds—they can't handle it. Any dog who fucks a woman is finished as an animal.' I respected Chuck for that. I have the courage of my convictions, he has the courage of his. Don't you get the idea yet? Nobody is putting these people in chains! I am taking them *out* of their chains! I am a monster with something to offer! I am changing American fucking forever! I am setting this country free!"

A third Percodan and the stupor began. Suddenly no words would stick in his mind, all the words were flying apart and no two seconds would hold together. To know what he was thinking required an enormous effort. By the time he found an answer, he could no longer remember the question. Laboriously he had to begin again. Beyond the fog there was a moat and beyond the moat an airy blankness. Don't ask how, but beyond that, out of the window and above the lake, he saw a marvel of gentle inaudible movement: snow falling. There was nothing that could ever equal coming home through the snow in late afternoon from Chancellor Avenue School. That was the best life had to offer. Snow was childhood, protected, carefree, loved, obedient. Then came audacity, after audacity doubt, after doubt pain. What does chronic pain teach us? Step to the front of the class and write your answer on the board. Chronic pain teaches us: one, what well-being is; two, what cowardice is; three, a little something of what it is to be sentenced to hard labor. Pain is work. What else, Nathan, what above everything? It teaches us who is boss. Correct. Now list all the ways of confronting chronic pain. You can suffer it. You can struggle against it. You can hate it. You can attempt to understand it. You can try running. And if none of these techniques provide relief? Percodan, said Zuckerman; if nothing else works, then the hell with consciousness as the highest value: drink vodka and take drugs. To make so much of consciousness may have been my first mistake. There is much to be said for irresponsible stupefaction. That is something I never believed and am still reluctant to admit. But it's true: pain is ennobling in the long run, I'm sure, but a dose of stupefaction isn't bad either. Stupefaction can't make you a hero the way suffering can, but it certainly is merciful and sweet.

By the time the limousine drew up in front of Bobby's town house, Zuckerman had emptied the last drop from his flask and was ready for the cemetery. On the front steps, in fur hat, storm coat, and buckled black galoshes, an old man was trying to sweep away the snow. It was falling heavily now, and as soon as he got to the bottom step, he had to start again at the top. There were four steps and the old man kept going up and down them with his broom.

Zuckerman, watching from the car: "It's not called the vale of tears for nothing."

Later: "You don't want to be a doctor, you want to be a magician."

Ricky came around to open his door. As he could barely think what he was thinking, he couldn't begin to surmise what she might be thinking. But that was fine—to be dumb to all that was a blessing. Especially as what you thought they were thinking wasn't what they were thinking, but no less your invention than anything else. Oh, ironic paranoia is the worst. Usually when you're busy with your paranoia at least the irony is gone and you really want to win. But to see your roaring, righteous hatred as a supremely comical act subdues no one but yourself. "Be out in ten minutes," he told her. "Just going in to get laid."

He started toward the old man still vainly sweeping the stairs.

"Mr. Freytag?"

"Yes? Who are you? What is it?"

Even in his stupor, Zuckerman understood. Who is dead, where is the body? What savage catastrophe, the old man was asking, had overtaken which of his beloved, irreplaceable kin? They belong to another history, these old Jewish people, a history that is not ours, a way of being and loving that is not ours, that we do not want for ourselves, that would be horrible for us, and yet, because of that history, they cannot leave you unaffected when their faces show such fear.

"Nathan Zuckerman." Identifying himself required a difficult, concentrated moment of thought. "Zuck," Zuckerman said.

"My God, Zuck! But Bobby's not here. Bobby's at school. Bobby's mother died. I lost my wife."

"I know."

"Of course! My thoughts are everywhere! Except where I am! My thoughts—they're so scattered!"

"I'm taking you to the cemetery."

Mr. Freytag nearly tripped over himself backing into the stairs. Maybe he smelled the drink or maybe it was the sight of the long black car.

"The car is mine."

"Zuck, what a boat. My God."

"I hit the jackpot, Mr. Freytag."

"Bobby told me. Isn't that wonderful. Isn't that something."

"Let's," said Zuckerman. "Go. Now." If he got back into the car he wouldn't collapse.

"But I'm waiting for Gregory." He pushed up his sleeve to check the time. "He should be home any minute. I don't want him taking a fall. He runs everywhere. He doesn't *look*. If anything should happen to that boy—! I have to get salt to sprinkle—before he gets home. Ice will never form once you get the salt in under the snow. It eats from beneath. Hey, your hat! Zuck, you're standing here without a hat!"

Inside, Zuckerman made for a chair and sat. Mr. Freytag was speaking to him from the kitchen. "The thick crystal salt—the kosher salt—" A very long disquisition on salt.

Navajo carpet. Teak furniture. Noguchi lamps.

Hyde Park Shakerism.

Yet things were missing. Pale shadows at eye level of paintings that had been removed. Holes in the plaster where hooks had been. The property settlement. The wife got them. Took the records too. In the shelves beneath the phonograph only four records left, their jackets torn and tattered. The living-room bookshelves looked plundered as well. All that Bobby had got to keep intact seemed to be Gregory.

Zuckerman was working hard to see where he was— to *be* where he was—when he was somewhere else. Gregory's bedroom. Mr. Freytag was holding open the door to the boy's closet. "He is not one of those kids you see around today who isn't neat and clean. He's neat as a pin. Beautifully combed. A lovely dresser. Just look at the shirts. The blues all together, the browns all together, the striped shirts at one end, the checked shirts at the other, the solids in between. Everything perfect."

"A good boy."

"In his heart a *wonderful* boy, but Bobby is a busy man and from his mother, unfortunately, the child got no direction. She couldn't give herself any, how could she give him? But I've been working on him since I'm here, and I tell you, it's having some influence. We sat yesterday morning, just the two of us right in this room, and I told him about his father. How Bobby used to study. How he used to work in the store. And you should have seen him listening. 'Yes, Grandpa, yes, I understand.' I told him how I started out in the handbag business, how with my brother I left school and worked in the tannery to help my father support a family of eight. At fourteen years of age. After the Crash, how I got a pushcart and on weekends and at night went door-to-door, selling imperfect handbags. During the day I twisted challahs in a bakery, and at night I went out with the pushcart, and you know what he said to me, when I finished? He said to me, 'You had a rough life, Grandpa.' Bobby has got his job and I've got mine. That's what I realized sitting with that boy. I am going to be a father again. Someone has to do it and it's going to be me!" He took off his storm coat and looked again at his watch. "We'll wait," he said. "Fifteen more minutes, till it's ten on the button, and if he's not here, we go. I don't understand it. I called all his friends. He's not there. Where does he go all night? Where does he drive to? How do I know if he's all right? They drive, and where are they going, do *they* even know? That car of his: mistake number fifty-six. I told Robert, 'He must not have a car!'" Then he burst into tears. He was a strong, heavyset man, dark-complexioned like Bobby, though now sickly gray from grief. He fought the tears with his entire torso: you could see in his shoulders, in his chest, in the meaty hands that had twisted those Depression challahs, how much he despised his weakness: he looked ready to tear things apart. He was wearing a checkered pair of slacks and a new red flannel shirt— the outfit of a man who wasn't submitting to anything if he could help it. But he couldn't help it.

They were sitting on Gregory's bed, beneath a large poster of a tattooed ten-year-old in mirrored glasses. The room was small and warm and Zuckerman wanted only to get into the bed. He was riding the waves, coasting up the crest and into the light, then down into the stupor's swell.

"We were playing cards. I said, 'Honey, watch my discards. You're not paying attention to my discards. You should never have given me that three.' A three of diamonds. A three of diamonds—and that's it. There's no way to grasp it. Urine coming out of her, out of this woman so spotless all her life. Onto her living-room rug. I saw the urine and I knew it was over. Come in here, come with me, I want to show you something beautiful."

Another closet. A woman's fur coat. "See this?"

He saw, but that too was it.

"Look how she cared for this coat. Still in mint condition. The way she looked after *everything*. You see? Black silk lining with her initials. The best bone buttons. Everything the best. The only thing she let me buy her all her life. I said to her, 'We're not poor people anymore, let me get you a diamond pin.' 'I don't need diamonds.' 'Let me get you a beautiful ring then, with your birthstone in it. You worked in the store all those years like a dog, you deserve it.' No, her wedding ring is enough. But twelve years ago this last fall, her fifty-fifth birthday, I forced her, literally *forced* her to come with me to buy the coat. During the fitting you should have seen her— white as a ghost, as though it was our last penny we were throwing away. A woman who for herself wanted *nothing*."

"Mine too."

Mr. Freytag didn't seem to hear him. Could be that Zuckerman hadn't spoken. Possible he wasn't even awake.

"I didn't want a coat like this sitting in that empty apartment where somebody could break in. She got it out of storage, Zuck, the day . . . the same day . . . the *morning* . . ."

Back in the living room he stood by the front window and looked out at the street. "We'll give him five more minutes. Ten."

"Take your time."

"I see little signs now of how ill she was. She would iron half a shirt and have to sit down for fifteen minutes. I couldn't add two and two. I thought the exhaustion was all in her head. Oh, am I angry! Am I furious! Okay, damn it, we go! We're going. I get you a hat and we go. And boots. I'll get you a pair of Bobby's boots. How does a grown man go out in this weather without a hat, without boots, without anything? All you need is to get sick!"

In the car to the cemetery, what is there to think? On the road to the cemetery, stupefied or wide awake, it's simple: what is coming. No, it stays unseen, out of sight, and you come to it. Illness is a message from the grave. Greetings: You and your body are one— it goes, you follow. His parents were gone and he was next. Out to the cemetery in a long black car. No wonder Mr. Freytag had fallen back in alarm: all that was missing was the box.

The old man bent forward, his face in his hands. "She was my *memory*."

"Mine too."

"Stop!" Mr. Freytag was hammering his fist on the glass partition. "Pull over! Here!" To Zuckerman he cried, "That's it, the store, my friend's store!"

The car edged to the side of a wide bleak boulevard. Low warehouses, vacant shops, auto wreckers on three corners.

"He used to be our janitor. A Mexican boy, a sweet lovely boy. He bought this place with his cousin. Business is murder. Whenever I come by, I buy something, even if I don't need it. Three beautiful little children and the poor wife is a double mastectomy. A girl of thirty-four. Awful."

Ricky kept the motor idling as Mr. Freytag and Zuckerman passed across the pavement arm-in-arm. The snow was covering everything.

"Where's Manuel?" Mr. Freytag asked the girl at the checkout counter. She pointed through the dimness to the rear of the store. Passing the rows of canned goods, Zuckerman became terrified: he would fall and pull everything down.

Manuel, a roundish man with a fleshy dark Indian face, was kneeling on the floor, stamping the price on breakfast cereal boxes. He greeted Mr. Freytag with a hearty laugh. "Hey, Big Man! What do you say, Big Man?"

Mr. Freytag motioned for Manuel to leave what he was doing and come close. Something he had to confide.

"What is it, Big Man?"

His lips to Manuel's ear, he whispered, "I lost my wife."

"Oh, no."

"Lost my wife of forty-five years. Twenty-three days ago."

"Oh, no. That's no good. That's bad."

"I'm on my way to the cemetery. A storm is coming."

"Oh, that was such a nice lady. Such a good lady."

"I stopped to buy some salt. I need the coarse kosher salt."

Manuel led him to the salt. Mr. Freytag removed two boxes from the rack. At the register Manuel refused his money. After bagging the boxes himself he accompanied them out into the snow in his shirt sleeves.

They shook hands to part. Mr. Freytag, close to tears, said, "You'll tell Dolores."

"It's no good," said Manuel. "No good."

Back in the car, remembering something more to say, Mr. Freytag reached to roll down the window. When he couldn't find a handle anywhere on the door, he began to pound at the glass. "Open it! I can't open it!"

Ricky pushed a button and, to the old man's relief, the window slid away. "Manuel!" he called out, into the snowfall. "Hey, Manuel—come here!"

The young grocer, turning in the doorway, wearily passed a hand back through his dark hair to brush away the snow. "Yes, sir."

"You better shovel this, Manuel. All you need on top of everything is for somebody to slip."

Mr. Freytag wept the rest of the way. In his lap he held the two boxes of coarse kosher salt, cradling the bag as though it contained Mrs. Freytag's remains. The snow whacking against the car windows, heavy whirling clots of it, caused Zuckerman to wonder if he shouldn't tell Ricky to turn back. The storm was here. But Zuckerman was feeling like a clean table, like an empty table, like a pale scrubbed wooden table, waiting to be set. No force left.

They passed beneath a railway bridge sprayed in six colors with mongoloid hieroglyphs. "Hateful bastards," said Mr. Freytag when he saw the public property defaced. The underpass was riddled with potholes, the potholes awash with black water. "Criminal," said Mr. Freytag as Ricky took the roadway at a crawl. "Funerals drive under here. Hearses, mourners, but Daley lines his pockets and everybody else can go to hell."

They passed through the tunnel, turned sharply along a steep railroad embankment littered with rusted chunks of abandoned machinery, and there, across the road, beyond a high black fence of iron palings, the gravestones began, miles and miles of treeless cemetery, ending at the far horizon in a large boxlike structure that was probably nothing but a factory, but that smoking foully away through the gray of the storm looked like something far worse.

"Here!" Mr. Freytag was rapping on the partition. "This gate!" And saw for the first time that their driver wasn't a man. He pulled at Nathan's sleeve but Nathan wasn't there. Out where everything ended, he had ended too. He was no longer even that table.

Ricky had unfurled a black umbrella and was shepherding the two passengers to the cemetery gate. A job to do and she did it. Dignity. For whomever.

"I saw the braid, a girl's braid, and it didn't even register." Mr. Freytag had struck up a conversation. "All I see is grief."

"That's all right, sir."

"A young girl. With a car this size. In weather like this."

"I began my career for a Jewish funeral home. My first position as a chauffeur."

"Is that so? But—what did you drive?"

"The relatives of the deceased."

"Amazing."

"I always used to say to my husband that there must be Jewish ESP, the way the word gets out when a Jewish person dies. The mourners come in droves, they come from everywhere to comfort the bereaved. It was my first experience of Jewish people. My respect for Jews began right there."

Mr. Freytag burst into tears. "I got three shoeboxes filled with condolence cards."

"Well," Ricky said to him, "that shows how much she was loved."

"You have children, young lady?"

"No, sir. Not yet."

"Oh, you must, you must."

Along a whitening path, alone, the two men entered the Jewish burial ground. They stood together before a mound of raw earth and a headstone bearing the family name. Now he was in a rage. "But this is not what I wanted! Why haven't they flattened it! Why hasn't this been leveled off? They left it like a garbage dump! Three whole weeks and now it's snowing and they still haven't made it *right*! Here it is—I don't get it. Julie's grave. I say the words, they have no meaning. Look how they left it!" He was leading Zuckerman by the hand from one family plot to the next. "My brother is here, my sister-in-law here, then Julie"—the pile left like a garbage dump—"and I'll be here. And there," he said, waving toward the smoking factory, "off there, the old part—her father and mother, my father, my mother, my two beautiful young sisters, one of them age sixteen years, dying in my arms..." They were standing again before the footstone engraved "PAUL FREYTAG 1899–1970." "You got pockets in there, Paul? My stupid brother. Made his money in gloves. Wouldn't spend a penny. Bought day-old bread all his life. All he thought about was his money. His money and his pecker. Pardon me but that's the truth. Always on his wife. No consideration. Wouldn't leave his poor wife alone, not even when she had cancer of the vagina. Little guy who looked like a candy-store owner. And she was a doll. The sweetest nature. A clever woman too. The best card player, Tilly— she could beat 'em all. What times we had, the four of us. Sold his business in 1965 for a hundred thousand

and the building for another hundred. They paid him three, four thousand a year just to stay on and look after his accounts. But he wouldn't give that wonderful woman a nickel to buy a thing. For the two years he was sick wouldn't even buy himself a remote-control switch so he doesn't have to get out of bed to change the channels. Saving it right to the end. The end. The end, Paul! You got pockets in there, you tight bastard? He's gone—they're all gone. And I stand on the edge and wait to be pushed. You know how I live with death now? I go to bed at night and I say, 'I don't give a shit.' That's how you lose your fear of death—you don't give a shit anymore."

He drew Nathan back to the upturned chunks of frozen earth heaped up over his wife. "Her Bobby. Her baby. How she nursed him in that dark room. How that kid suffered with those mumps. And that's what changes a life. I don't believe it. Zuck, it's idiotic. Would Bobby have chosen that girl for a wife if he had known he was a hundred percent? Not in a million years. He actually didn't think he was good enough for anything better. That Julie's Robert should have such a thought! Yet this, I believe, is what happened. With what that kid had to offer, with all his achievements, the respect and admiration he has in his field—and his downfall? The mumps! And a son who tells his father to eat shit! Would Bobby have produced, on his own, a boy so full of contempt? He would have had a child who has *feelings*, feelings like *we* have feelings. A child who worked and who studied and stayed home, and who wanted to excel like his father. Is that what death and dying is supposed to be about? Is that what the hardship and the struggle is for? For a piece of contempt who gets on the phone with his father and tells him to go eat shit? Who thinks to himself, 'This family, these people, I'm not even theirs and look what they do.' Who thinks, 'Watch me bend them around my finger with all their stupid Jewish love!' Because who is he? Do we even know where he comes from? She wanted a baby, right away, off the bat, had to have a baby. So they found a little orphan baby, and what in his roots that we don't know makes him behave this way to Bobby? I have a brilliant son. And all that brilliance locked in his genes! Everything we gave him, trapped like that in Bobby's genes, while everything we are *not*, everything we are *against*— How can all of this end with Gregory? Eat shit? To his *father*? I'll break his neck for what he's done to this family! I'll kill that little bastard! I *will*!"

Zuckerman, with what strength remained in his enfeebled arms, pounced upon the old man's neck. *He* would kill—and never again suppose himself better than his crime: an end to denial; of the heaviest judgment guilty as charged. "Your sacred genes! What do you see inside your head? Genes with JEW sewed on them? Is that all you see in that lunatic mind, the unstained natural virtue of Jews?"

"Stop!" Mr. Freytag began pushing him off with his thick gloved hands. "Stop this! Zuck!"

"What's he do all night long? He's out studying fucking!"

"Zuck, no—Zuck, the dead!"

"*We* are the dead! These bones in boxes are the Jewish living! These are the people running the show!"

"Help me!" He struggled free, turned to the gate, stumbled—and Zuckerman slid after him. "Hurry!" Mr. Freytag called. "Something's happened!" And wailing for help as he ran, the old man to be strangled was gone.

Just white snow whirling now, all else obliterated but the chiseled stones, and his hands frantically straining to throttle that throat. "Our genes! Our sacred little packet of Jewish sugars!" Then his legs flew off and he was sitting. From there he began his recitation, at the top of his voice read aloud the words he saw carved all around him in rock. "Honor thy Finkelstein! Do not commit Kaufman! Make no idols in the form of Levine! Thou shalt not take in vain the name of Katz!"

"He—he—snapped!"

"O Lord," cried Zuckerman, sledding inch by inch on his palms and his knees, "who bringeth forth from the earth the urge to spurt that maketh monkeys of us all, blessed art thou!" Eyes all but blinded by the melting snow, icy water ringing his collar and freezing slush filling his socks, he continued to crawl toward the last of the fathers demanding to be pleased. "Freytag! Forbidder! Now I murder *you*!"

But the boots stopped him: two tall cavalry boots burnished with oil and shedding the snow, ominous powerful sleek splendid boots that would have prompted caution in his bearded forebears too.

"This"—Zuckerman laughed, spewing flakes of burning ice—"this is your protection, Poppa Freytag? This great respecter of the Jews?" He strained to find the power to leave the graveyard ground. "Out of my way, you innocent bitch!" But against Ricky's boots got nowhere.

He awoke in a hospital cubicle. Something was wrong with his mouth. His head was enormously large. All he was aware of was this huge echoing hole which was the inside of his head. Within the enormous head there was something barely moving that was just as enormous. This was his tongue. The whole of his mouth, from ear to ear, was just pain.

Standing beside his bed was Bobby. "You're going to be all right," he said.

Zuckerman could begin to feel his lips now, lips swelled nearly to the size of his tongue. But below the lips, nothing.

"We're waiting for the plastic surgeon. He's going to sew up your chin. You've burst all the skin on the underside of your jaw. We don't know whether you've broken it, but the gash under your chin he can put together, and then we'll get some X-rays of your mouth and see the extent of the damage. Also of your head. I don't think the skull's fractured, but we better look. So far it seems you got off lightly: the gash and a few smashed teeth. Nothing that can't be fixed."

Zuckerman understood none of this—only that his head was getting larger and was about to roll off. Bobby repeated the story: "You were out on the heath with King Lear. You keeled over. Face forward, straight out, onto my Uncle Paul's footstone. My father says it sounded like a rock hitting the pavement. He thought you'd had a heart attack. You took the impact on the point of your chin. Burst the skin. Your two front teeth snapped just below the gum line. When they picked you up, you came around for a few seconds, completely came to, and said, 'Wait a minute, I've got to get rid of some teeth.' You spat the bits of teeth into your hand, then blacked out again. Doesn't look to be a fracture, no intracranial bleeding, but let's be sure of everything before we take the next step. It'll hurt for a while, but you're going to be fine."

The gloved fist that was Zuckerman's tongue went off in search of his front teeth. The tongue found instead their spongy gritty sockets. Otherwise, within his head, he felt giddy, echoing, black.

Patiently, Bobby tried a third explanation. "You were at the cemetery. Remember that? You took my father to visit my mother's grave. You turned up in a car about nine-thirty this morning. It's now three. You drove out to the cemetery, the driver parked by the embankment, and you and my father went in. He got a little over-wrought from the sound of it. So did you. You don't remember any of this? You went a little haywire, Zuck.

At first my old man thought it was a fit. The driver was a woman. Strong as a little ox. You apparently tried to knock her down. That's when you fell. She's the one who carried you out."

Zuckerman indicated, by a dim croak, that he still didn't remember a thing. All this damage had happened and he didn't know how. His jaw wouldn't come undone to allow him to speak. Also his neck had begun stiffening up. He couldn't move his head at all. Imprisonment complete.

"A little temporary amnesia, that's all. Don't panic. Not from the fall. No brain injury, I'm sure. It's from the stuff you were on. People have these blackouts, especially if there's a lot of alcohol involved. I'm not surprised to hear that you lost your manners with the lady. They went through your pockets. Three joints, about twenty Percodan tablets, and a beautiful monogrammed Tiffany flask completely emptied of NZ's booze. You've been flying for quite some time. The driver had some story you'd given her all about you and Hugh Hefner. Is this what is known as irresponsible hedonism, some sort of recreational thing, or is it a form of self-treatment for something?"

He discovered an intravenous tube in his right arm. He felt himself beginning to inch back from some black place of which he knew nothing. With the index finger of the free hand he traced the letter "P" in the air. The fingers worked, the arm worked; he tested the legs and the toes. They worked. Below his collarbone he was completely alive, but he himself had become his mouth. He had turned from a neck and shoulders and arms into a mouth. In that hole was his being.

"You were treating pain with all this stuff."

Zuckerman managed to grunt—and tasted his own blood. He'd progressed from vodka to blood.

"Show me where it hurts. I don't mean the mouth. The pain you were treating on your own, before the morning's fun began."

Zuckerman pointed.

"Diagnosis?" asked Bobby. "Write down the diagnosis. In that book."

There was a pad on the bed beside him, a large spiral note pad and a felt-tipped Magic Marker. Bobby uncapped the Magic Marker for him and put it into Zuckerman's hand. "Don't try to speak. It'll hurt too much. No talking, no yawning, no eating, no laughing, and try not to sneeze—not for a while yet. Write for me, Zuck. You know how to do that."

He wrote a word: NONE.

"No diagnosis? How long has this been going on? Write that down."

He preferred to show him the number with his fingers—to prove again that the fingers could move and that he could count and that his head hadn't rolled away.

"Eighteen," said Bobby. "Hours, days, months, or years?"

In the air, with the tip of the marker, Zuckerman formed an "M."

"That's a little too long to suit me," Bobby said. "If you've had pain for eighteen months, something's causing it."

The sensation of being brainless continued to lift. He still couldn't remember what had happened, but for the moment he didn't give a fuck: all he understood was that he was in trouble and it hurt. It had become excruciating.

Meanwhile, he gave off a harsh, growling sound: yes (the growl was intended to suggest), more than likely something is causing it.

"Well, you're not leaving here till we find what it is."

Zuckerman snorted, downing in the process a second shot of old blood.

"Oh, you've made the medical rounds, have you?"

With one finger Zuckerman indicated that he'd been round and round again. He was getting sardonic. Angry. Furious. I did *this* to myself too! Forcing the world to pay attention to my moan!

"Well, that's over. We're going to put you through a multidisciplinary examination right here in the hospital, we're going to track it down, and then we're going to get rid of it for you."

Zuckerman had a clear compound thought, his first since the morning. Since leaving New York. Maybe in eighteen months. He thought: The doctors are all confidence, the pornographers are all confidence, and, needless to say, the oxlike young women who now drive the limousines live far beyond the reach of doubt. While doubt is half a writer's life. Two-thirds. Nine-tenths. Another day, another doubt. The only thing I never doubted was the doubt.

"We're also going to get you off the medication merry-go-round. As long as you're not on it for kicks, we can break your habit easily enough. Medical addiction, no real problem. As soon as your mouth is fixed and the trauma subsides, we're going to phase you out of all your pain-killers and away from the alcohol. The grass too. That's *really* childish. You're going to stay here as my patient until you're no longer addicted. That means three weeks at least. There's to be no cheating, Zuck. The cure for alcoholism isn't two little martinis before dinner. We're going to eliminate the drugs and the drink and we're going to do our best to find the cause and eliminate the pain that causes the need to get blotto. Is that clear? I'm going to oversee your withdrawal myself. It'll be gradual and painless, and if you cooperate and don't cheat, it'll be lasting. You'll be back where you were before it all began. I wish you'd told me you were in this when I saw you yesterday. I'm not going to ask why you didn't. We'll save that. I thought something was up, you looked so God damned gaga, but you said no, and it just didn't occur to me in my office, Zuckerman, to look you over for needle tracks. Are you in bad pain right now? From the mouth?"

Zuckerman indicated that he was indeed in pain.

"Well, we're just waiting for the plastic surgeon. We're still in emergency. He'll come down and trim up the wound and get all the grit out and stitch you up so there's hardly a scar. I want him doing it so that afterwards it looks right. Then we'll get some pictures. If your mouth needs work right away, we'll get the jaw man down. He knows you're here. If they have to wire anything together, he's the best. He's the guy who wrote the book. I'll stay with you all the way—but one thing at a time. I can't give you anything for the pain right now, not after what you've come off of. Don't want more 'fits.' Just go with it. Ride it out. It'll end like everything else. The whole thing won't be the shortest journey imaginable, but it won't last forever either."

Zuckerman found the Magic Marker and, with fingers as awkward as a first-grader's, wrote four words in the spiral notebook: CAN'T STAY THREE WEEKS.

"No? Why not?"

CLASSES BEGIN JAN. 4.

Bobby tore out the sheet, folded it in half, and stuck it in the pocket of his smock. He rubbed the edge of his hand slowly back and forth across his bearded chin—clinical detachment—but his eyes, examining the patient, showed only exasperation. He is thinking—thought Zuckerman—"What's become of this guy?"

A doctor named Walsh appeared in Zuckerman's cubicle, how long after Bobby left Zuckerman had no way of telling. He was a tall, bony man in his fifties, with a long, pouchy, haggard face, wispy gray hair, and a smoker's hoarse catch in his voice. He sucked continuously at a cigarette as he spoke. "Well," he said to Zuckerman, with a disconcerting smile, "we see thirty thousand people a year down here, but you're the first I know of to cross the threshold in his lady chauffeur's arms."

Zuckerman wrote on a clean notebook page: WHEN HE IS SICK EVERY MAN NEEDS A MOTHER.

Walsh shrugged. "The hoi polloi generally crawl through on their knees or roll in comatose on the stretcher. Especially hopheads like yourself. The lady says you gave a real fine show before you left for the Land of Oz. Sounds like you were nice and wacky. What all were you on?"

WHAT YOU FOUND. PERCODAN VODKA POT. KILLING PAIN.

"Yep, that'll do it. If it's your maiden voyage, three or four tablets of Percodan, a couple highballs, and if you don't have much tolerance, you're out for the count. People start overtreating pain, and next thing they either set fire to the mattress or they're under the wheels of a bus. We had a guy in here the other night, smashed like you and feelin' groovy, whammo, ass over skull down four flights. Only thing he *didn't* break was his teeth. You got off lucky. From a straight fall like yours you could have done worse. You could have brained yourself but good. You could have bitten off your God damn tongue."

HOW FAR GONE WAS I?

"Oh, you were zonked, bud. You weren't breathing very hard, you'd thrown up all over yourself, and your face was a mess. We drew some blood to see what you had in you, we passed a tube down your stomach to wash you out, we injected a narcotic antagonist, we got you breathing and hooked up to the IV. We're waiting for the surgeon to come down. We cleaned out the wound but he's going to have to stick you together if you still want to turn on the girls."

WHAT'S IT LIKE TO BE AN EMERGENCY-ROOM DOCTOR? NEVER KNOW WHAT'S COMING THROUGH THE DOOR. CALLS FOR QUICK THINKING. LOTS OF SKILLS.

The doctor laughed. "You writing a book or what?" He had a funny, honking sort of laugh and a vast array of jittery gestures. A doctor with doubts. There had to be one somewhere. You might have taken him for the orderly—or for a psychiatric patient. His eyes looked scared to death. "I never read anything, but the nurse knew who you were. Before you get out of here, she's going to get your autograph. She says we got a celebrity here."

QUESTION SERIOUS. He was trying to think of something other than the ear-to-ear pain. ABOUT TO ENTER MEDICAL SCHOOL, EMERGENCY-ROOM MEDICINE REWARD-ING?

"Well, it's a God damn tough way to earn a living, if you want to know. Average guy burns out at this job in about seven years. But I don't know what you mean, entering medical school. You're the famous writer. You wrote the dirty book."

MUST SAVE LOTS OF LIVES. MUST MAKE THE HARD WORK WORTH IT.

"I suppose. Sure there are two or three cliff-hangers in a day. People come in here on the rack and you try to do something for them. I can't say everyone leaves with a smile, it doesn't work out that way. You, for instance. You come in here OD'd and three, four hours after admission, you begin to lighten up. Sometimes they *never* wake up. Look, you pulling my leg? You write these hilarious best-sellers, from what they all tell me— what are you trying, to put me in one?"

HOW DID YOU BECOME AN EMERGENCY-ROOM DOCTOR? Another nervous honk. "Monkey on my back," he said, and then was seized by a shattering cough that seemed of itself to hurl him out of the room. A moment later Zuckerman heard him call down the corridor, "Where the hell'd they put the diabetic?"

Zuckerman had no idea how much more of the day had passed before Walsh appeared at his bedside again. He had something urgent to say, something to make clear about himself before he (or the writer) went back on duty. If he was going to wind up in a hilarious best-seller, Zuckerman might as well get it right.

A book machine is what they see when they meet me. And appalling as it is, they're right. A book machine consuming lives—including, Dr. Walsh, my own.

"Most every emergency-room doctor I know has something on his back," he said. "Alcoholism. Mental disorder. No spika dee English. Okay, with me it was Demerol. Percodan turns me off, morphine turns me off, even alcohol disagrees with me. But Demerol—it's a good thing you didn't find out about Demerol. It's a great favorite with us folks whose pain drags on and on. Gives a lot of elation. Relaxation. No more problems."

WHAT PROBLEMS WERE YOURS?

"Okay," he said, his anger raw now and undisguised. "I'll tell you, Zuckerman, since you want to know. I used to have a practice over in Elgin. A wife, a child, and a practice. Couldn't handle it. You'll understand that. You wouldn't be here if you didn't understand that. So I got through on Demerol. Ten years ago this is. The big problem for me in dealing with patients is getting someone out of a difficult situation over a period of time. Down here in emergency, we just light the fuse and run. We put our finger in the dike for a while and that's it. But if a guy gets a tough case up on the floors, a case that goes on day after day, you've got to push the right buttons over the long haul. You've got to watch them die without falling apart. I can't do that. With my history, and pushing sixty, I'm lucky I can do this. I work forty hours a week, they pay me, and I go home. That's about all Gordon Walsh can handle. Now you know."

But that sounded to Zuckerman like all a man could want, an end to the search for the release from self. After Walsh had left for the second time, he tried to imagine those forty-hour weeks in order to forget what was happening in his mouth. Car accidents. Motorcycle accidents. Falls. Burns. Strokes. Coronaries. Overdoses. Knife wounds. Bullet wounds. Dog bites. Human bites. Childbirth. Lunacy. Breakdown. Now, there's *work*. They come in on the rack and you keep them alive till the surgeon can wire them together. You get them off the rack and then you disappear. Self-oblivion. What could be less ambiguous than that? If the dean were to say to him over at the medical school, "No, no room, not with your history, not at your age, not after the stunt you pulled out here," he'd reply that he wanted only to be another emergency-room doctor with a monkey on his back and an exemplary record of doubt. Nothing in the world could make him happier.

It was dark in Chicago when the plastic surgeon arrived. He apologized for being late but he'd driven in through the blizzard from Homewood. He sewed him up right in the room, stitched him up from inside the flesh so there'd be nothing afterwards but a hairline scar. "If you want," he said—a joke to lift the patient's spirits—"we'll take another tuck right here and nip that dewlap in the bud. Keep you young for the ladies." Whether he was given a local anesthetic Zuckerman had no idea. Maybe everything just hurt too much for him to feel the stitching.

The X-rays showed a fracture of the jaw in two places, so the maxillo-facial surgeon was called down, and at about the dinner hour Zuckerman was wheeled into the operating room. The elderly surgeon explained everything beforehand—in the quietest voice, like the TV announcer at the tennis match, described for Zuckerman what was next. Two fractures, he explained: an oblique fracture at the front, a thin vertical line running from between where the teeth had broken off down to the point of the chin, and a second fracture up by the hinge. Because the fragments weren't in a very good position running down to the chin, he'd have to make a small incision just beneath the chin to go in and get them aligned, then take very fine wire, drill some holes, and wire the bone together. Up by the hinge no surgery necessary. They'd put metal bars on his upper and lower teeth, crisscross rubber bands to hold the bars fastened together, and that's all it would take to heal the second fracture and give him an even bite. He shouldn't be alarmed when he woke up if he experienced a slight choking sensation—it would only be from the rubber bands clamping his mouth "more or less shut." They would be loosening that up as soon as they could. And then, for the twentieth time that day, Zuckerman was assured that after his face was all fixed, he'd still be able to wow the girls.

"Yes, it's a clean fracture, but not quite clean enough to suit me." These words of the surgeon's were the last that he heard. Bobby, there to administer the anesthesia, patted his shoulder. "Off to Xanadu, Zuck," and off he went, to the tune of ". . . not quite clean enough . . ."

Bobby was there to put him out and was there in the recovery room to check up on him when Zuckerman came to, but when the Xylocaine wore off sometime during the night, Zuckerman was alone and at long last he found out just what pain could really do. He'd had no idea.

One of the maneuvers he adopted to get from one minute to the next was to try calling himself Mr. Zuckerman, as though from the bench. Chasing that old man around those tombstones, Mr. Zuckerman, is the dumbest thing you have ever done. You have opened the wrong windows, closed the wrong doors, you have granted jurisdiction over your conscience to the wrong court; you have been in hiding half your life and a son far too long — you, Mr. Zuckerman, have been the most improbable slave to embarrassment and shame, yet for sheer pointless inexcusable stupidity, nothing comes close to chasing across a cemetery, through a snowstorm, a retired handbag salesman understandably horrified to discover grafted upon his own family tree the goy who spoils everything. To fix all that pain and repression and exhaustion on this Katzenjammer Karamazov, this bush-league Pontifex, to smash him, like some false divinity, into smithereens . . . but of course there were Gregory's inalienable rights to defend, the liberties of a repellent mindless little shit whom you, Mr. Zuckerman, would loathe on sight. It appears, Mr. Zuckerman, that you may have lost your way since Thomas Mann last looked down from the altar and charged you to become a great man. I hereby sentence you to a mouth clamped shut.

When the lighthearted approach proved ineffective — and then the distraction of reciting to himself what he could remember from high school of the *Canterbury Tales* — he held his own hand, pretending that it was somebody else. His brother, his mother, his father, his wives — each took a turn sitting beside the bed and holding his hand in theirs. The pain was amazing. If he could have opened his mouth, he would have screamed. After five hours, if he could have got himself to the window, he would have jumped, and after ten hours the pain began to subside.

For the next few days he was nothing but a broken mouth. He sucked through a straw and he slept. That was it. Sucking would seem to be the easiest thing in the world to do, something nobody had to be taught, but because his lips were so bruised and sore and the

overall swelling so bad, and because the straw only fit
sideways into his mouth, he couldn't even suck right,
and had to sort of draw in from down in the stomach to
get the stuff to begin to trickle through him. In this
way he sucked in carrot soup and mushed-up fruit, and
a milky drink, banana-flavored and extolled as highly
nutritious, that was so sweet it made him gag. When
he wasn't sucking liquid pulp or sleeping, he went ex-
ploring his mouth with his tongue. Nothing existed but
the inside of his mouth. He made all sorts of discoveries
in there. Your mouth is who you are. You can't get very
much closer to what you think of as yourself. The next
stop up is the brain. No wonder fellatio has achieved
such renown. Your tongue lives in your mouth and your
tongue is you. He sent his tongue everywhere to see what
was doing beyond the metal arch bars and the elastic
bands. Across the raw vaulted dome of the palate, down
to the tender cavernous sockets of the missing teeth, and
then the plunge below the gum line. That was where
they'd opened him up and wired him together. For the
tongue it was like the journey up the river in "Heart of
Darkness." The mysterious stillness, the miles of silence,
the tongue creeping conradianly on toward Kurtz. I am
the Marlow of my mouth.

Below the gum line there had been bits of jawbone
and teeth smashed up, and the doctor had spent some
time, before setting the fracture, picking around in there
to take out all the tiny fragments. Giving him new front
teeth was still to come. He couldn't imagine ever again
biting into anything. The idea of anyone touching his
face was horrible. He slept at one point for eighteen
hours and afterwards had no recollection of having his
blood pressure taken or his IV changed.

A young night nurse came by to cheer him up with
the *Chicago Tribune*. "Well," she said, flushed a little
with excitement, "you really are somebody, aren't you?"

He motioned for her to leave the paper beside his sleeping pill. In the middle of the night—some night or other— he finally picked up the copy she'd left him and looked at it under the bed light. The paper was folded back to an item in one of the columns.

Latest from our celebrity chauffeur: How time jets! Sixties rebel, Novelist Nathan ("Carnovsky") Zuckerman recouping at Billings from cosmetic surgery. Just a nip and a tuck for the fortyish Romeo, then back to "Elaine's" and the NY scene. Nathan slipped into town incognito to party at the Pump Room on the eve of the lift...

A card arrived from Mr. Freytag. On the envelope's return-address sticker, where it read "Mr. and Mrs. Harry Freytag," Mr. Freytag had put a line through "and Mrs." Drawing that line would have taken some doing. The card read "Hurry and Get Well!" On the back he had handwritten a personal message.

Dear Nathan,
    Bobby explained about the death of your beloved parents that I did not know about. Your terrible grief as a son explains whatever happened and nothing more has to be added. The cemetery was the last place in the world for you to be. I only kick myself that I didn't know beforehand. I hope I didn't make it worse with anything I said.
    You have made a great name in life for which all my congratulations. But I want you to know you are still Joel Kupperman ("The Quiz Kid") to Bobby's Dad and always will be. Hurry and get well.
                    Love from the Freytags,
                    Harry, Bobby, and Greg

The last of the old-fashioned fathers. And we, thought Zuckerman, the last of the old-fashioned sons. Who that follows after us will understand how midway through the twentieth century, in this huge, lax, disjointed democracy, a father—and not even a father of learning or eminence or demonstrable power—could still assume the stature of a father in a Kafka story? No, the good old days are just about over, when half the time, without even knowing it, a father could sentence a son to punishment for his crimes, and the love and hatred of authority could be such a painful, tangled mess.

There was a letter from the student paper, *The Maroon.* The editors wanted to interview him about the future of his kind of fiction in the post-modernist era of John Barth and Thomas Pynchon. Since they understood that because of his surgery he might not wish to be seen, would he please answer, at whatever length he chose, the ten questions on the sheet attached.

Well, they were kind not to show up and just grill him on the spot; he didn't feel ready quite yet for the social pleasures of an author's life.

1. Why do you continue to write? 2. What purpose does your work serve? 3. Do you feel yourself part of a rearguard action, in the service of a declining tradition? 4. Has your sense of vocation altered significantly because of the events of the last decade?

Yes, yes, said Zuckerman, very much so, and dropped back below the gum line.

The fourth morning he got up and looked in the mirror. Until then he hadn't been interested. Very pale, very drawn. Surgical tape under his chin. Hollow cheeks that a movie star would envy, and around the surgical tape a scraggly growth of beard that had come in all white. And balder. Four days in Chicago had undone four months of trichological treatment. The swelling had subsided, but the jaw was alarmingly lopsided and even through the whiskers looked badly bruised. Mulberry, like a birthmark. His cracked and spotted lips had also turned colors. And two teeth were indeed gone. He realized that his glasses were gone. Under the snow in the cemetery, buried till spring with Bobby's mother. All the better: for now he didn't care to see clearly the clever jokes that mockery plays. He'd been considered a great mocker once himself, but never as diabolically inspired as this. Even without the aid of his glasses, he understood that he didn't look like he was on the ball. He thought, Just don't make me write about it after. Not everything has to be a book. Not that, too.

But back in bed he thought, The burden isn't that everything has to be a book. It's that everything *can* be a book. And doesn't count as life until it is.

Then the euphoria of convalescence—and the loosening of his rubber bands. During the weeks that followed the successful operation, in the excitement of giving up each day a little more of the narcotic support, full of the pleasure of learning for the second time in forty years to form simple monosyllabic English with his lips and his palate and his tongue and his teeth, he wandered the hospital in his robe and slippers and the new white beard. Nothing he pronounced, in his weakened voice, felt timeworn—all the words seemed rapturously clean, and the oral catastrophe behind him. He tried to forget all that had happened in the limousine, at the cemetery, on the plane; he tried to forget everything that had happened since he'd come out to go to school here the first time. *I was sixteen, intoning ". . . shantih, shantih, shantih" on the El. That's the last I remember.*

The first-year interns, young men in their mid-twenties, mustaches newly cultivated and eyes darkly circled from working days and nights, came around to his room after supper to introduce themselves and chat. They struck him as artless, innocent children. It was as though, leaving the platform with their medical-school diplomas, they'd taken a wrong turn and fallen back headlong into the second grade. They brought their copies of *Carnovsky* for him to autograph and solemnly asked if he was working on a new book. What Zuckerman wanted to know was the age of the oldest member of their medical-school class.

He began helping the post-operative patients just up out of bed, slowly wheeling along the corridor the poles slung with their IV bags. "Twelve times around," moaned a forlorn man of sixty with a freshly bandaged head; dark pigmented moles could be seen at the base of his spine where the ties to his gown had come undone. ". . . twelve times around the floor," he told Zuckerman, ". . . supposed to be a mile." "Well," said Zuckerman, through a rigid jaw, "you don't have to do the mile today." "I own a seafood restaurant. You like fish?" "Love it." "You'll come when you're better. Al's Dock. 'Where lobsters are the Maine thing.' Spelled M-a-i-n-e. You'll have dinner on me. Everything fresh that day. One thing I learned. You can't serve frozen fish. There are people who can tell the difference and you can't get away with it. You have got to serve fresh fish. The only thing we have that's frozen is the shrimp. What do you do?" Oh, God— should I now do my number? No, no, in their weakened condition too alarming for both of them. Donning that mask wasn't a joke: all the while he was enjoying it, his exuberant performance was making even more unrelenting all the ghosts and the rages. What looked like a new obsession to exorcise the old obsessions was only the old obsessions merrily driving him as far as he could go. As far? Don't bet on it. Plenty more turmoil where that came from. "Out of work," said Zuckerman. "A bright young guy like you?" Zuckerman shrugged. "Temporary setback, that's all." "Well, you ought to learn the seafood business." "Could be," said Zuckerman. "You're young—" and with those words, the restaurateur was choking back tears, suddenly fighting down the convalescent's pity for all vulnerable things, including himself now and his bandaged head. "I can't tell you what it was like," he said. "Close to death. You can't understand. How it draws you to life. You survive," he said, "and you see it all new, *everything*," and six days later he had a hemorrhage and died.

The sobbing of a woman, and Zuckerman was transfixed outside her room. He was wondering what, if anything, he should do—*What is the matter? What does she need?*—when a nurse popped out and rushed right past him, muttering only half to herself, "Some people think you're going to torture them." Zuckerman peered inside. He saw the graying hair spread across her pillow, and a paperback copy of *David Copperfield* open on the sheet that covered her chest. She was about his age and wearing a pale blue nightgown of her own; the delicate shoulder straps looked absurdly fetching. She might have been lying down to rest for a moment before rushing off to a dinner party on a summer evening. "Is there anything—?" "This cannot be!" she shouted. He came farther into the room. "What is it?" he whispered. "They're removing my larynx," she cried—"go away!"

In the lounge at the end of the ear, nose, and throat floor he checked the relatives of the surgical patients waiting for the results. He sat and waited with them. Always somebody at the card table playing solitaire. All there was to worry about, yet not one forgot to give the deck a good shuffle before dealing a new game. One afternoon Walsh, his emergency-room doctor, found him there in the lounge, on his lap a yellow pad where he'd been able to write nothing more than "Dear Jenny." Dear Diana. Dear Jaga. Dear Gloria. Mostly he sat crossing out words that were wrong in every possible way: *overwrought . . . self-contempt . . . weary of treatment . . . the mania* of sickness . . . the reign of error . . . hypersensitized to all the inescapable limits . . . engrossed to the exclusion of everything else . . . Nothing would flow with any reality—a mannered, stilted letter-voice, aping tones of great sincerity and expressing, if anything, his great reservations about writing to explain at all. He couldn't be intelligent about having failed to make good as a man on his back, and he could not be apologetic or ashamed. Wasn't emotionally persuasive any longer. Yet as soon as he sat down to write, out came another explanation, causing him to recoil from his words in disgust. The same with the books: however ingenious and elaborate the disguise, answering charges, countering allegations, angrily sharpening the conflict while earnestly striving to be understood. The endless public deposition—what a curse! The best reason of all never to write again.

While they rode the down elevator, Walsh savored the last of his cigarette—savoring, Zuckerman thought, some contempt for me too.

"Who set your jaw finally?" Walsh asked.

Zuckerman told him.

"Nothing but the best," said Walsh. "Know how he rose to the white-haired heights? Studied years ago with the big guy in France. Experimented on monkeys. Wrote it all up. Bashed in their faces with a baseball bat and then studied the fracture lines."

To then write it up? Even more barbaric than what went on in his line. "Is that true?"

"Is that how you get to the heights? Don't ask me. Gordon Walsh never got to do much bashing. How about the five-dollar habit, Mr. Zuckerman? Remove you from your Percodan yet?"

Because of his habit Zuckerman was handed a drink twice a day looking and tasting like a cherry soda—his "pain cocktail" they called it. It was delivered routinely—early morning, late afternoon—by the nurse who put the addict through his paces. Taken at fixed times and not in response to the pain, the drink furnished the opportunity to "relearn" facing his "problem." "Give us this day," she said, "our daily fix," while obedient Zuckerman emptied the glass. "Not taking anything on the sly, are we, Mr. Z.?" Though for the first several days off the pills and the vodka he'd been feeling unpleasantly jittery and nervous—at moments shaky enough to wonder who he could find in the hospital to help him break Bobby's rules—the answer was no. "Nothing surreptitious about Mr. Z.," he assured her. "That's the boy," she said, and with a conspiratorial hospital wink ended the pseudo-seductive little game. The changing proportion of active ingredients to cherry syrup was known only to the staff; the cocktail was the centerpiece of Bobby's deconditioning plan, a gradual fading process to reduce Zuckerman's medication to zero over a period of six weeks. The idea was to phase Zuckerman out of physiological dependence on pain-killers as well as the "pain behavior syndrome."

As for the investigation into the pain so conducive to the behavior, it had yet to be ordered. Bobby didn't want Zuckerman, whose morale after a year and a half required a certain tactful treatment of its own, to drop into a state of confused depression because of too many fingers of too many doctors poking around to see what was wrong. Zuckerman's energy was to be engaged for now in overcoming the long-standing addiction to the drugs and the strength-sapping trauma to the face, especially as the occlusion of the jaw wasn't exactly as it should be and there were two front teeth still to come.

"So far so good," reported Zuckerman on the subject of his habit.

"Well," Walsh replied, "we'll see when you're out from under surveillance. No armed robber breaks into a bank while still a guest of the state. That happens the week he gets sprung."

At the ground floor they left the elevator and started down the corridor to the emergency ward. "We just admitted a woman of eighty-eight. Ambulance went to get her eighty-one-year-old brother—a stroke. They took one whiff and brought her along too."

"What'd they smell?"

"You'll see."

The woman had only half a face. One cheek, up to the eye socket, and the whole side of her jaw had been eaten away by cancer. Ever since it had begun, as just a blister, four years before, she had been treating it on her own with Mercurochrome and dressing it with a bandage that she changed once a week. She lived with her brother in one room, cooked for him and cleaned for him, and no neighbor, no shopkeeper, no one who saw it had ever looked under the bandage and called a doctor. She was a slight, shy, demure, well-spoken old woman, poor but a lady, and when Zuckerman came in alongside of Walsh, she pulled her hospital nightie around her bare throat. She lowered her eyes. "How do you do, sir?"

Walsh introduced his companion. "This is Dr. Zuckerman. Our resident humanist. He'd like to take a look, Mrs. Brentford."

Zuckerman was dressed in the hospital robe and slippers and his beard was, as yet, without distinction. He lacked two front teeth and had a mouth full of metal. Yet the woman said, "Oh, yes. Thank you."

To Zuckerman, Walsh explained the case. "We've been cutting the scabs away and draining pus for an hour—all cleaned up for you, Doc." He led the resident humanist to the far side of the bed and shined a pocket light on the wound.

There was a hole in her cheek the size of a quarter.

Through it Zuckerman could see her tongue as it nervously skittered about inside her mouth. The jawbone itself was partially exposed, an inch of it as white and clean as enamel tile. The rest, up to the eye socket, was a chunk of raw flesh, something off the butcher's floor to cut up for the cat. He tried not to inhale the smell.

Out in the hallway Walsh was racked with the cough ignited by his laughter. "You look green, Doctor," he said when finally he could speak. "Maybe you're better off sticking to books."

By midmorning each day the large canvas bins along the corridor were stuffed with the night's soiled linen. Zuckerman had been eyeing these bins for weeks, each time he passed beside one tempted by the strangest yearning. It was on the morning after Walsh's caper, when there was no one anywhere nearby to ask what the hell he thought he was doing, that finally he plunged his arms down through the tangle of sheets and bed wear and towels. He never expected so much to be so damp. The strength rushed from his groin, his mouth filled with bile—it was as though he were up to his elbows in blood. It was as though the reeking flesh of Mrs. Brentford's face was there between his two hands. Down the corridor he heard a woman begin to howl, somebody's mother or sister or daughter, the cry of a survivor—"She pinched us! She hit us! The names that she called us! Then she went!" Another catastrophe—every moment, behind every wall, *right next door*, the worst ordeals that anyone could imagine, pain that was ruthless and inescapably real, crying and suffering truly worthy of all a man's defiance. He would become Mrs. Brentford's physician. He would become a maxillo-facial surgeon. He would study anesthesiology. He would run a detoxification program, setting his patients the example of his own successful withdrawal.

Until someone down the corridor shouted, "Hey, *you*!

You all right?" Zuckerman remained submerged to his shoulders in the sheets of the healing, the ailing, and the dying—and of whoever had died there during the night—his hope as deep as the abiding claim of his remote but unrelinquishable home. *This is life. With real teeth in it.*

From that evening on, whenever the interns dropped by to say hello, he asked to accompany them on their rounds. In every bed the fear was different. What the doctor wanted to know the patient told him. Nobody's secret a scandal or a disgrace—everything revealed and everything at stake. And always the enemy was wicked and real. "We had to give you a little haircut to get that all cleaned out." "Oh, that's all right," the enormous baby-faced black woman replied in a small compliant voice. The intern gently turned her head. "Was it very deep, Doctor?" "We got it all," the intern told her, showing Zuckerman the long stitched-up wound under the oily dressing just behind her ear. "Nothing there to worry you anymore." "Yes? Well, that's good then." "Absolutely." "And—and am I going to see you again?" "You sure are," he said, squeezing her hand, and then he left her at peace on her pillow, with Zuckerman, the intern's intern, in tow. What a job! The paternal bond to those in duress, the urgent, immediate human exchange! All this indispensable work to be done, all this digging away at disease—and he'd given his fanatical devotion to sitting with a typewriter alone in a room!

For nearly as long as he remained a patient, Zuckerman roamed the busy corridors of the university hospital, patrolling and planning on his own by day, then out on the quiet floor with the interns at night, as though he still believed that he could unchain himself from a future as a man apart and escape the corpus that was his.

About the Author

Philip Roth was born in New Jersey in 1933. He studied literature at Bucknell University and the University of Chicago. His first book, *Goodbye, Columbus*, won the National Book Award for Fiction in 1960. He has lived in Rome, London, Chicago, New York City, Princeton, and New England. Since 1955, he has been on the faculties of the University of Chicago, Princeton University, and the University of Pennsylvania, where he is now Adjunct Professor of English. He is also General Editor of the Penguin Books series "Writers from the Other Europe." Recently he has been spending half of each year in Europe, traveling and writing.